A QUIET DRINK

Claudia has always been independent – own flat, absorbing job, a husband so devoted he is almost a housewife. Until she finds herself an abruptly and uneasily liberated woman.

Steve Mullen deals in faces – and is perhaps too well fitted for his job as a cosmetics rep. His wife June is a perfect model for his firm's products. Yet after a year of marriage, life is proving rather less than perfect.

It is a sly stroke of chance which brings Claudia and Steve together. Yet neither could know how far the consequences of a quiet drink would reach . . .

Also by Deborah Moggach
available from Mandarin Paperbacks

*Stolen
*You Must Be Sisters
Hot Water Man
Porky
To Have And To Hold
Driving In The Dark
Smile And Other Stories
The Stand In

DEBORAH MOGGACH

A Quiet Drink

Mandarin

A Mandarin Paperback
A QUIET DRINK

First published in Great Britain 1980
by William Collins Ltd
This edition published 1991
by Mandarin Paperbacks
Michelin House, 81 Fulham Road, London SW3 6RB

Mandarin is an imprint of the Octopus Publishing Group,
a division of Reed International Books Limited

Copyright © Deborah Moggach 1980

This is a work of fiction. All the characters are imaginary.

A CIP catalogue record for this title
is available from the British Library
ISBN 0 7493 0924 5

Printed and bound in Great Britain
by Cox and Wyman Ltd, Reading, Berks

To Audrey and Eileen,
who cared for the children

ONE

It was far from dignified, she knew it. Besides, it was chilly standing here in the drizzly street. She gazed up at the block of flats. She should be home cooking her supper.

Claudia did not move. She shifted on to the other foot and inspected the rows of windows, some dark, some lit, all those evenings beginning. It was a large block of flats, larger than she had imagined; Edwardian, with a decorated porch, on its glass in Gothic script *Albion Court*.

16 Albion Court, Muswell Avenue, N10 4 LR. Her husband, punctilious to the last, had typed out the address including the postcode. She had sellotaped the piece of paper to the fridge. She did not need to, of course; for three weeks now the words had been tinkling around her head like the chorus of her marriage, the closing chorus sung by a single piping voice. So insistent, the little tune, that she had looked up the street in her *A-Z*. So insistent, that for three weeks she had carried the *A-Z*, bulky in her handbag, to work and home again. It nudged her, tempted her, every time she reached for her wallet. She would not go there; she would resist.

It was an ordinary street, rather suburban, in a part of London unknown to her. 'Beth has her own flat,' he had said, 'in Muswell Hill.' Her husband had spoken of Beth's most unremarkable attributes with a note of shy pride in his voice, a note new to him.

A bus splashed past. She stepped back, wiping her coat. It was cold and wet for October; in Albion Court, no doubt, the central heating would be switched on. *Not that they'll need it.*

No, that would not do. Any nudge-nudge stuff seemed inappropriate to Adrian and Beth. Beth seemed such a dowdy name; indeed, by all accounts Beth was a remarkably dowdy girl. 'You know, Claudia, she's not half as good-looking as you. Or as intelligent.' This had hurt, for some reason, more than anything else. (Why?)

Adrian and Beth. Already the names sounded married. Adrian and Claudia had always sounded clumsy. Adrian and Beth did not sound exciting; they did not sound as if they were having an affair; they sounded sincere.

Two figures emerged from the entrance hall; they hesitated on the step. Claudia tensed. She clutched her handbag; the *A-Z* dug into her stomach.

The couple turned and walked down the street. No, they were unfamiliar. Claudia relaxed; her hands loosened. She smiled to herself; it was years since her heart had thudded like this for her husband.

She stood behind the pillar-box and studied the windows. What did Flat 16 look like? Was there a little heap of silver upon Beth's chest-of-drawers? Adrian always emptied out his loose change when he returned from work. Would he be asking *Something nice for supper*? Mutual greed, both for food and drink, had been one of her strongest bonds with Adrian. But he would not be waiting in the living-room. In the kitchen of number 16, no doubt, he would be standing close to Beth, his hands on her shoulders, sniffing the steaming saucepans. A husband in an Oxo Cube ad, already distanced and altered.

At moments it had hurt. 'Describe her,' she had said. Adrian had paused, looking out of the window at the darkening sky. 'Claudia, she's like one of the women in those paintings. What's his name – Vermeer? Sort of roundish – brown hair – comfortable at small tasks.'

Oh, it had hurt. She had never heard Adrian talk of painters before.

Claudia took the bus home. She did not investigate further, she did not inspect the entrance hall, the wooden board with the numbers of the flats, she did not calculate which row of windows belonged to Flat 16. Certainly she did not knock on the door. This had not been her intention. All she had needed was to place Adrian, to give him a street and a locality. No longer need she scrawl an address upon his letters and send them into a void. The words were solid now, a big building with a stone-scrolled porch. When he wrote to her, as soon he must, the envelope would be posted in the pillar-box against which she had rested.

'Yes miss?'

She fumbled for her fare. Miss now, was it? To all intents and purposes she was no longer Claudia Ensor, a name unremarkable and indeed rather distinguished, but her maiden name, Claudia Cockshutt. She thought she had got rid of this for good. Returning to it was like returning to an old school friend one has long outgrown – familiar, a sharer of the past, indeed absorbed into one's very blood-stream, but in company embarrassing. Now that she was thirty and matured by seven years, she should cope better with the burden of her surname; better than the days of first, hesitant introductions to first, hesitant boys.

It was eight o'clock. The bus filled up; people sat in the seats in front, the seats behind, wet raincoats rustled. 'Mum in tonight?' 'Think I'll wash my hair.' People returned to lit rooms, scents of dinner. Her house, unlit, lay on the other side of the river, a fair distance across London. Adrian's office had been in this direction – even further, in fact; a good eight miles into suburbia. Convenient enough for their own flat, it was a good deal less convenient for Beth's.

How was he taking a cramped, hour-long car journey twice a day, across London and practically out the other side?

She need no longer concern herself with this, the length or discomfort of his journey. Nor whether he should invest £300 in that apparently necessary dentistry. Nor that now his father was dead his mother could be persuaded to go into a Home. Upon Beth these problems now devolved. Beth's brown head would now tilt and nod over the pros and cons of temporary and permanent bridgework; Beth's rounded body would now accompany Adrian on the dutiful trips to Chelmsford, the Sunday teas in the front room, the eating of the rock cakes that grew progressively rockier as the hand that cooked them grew more uncertain, but which must be finished, the plate left empty, satisfied murmurs made. Would Beth know the right things to say about the medals, and would she ask to see the photographs? Beth had taken on a forty-year-old man with a past, with a body thickened by many thousand meals she had not shared; his hair threaded with grey from a thousand decisions in which she had had no part. She would never know the younger Adrian that Claudia had married. But then for Beth perhaps he had become young again.

It was late-night shopping in the West End. The bus crossed Oxford Street; the conductor pushed past bulging carrier-bags to reach the outstretched coins. He looked very young, with clear girlish skin. When he passed Claudia he winked; by now she was the veteran of the upper deck, people had arrived, others were already leaving and only she remained in her seat. She thought: I could take any bus, any train. I could go anywhere and nobody would notice that I had lit no lamps.

The windows were steamed up; she rubbed them with her hand. Below was black nothingness. They must be crossing the Thames. Then the bulk of Battersea Power Station, its thick legs pointing into the suffused, city sky. And beyond that? All the little houses.

The bus drove down a long straight road, rain-washed, lit with orange sodium lights. At each stop people got up, easing their shopping bags down the stairs. The bus passed the houses on a level with their bedrooms; from the upper deck Claudia could see the windows, dark as yet, for the evening was early. When he ran away with Beth, from what was Adrian running?

'What are you smiling at, then?'

The conductor sat down on the seat in front of her. He had finished his fares.

I am smiling at the words. Run away. What could be less like running away than Adrian's weeks of thoroughly sorting out his paperwork, his painstaking fairness? *Nothing in his marriage became him like the leaving of it*. He had never been a mean man but neither had he been over-generous. He had always been conscious of the value of objects – indeed, this had been one of his traits that Claudia had found both useful and dispiriting, depending on circumstance. But there he sat, settling electricity bills, ringing up the bank, writing out a cheque for her television rental twelve months in advance. He had made a lengthy list of the objects that they shared but he had taken few of them, leaving her his desk, his stereo, countless things that by rights he should remove. All this meekly, methodicially. Beth had made a better man of him. Or perhaps she had just found an Adrian that Claudia had long ago forgotten to seek, or no longer had the power to summon.

No doubt guilt had helped. Guilt had stirred his generosity and made him emotional, for he was by nature an undemonstrative man. Stirred, too, an almost trembling appreciation of herself, his wife. Looking up from his desk, pen poised: 'Claudia, I can't tell you how terribly grateful I am. You know, at the way you're taking this.' His tone loving, even passionate. She had surprised him, she had surprised herself, this new Claudia; smiling, understanding.

11

'I'm not smiling,' she said.

'Bleeding night like this, don't blame you. Best thing, draw the curtains, switch on the telly and snuggle down with someone nice.'

'This is my stop,' she said, rising. 'You married?'

'For my sins. Two kiddies, little bruisers. And you?'

'No,' she said. 'No kiddies.'

TWO

'Twist my arm,' said Vincent Crosbie, 'and I'll take six. Only for you, mind.'

'Be a devil and make it a dozen. Look, it's got a lovely little atomiser.'

'Steve, they won't buy it. Not round here. Not at £4.50.'

'The atomiser's thrown in.' Steve pointed to the cardboard presentation pack. 'It's part of our launch, see. Four for the price of three, special for Christmas. Got you this lovely display stand here. Then there's the back-up, the whole *Liberesse* range – sprinkler talc, body lotion, skin dew, bath gel –'

'Bit funny, isn't it, that French name? I mean, they can twig to *Reverie* and *Amour*.'

'And then the cosmetics, Vince – Two-Tone Blusher, Hardly-There Foundation, Come Closer Lip Gloss –'

'What's it mean anyway?'

'Go on, Vince. It's your new woman, isn't it. *Liberesse*, your liberated lady of the eighties. She's going to go mad about this.' He lifted the display stand with its grainy, soft-focus photo. It showed a girl sitting on a packing case; she wore khaki combat gear, the shirt unbuttoned to the waist, the trousers rolled up to reveal two slender tanned legs. *Liberesse*, it said. *It's Not Just Yourself You'll Be*

12

Changing. 'Seemed to think you liked it at our show. Must've been the free liquid refreshment.' Steve shook his head. 'What we do for you lot, I don't know. Fill you up with Carlsberg Specials and what do you say? Half a dozen. I'm telling you, Vince, this'll go down a bomb.'

'Don't talk to me about bombs. Read about that rally they had just down the road? They –'

'See, Vince, we're spending over half a million on Christmas promotion. Magazines, TV, the lot. You've got to get the stock in. Remember, it's November in a couple of weeks. They'll be pouring through the door.'

'Bet they won't look like that.' Vincent gazed at the photo. 'Wouldn't mind a few skirmishes with her.'

Vincent Crosbie ran a small chemist's business behind Lewisham High Street; he had the stance of a man who has witnessed, day after day, the gulf between dreams and reality. On all sides the cardboard temptresses crowded in, tiers of them. Through thickly-fringed lashes they gazed at him, half-smiling, as he stood behind his counter. They were the sensual sharers of his working hours. Over their rows of pots and tubes their moistened, crimson lips were parted. Then the bell pinged, the door opened and it was old Mrs Philpot come in for her suppositories.

'All right, all right, Sunny Jim,' said Vince. 'Just to keep you happy I'll take twelve. Don't know where I'll put them . . .'

'No problem.' Steve moved swiftly.

'Hey, don't you move my Elizabeth Hard-Ons. Sell a lot of those.'

'Trust me, Vince. Look, if we just shift them to the left. Plenty of room.'

'Careful with my Max Factors. You reps are all the same.'

Steve stepped down from the window ledge. At that moment the door opened and a customer entered. Steve moved aside. Vincent took the piece of paper the woman

13

gave him. He inspected it, scratching his nose, his scalp, again his nose. He had the seedy air of someone permanently under par; never quite ill but suffering from the very same minor discomforts – flaky scalp, eczema-pickened skin, halitosis – that his bottles should prevent. While Vincent was busy Steve inspected the display stands. Pintaubaum International, formerly just a fragrance house, had branched out into cosmetics, first with its teenage *Diana* then its *Liberesse* range, and the competition was fierce. Packaging, presentation, marketing, it all depended on that. Steve cast his eye over the rivals – Revlon, Coty, Mary Quant. Neatly-slotted products, fronted by a row of little smudged testers. One stand had the lipsticks slotted into a mounting zig-zag, pilgrims working their way up the plastic hillside to the goddess face at the summit. Across her forehead the cardboard was creased.

Steve opened his dispatch case and produced his order forms. He shifted on to the other foot. Vincent had gone into his dispensary. It was connected to the shop by a window. Crosbie, grave in his white coat, moved to and fro, reaching for a bottle, bending down, moving out of sight. A faint rattle as he measured out the pills. His face reappeared, intent; from this distance his inflamed skin was not apparent. Trained in cosmetics, Steve had no knowledge of pharmaceuticals; after three years in this job it could still intrigue him, the change that came over someone like Vince when he stepped into his shrine. There were shelves of tinted bottles with Latin labels. Housewives waited seriously while their alchemist, their Lewisham medicine man, got to work.

Vincent was back. 'Where have we got?' He scratched, thoughtfully, the crimsoned lobe of his ear.

'Just looking at your aftershaves. Your *Monsieur Pintaubaums*.' Steve indicated the packets on the shelves. 'Moving all right?'

'Mister Pointy-Bums? Sluggish, very sluggish. See,

14

we've got the *Brut* here at £2.45 and the *Old Spice* at £2.50. Yours are blooming pricey, Steve.'

'They're class stuff, that's why. Vince, wait till you see our special Christmas offer. This other stuff's pathetic.' He took something out of his dispatch case. 'Take a look at this, Vince. You saw it at our show. Very distinguished, very male. Our *Monsieur Pintaubaum* Pochette.'

Steve held it out. Tied with a drawstring, it was a little bag made of the thinnest, supplest beige leatherette. 'Isn't it lovely? Give it a feel. There's 10 ml. of splash cologne in there.' He took out the display holder: *Give Him A Christmas Neither Of You'll Forget*. 'You can hang ten on this; twelve at a pinch.'

Vincent held the small, dangling bag. 'Still, can't be worse than some of the other rubbish. Seen this?' He reached down something from a shelf. It was a stout pink deodorant with a knob-like top. *Nudge*, it was called. 'I ask you. Never knew you could do *that* with 'em.'

'Know what we're working on?' Steve paused, then lowered his voice. 'Vibrating mascara.'

Vince looked at him sharply, then relaxed. 'Yes, well, I wouldn't put anything past you lot.'

'Twenty pochettes, right? We're doing this fantastic pochette slot on Capital Radio.'

'Steve, there'll be no call for it. They're all wogs and welders around here. Imagine one of them with this hanging from his finger.' He paused. 'Ten, then.'

Half an hour later, business concluded, Steve picked up his case. As he moved towards the door a familiar figure entered.

'Well, well.' Vince looked up. 'The man from the Launderette.'

Steve stood back to let him pass. Ray worked for Estée Lauder; between himself and Ray, as between himself and the other agency reps who covered this area (South London, into Kent and Surrey), Steve felt both companionship

15

and rivalry. After all, he shared more with them than he shared with the reps on his own firm, whom he saw only at six-weekly intervals when they reported back to base. With Ray and his like, Steve shared the same fume-filled high streets, the same back-alley parking meters. At different hours of the week they straightened their ties outside the same Boots window displays – summer's racks of suntan oil, winter's furry hot water bottles. They made their way through the same dawdling housewives who would soon go in to buy. They shared the same frustrations – Dulwich's dour Mr Cox who was always out to lunch, the Underwoods manageress who got their names wrong, the standing for hours while the customers were served, Lambeth with its double yellow lines and wardens clinging to the cars like wasps, the Camberwell congestion which had them tapping the dashboard, four more calls to make before they could knock off.

Half past ten. Steve walked past the shops, *Sunny Isle Discs* with its thumping reggae, *Miss Sophisticate* with its racks of nylon nighties that brushed his arm as he passed. Yet he felt rivalry too, for the repetition of his own scene once he himself was absent – Ray moving back the Pintaubaum stand, Ray being handed *Nudge* by a sorrowing, scurfy Vince.

'It's enprints I want,' said the woman, 'two of this one and two of this one wherever it is.' Black negatives fluttered to the floor. 'It's a lovely likeness. He's wearing his sailor suit and all. And then there's a couple Bill wants nice and large.'

Mr Patel indicated the board of Kodak samples. Both in colour and black-and-white, they depicted happy scenes: two little girls in party hats, a beribboned kitten, an olde worlde cottage burdened with Kodachrome roses. Steve, by nature an optimist, gazed at them as he waited.

'Hang on, there's another one here.' She rummaged in

the envelope.

Vincent would have glanced at Steve over the bent head and wiggled his eyebrows. Mr Patel was too respectful for this. 'Myself, I hail from Bombay,' he once told Steve. His moist brown eyes held such sadness. Dispensing his medicines, he passed over the counter the bottled mysteries of the East.

She paused, considering. 'I'll have two little girls, then, and an Alsatian.'

'I beg your pardon?'

'Two the size of the kiddies,' she explained slowly; after all, he was a darkie. 'And one like the dog.'

Mr Patel gazed at her with his treacly eyes; he wrote out the processing order. Steve had only been married a year and he was always photographing June; he leapt around the flat, popping flashbulbs, crouching, poised, like David Baily. 'Steve, don't,' she would say, hand going to her hair, face already stiffening into a smile. 'Don't. I haven't got my make-up on.' 'Cool, baby, that's cool.' His voice clipped, mid-Atlantic. 'Jesus sweetie, that's just so *right*,' flinging himself to the ground, rolling over, Praktica clamped to his eye. 'Wow, you're beautiful.' Indeed she was – willowy; lovely long blonde hair. 'Steve, you're scuffing the settee.'

'Yes, Mr Mullen?'

The chemist turned. Even after three years it was all your Mr Mullens and Mr Patels here; during the very first visit, in fact, Steve knew which it was going to be. He clicked open his case and drew out the *Liberesse* presentation pack. Its photograph gazed up at him. He glanced from the combat female on the packing case to the elderly sari-clad lady who was sitting beside the stockroom door. Draped in mauve rayon, she had sat there, it seemed, since time began. Mr Patel's mother or his wife?

Steve adjusted his patter. No, not patter; he meant every word. To be precise, when he was speaking it he meant every word. (This had got him into some complications in

17

the past, what with girls and things. One called Gloria, sobbing into her Bacardi and coke: 'Steve, I can't believe you any more. Not now I've heard about *her*.' Raising her streaming face. 'You don't love me.' 'I do, I do.' When I'm with you, I do.)

Just now he believed every word he was telling Mr Patel, though the words were different from those he had used with Vince an hour earlier. *Liberesse* is so fresh, he said, so feminine. Still, as the perfume altered with the differing skins upon which it was sprayed, so for Steve it altered with each face he was addressing. He could make it anything; in the heat of the sell he could become anything. 'Steve, you could flog the last half of your Spam sandwich,' said Bruce, who covered Herts and Beds. 'Know why? You're so blooming charming and passionate.' After all, underneath the ribbed, frosted or tinted glass it was all the same – a few drops of this, a few drops of that.

Steve loosened his tie. He pressed his nose against the glass and gazed at the little fishes.

They swam to and fro, a shoal of tetras; they turned with a flick of their silver bellies. It was quiet in the shop, so quiet that the lorries outside seemed very far away, seemed in another city. As he gazed into the bright water, he heard the muffled grinding of their gears.

The shop was dark; its windows were so dirty that, outside, the pedestrians were shifting smudges. None of them paused to enter. Only the windows of the little aquariums were polished. Steve watched the tetras; tiny, translucent, they hung in the water, only their fins flickering. They were so frail that he could see the darker, bunched beating within. Then a flurry; they darted, turned, then again hung suspended, shimmering, trembling against the swaying ribbons of weed.

Steve straightened up. In the interior of the shop nothing moved except for the fishes and the pumping bubbles in the

18

six aquariums. Mr Sims was sitting behind his desk, probably reading. He was as motionless as the fan-shaped corals and the lumps of granite on the shelves behind him; an old man of the rocks. Beside him, glass-fronted drawers held gravel tinted red and blue.

(Boots, Steve's last call – jostling shoppers, flustered girls in puce nylon overalls, no corals there but sponges, *Squeeze Me* sponges wrapped in cellophane.)

The man looked up. 'Anything this time, sir?'

Steve loved this shop, he was humbled by it, the Boots people three doors up the road would not recognize him.

'A neon,' he said. 'Just the one.' He came here every month, regular as clockwork, every time he visited the Beckenham Boots. The old man got to his feet. This shop would never change; no promotion lines here, no thrusting marketing strategies. On the stand of booklets, the yellowing copy of *Enjoy Your Guppies* would always be priced at three shillings and sixpence.

When Steve left the shop it was dusk. He had finished for the day. Holding, very carefully, his small plastic bag, he crossed the road. On the opposite side stood *Rediffusion Rentals*. The big colour consoles were switched on, the screens flickering. Bright rectangles, bright as the fish tanks but they looked inane, faces mouthing silently. There were three different channels going on at the same time. On one a man held up a packet. The TV was faulty, he swayed as if under water; ripples ran up and down his body, his pointing hand rippled, his grinning, seller's face shifted and swayed.

THREE

No, no kiddies. Claudia switched on the light. The armchairs were illuminated; the sofa and the dead TV. Now that there was nobody else to pick things up and put things down the flat seemed as static as a stage-set. Down the corridor lay the far, unlit kitchen where her breakfast bowl would be waiting in the position she had left it that morning. Here in the living-room there were three cigarette ends in the ashtray and a biro on the floor. Unless she herself did something they would presumably remain for ever facing her with her past actions, the smoking of three Rothmans, the dropping of a ballpoint. When married she had seemed so independent. When married it was easy. In fact, in all her thirty years she had never lived alone.

Before Adrian there had been Verity, who dated from schooldays. They had shared the flat, which Claudia owned. It occupied the ground floor of a Victorian terraced house. Outside there was stained glass around the front door and a privet hedge, but inside it had been enlarged with an extension through the kitchen to the garden at the back. Had Adrian resented her owning it? Now it seemed too big for one, the passage too long with its five closed doors – bedroom, bedroom, boxroom, bathroom, lavatory.

She looked around the living-room. He had taken away little. Even so, the room looked curiously characterless. She had shifted her pot plants to hide the gaps in the bookshelves (*Wisden's Cricketer's Almanacs* he had taken; books on management accounting and on wine). Still, there seemed a lack. She had not yet claimed this place, made it hers rather than theirs. At present it had the poised, dispossessed air of a hotel room. Adrian had departed but she herself was not fully back in occupation.

Vacancy in the room, in herself. There were many things about the past few weeks that she could not have predicted. One was the speed of events, once the secret was out; their marriage, transformed suddenly into public property, had been caught up in a quickening tempo of telephone conversations, of startled queries, that had hastened its own dissolution. Another was the way in which she herself was left empty and undefined. The flat was easy to solve. Claudia paused at the door, gazing at the living-room. On Saturday she would paint the walls a different colour, rearrange the furniture. She could even throw out some stuff she had been meaning to get rid of and buy some more.

But what about herself, this partly-inhabited body that henceforth might be known as Claudia Cockshutt? It dressed itself and went to work, it dropped pencils and eventually picked them up again, it appeared remarkably brisk and bright – indeed, friends and colleagues had hinted at this, admiringly. But she had not yet caught up with it.

Claudia went into the bathroom; she turned on the taps and filled the basin with water. She scrubbed at her face, raising it to gaze in the mirror. Beneath the soapy skin, who was in residence? She knew the face, it was strong, blunt and freckled. It had a full rounded chin with full pale lips; at school the teachers thought she was sucking sweets. Around it grew brown hair – reddish when it caught the light. But beneath this, who? If only Adrian knew – as neither did then – how he had given her shape. How pleased he would be – he, who had always considered himself so powerless. She had not realized it then either. Too late to tell him now.

21

She dried her face and picked up the paper bag from Boots. All she had meant to buy was a tube of toothpaste; she had ended up producing her chequebook. Ah, those packages, rows of them, shelves of them sheeny with cellophane, promises, promises. Be a Wood Nymph, be the Girl Next Door, be a Woman About Town, be the Woman He Never Knew He Knew, be Innocent with a Hint of Sensuality, be Sensual with a Hint of Innocence, be Fresh, be Subtle, be Frosted, be Glossy, be Someone Special, Because You're Unique, You're a Woman, You're *You*.

Had Adrian felt it, the almost honeymoon atmosphere of the last few weeks of their marriage? They had drunk a good deal, working their way through Adrian's best claret, stored in the boxroom under the mutual clutter – the suitcases, the two-person tent which it was becoming wistfully, boozily apparent that they would never again share. Towards Claudia he had seemed alert in a way he had not been for years, returning promptly from work, glancing up when she moved around the room, talking at length about his feelings – an indulgence, this, that he had denied himself for the entire seven years they had been together. It seemed ridiculous that they had so much to say and that neither of them had ever said it. The television had remained switched off; his file of marketing strategies had remained closed away in his briefcase. Later she had tried to explain it to Verity. 'Remember what it was like when the exams were over that last summer? The way there were no rules – the way we wandered into labs and classrooms we'd never gone into before?'

And bed. There had been some hesitation about the spare room but finally they had climbed into their double bed as usual, Adrian tactfully placed well over on his side. Humble, thoughtful, pyjama-striped back. She had reached for him; he had lurched around, holding her, clinging. His passion had surprised them both; her body moved

22

in new ways for this new man. Afterwards he had buried his head in the pillow, and when he raised it his eyes were streaming with tears. For years he had done nothing afterwards but fall asleep, heavily. For a long while she had gazed at his face – his blurred face, for she, of course, was crying too.

Next morning, muttering into his shaving mirror: 'Sorry about that.' Was he ashamed of his passion or of his tears? Or had he just thought her body was Beth's? Perhaps she, Claudia, had been using him, making her body a final demonstration of all he would miss. Was it exciting, his limbs being touched and made strange by Beth?

Questions swam around her head nowadays. She had no one towards whom she would point them and find, even in her own speech, an answer. Living alone, she was discovering, meant she seldom heard the sound of her own voice and so her thoughts drifted, transparent and elusive. Only speech could make them solid and able to be handled.

When she was sixteen it had all seemed so clear. During that summer she was still at home. Her sister left for college; Claudia moved into the attic bedroom she had always craved. It was a large, redbrick house on the outskirts of a Kentish commuter town; from certain windows fields could still be glimpsed. Claudia was inward and adolescent; she spent most of the time in her slanting room. From her bird-like vantage point under the eaves she viewed her parents with a new detachment. Downstairs on the sunny square of landing, her mother, loaded with sheets, crossed to and fro between ironing-board and airing-cupboard. She was an intelligent woman and had been offered a place at Bedford College, but the war had come and then two children. In the evening Claudia's father returned from the City. The murmurs in the hall were no longer the voices of her parents but of two middle-aged adults. From above, their hair was grey.

She had realized several things. Her mother (Claudia saw this one day, with a thud), her mother was more intelligent than her father. She had a quick brain; she explored her children's homework books wistfully, eagerly, whereas Mr Cockshutt descended heavily twice a year to demand information about marks. When the children were older she started part-time work. This she enjoyed. 'Something to amuse Anne,' said Denis Cockshutt. 'Don't need the money, of course, but keeps her busy.' When the company expanded and she was offered full-time work, his surprise that she wanted it, his barely-concealed dismay, had buried the idea.

At sixteen, Claudia had deeply disapproved of him. Typically English, typically male, the way he combined an utter dependence upon his wife (without her he would die) with an equally profound refusal to take her seriously.

In August she listened to the swallows twittering outside her window; soon they would be flying south. Below in the kitchen came the clatters of cooking; from the front room the murmurs of the Test Match. The rattle of the tea trolley as it made its way from the back of the house to the front.

No, not for her, this baking of scones for the heavy, presuming male hand. Not for her, any of this. Outside an expanse of blue sky, looped with vapour trails.

And indeed it had been her very independence, her inability to serve and dote, that had first attracted Adrian. There she stood, tall and slender, her reddish hair long then and piled up. She had a man's job in the printing world. She had her own souped-up Spitfire whose tyres she could change without eager masculine aid.

'You make me feel so redundant,' Adrian had said that first time, fidgeting on the pavement. But he had been smiling; he found it piquant, her knowledge of mechanics. ('You make me feel so redundant,' he had said, six years later but not smiling now, standing at the mantlepiece

24

fingering the clock. 'You know, Claudia? You make me feel like your damned lodger.' She had jumped up and put her arms around this stocky man, his head hanging.)

No, at the beginning he had respected her for this.

'Marry me, marry me,' he had said.

'Why, when we can sleep together? Mmm, that's nice.'

'Claudia, you're not listening. Marry me.'

'Don't sit up, you're taking all the sheet.'

'Don't you understand?'

'Hey, you've got a little mole here. Anyone notice it before? Why?'

'Why? Because I love you. Claudia, I'm thirty-two.'

'I'm twenty-two. So?'

'So, I want you. Before anyone else gets you. I want all of you, I want to keep you –'

'Keep me?'

'Well, not keep you. You know what I mean. Just *be* with you – Claudia. Don't do that, you're putting me off. Just be with you all the time. Be here.'

'You can be here. Darling, darling, move in. You know Verity's getting married.'

'I don't want to be your lodger, I don't even want to be your lover. I want to be your husband.'

'Adrian, we're so happy like this.' It was a Saturday afternoon. 'Better than shopping in Tesco's.'

'Claudia darling, for goodness' sake.'

'I don't *want* you to make an honest woman of me – hey, don't get up.'

This conversation was repeated, with variations, in restaurants, in Adrian's flat, in his car, in her car. Once, while waiting at traffic lights:

'Claudia, this is ridiculous.' He sat beside her, staring at the red light. 'What do you want me to do – shout at you, drag you off? I'm so pathetically craven.'

'No, I like you are you are.' She revved the powerful motor under her foot.

'You women don't know what you want. You pretend you're all liberated – what you really want is some jack-booted thug to hurl you onto the cobblestones.'

'Mmm.'

'*Claudia*. Should I do that rather than sit here begging?' The lights changed to green. 'I want to marry you and give you children.'

'You want to fill me up like a balloon and then I'll never run away. Adrian, I love you and I love my work, don't you see?'

'We'll put off the children. I'll force you to take your pill.'

'Verity had a horse once that got ill. She gave it a bucket of carrots with a pill hidden in one of the carrots. It ate the lot and then after about ten minutes it spat out the pill – *psst* – with a smug look. It had kept it in the corner of its mouth all the time.'

He paused. 'There you are. You see, you really want a child.'

She changed into fourth gear. 'I don't, really I don't.'

(Ah, but the irony. Seven years later and she threw away her little foil card. That night he had come home and told her about Beth. Irony or coincidence?)

He needed her, this solid man. He was handsome; she took pleasure in looking at his kind, broad face and feeling his sandy hair. Over several months he concentrated all the energy in his packed, meaty body upon her. She needed him too, but more casually; at some point she might find herself slipping from him. In public Adrian was one for the proprieties; yet one night, in a Battersea kebab restaurant they frequented, he broke down and cried in front of the waiters, sobbing under the strings of plastic peppers. By nature a stiffish, passive man, his love made him alive and articulate, persuasive. He blossomed *in extremis*, he was at his best. He took her to concerts, he neglected his parents, his work suffered.

One summer's day she was conquered – less by him, it appeared at first, than by a pollen count of 190. She lay flat in her garden, her eyes streaming. He was sittting on her bikini'd rump rubbing Cooltan into her skin.

'I wish I could make you cry,' his voice above her head, 'like your flowers do.'

She sneezed into a Kleenex. Tissues lay scattered on the grass like scrumpled roses. 'You're too nice, Adrian. Nicer than me.'

'I'd make someone a wonderful wife. I can cook, you know.'

'I know.' She blew her nose.

'I'm a demon with a Hoover.'

'Darling, I know.' She preferred him like this, making light of it.

He rubbed cream into her shoulder blades, down her back, working it in. He did it in a dogged way, loving but unsuggestive. He said: 'Who else could be so thorough? Look, I'm even doing your elbows.'

Who else, indeed, would bother? He squeezed the tube and spread the Cooltan over every inch of her skin, usefully and carefully. Likewise in the least dramatic of ways he was spreading himself into her life. He had acquainted himself with her parents and even with her great-aunt Edie in Harrogate, where he sometimes went on business. He was always available, ferrying her friends across London and running errands. He was the man who remembered birthdays, who took the photos and actually sent copies to those featured in them; he was around. Gradually people, including Claudia, presumed him to be there; he became part of their evenings and weekends. He told Claudia it was because her friends interested him, anything about her interested him, and besides he had few friends of his own. Whatever the reason, he seeped into her life as the sun's rays were then, in the hot garden, seeping into her skin.

Claudia twisted her head and looked up at Adrian. He

was still sitting on her, in an unaccustomed position of superiority. He wore large, metal-rimmed sunglasses.

'You really ought to go indoors,' he said. 'Look, you're streaming.'

'I won't.' Hayfever would not beat her.

'Your eyes are all puffed up.'

She sneezed, loudly, wetly. She said, her voice muffled in Kleenex: 'You couldn't love me like this. Nobody could.'

'Right. You're quite a sight.' His head was against the sun; she could not see his expression, only the frames of his glasses glinting. Despite his bare torso they gave him a commanding, military look, like a holiday-making colonel. She lay there, humbled.

Then she heard his voice, mild as ever. 'You know, you could still have lovers. I'd let you, if only you would marry me.'

'Christ, Adrian!' She sat up, her watery eyes smarting. 'Stop being so sweet and reasonable and *soft*.'

'Soft? Soft? You're an idiot, Claudia. Prefer me like this?' He grabbed her shoulders and pushed her back on the grass. 'Like this better, do you?' He wrenched down the straps of her bikini, pulling them off her breasts. He pressed her down amongst the scattered tissues.

'Hey, that hurts!' Ah, but her blood surged.

'Like it, do you?'

'No, no.' Yes, yes. Ashamed, inflamed, she pulled him down against her; between her legs his swimming trunks were hard.

She fumbled at them, pulling at their elastic waistband. But Adrian rolled off. 'Oh Claudia.' His voice was muffled. 'Claudia, don't disappoint me.' Still she could not see his face.

He sat up, took off his sunglasses and rubbed his eyes. She drew up her straps. He took out a Kleenex and blew his nose; perhaps *he* was getting hayfever now.

Then he laughed shakily. 'Anyway, what would the

28

neighbours say?'

At the end of that hot, hayfever summer Claudia had married Adrian. Despite her seeming insouciance she loved this kind man. As he reminded her often, deprecatingly, he was indeed ten years older than herself. She did not mind. The younger men of her acquaintance seemed by contrast smooth and unused, insubstantial and fidgety. She liked a man with years behind him, who could look at her straight and admit his love.

FOUR

Marrying a girl as pretty as June, Steve had presumed that at some point he would cease to be surprised by her looks. Soon, surely, he would no longer glance up when she pushed a strand of hair behind her ear. Through sheer habit he would start to take her for granted; at some point she must look plain.

Before the wedding they had not lived together. They had managed to spend the odd, whole night, but those few times her face in the morning, lips blurred by love-making, cheeks flushed, eyes still spiked and darkened by make-up, had a temporary and lawless look. What would happen when habit set in, when as a wife she would be there all the time, when she would start to believe in nighties instead of nakedness, and thorough cleansing before she stepped into bed?

This had indeed been the case. Before the bouquet had withered in its silver foil June had reverted to what he realized was her normal routine, closing the bathroom door on him and, with a clatter of pots and the wheezing sigh of the mirrored cabinet, divesting her face of its daytime tinted layers. She had hid her scrubbed skin, nestling against him, but he had found the face on the morning

29

pillow lovely, her opening eyes pale and child-like, her skin like ivory. This bare face was his alone, the secret he shared with June. 'You're not so pretty,' he had said, running his finger over her dewy forehead, 'but, hey, you're beautiful.' He could see the palest fuzz along her jaw; disarming, the faint, smudgy freckles over the bridge of her nose. She had struggled from his arms to get to the bathroom. 'Steve, you're having me on.'

June was twenty-two. Her hair was long, pale and silky as a child's; it was rare to see such hair on a woman. Her face, too, was delicate as a child's, but sensual; achingly lovely, her head tilting down as she painted her nails, tilting up as she reached to pull off a piece of kitchen roll. A year of marriage, and though in some ways she herself had ceased to surprise him, her body still could – forever, it seemed. He could gaze at it as she talked.

She was talking now about her day at work. He sat beside her, a can of McEwan's in one hand, the other massaging the small of her back.

' . . . you see, Steve, I can't face it then, that early. None of us can. I always like to have a salad – they do nice ones in the canteen – cottage cheeese – but even a salad doesn't taste right at half past eleven. I mean, how could it?'

June worked in a big Oxford Street store; she was a cosmetics consultant. They had met this way.

' . . . so I asked Miss Finch and she said everyone had to take their turn with the early lunch hours. Steve, I wish you'd use a glass. Anyway, I kept on getting these awful migraine pains – you know, like last week – the real cramping ones and I was just longing for somewhere to sit down, only for five minutes, but you know we're not allowed to. . .'

'It's ridiculous, that. You ought to all organize yourselves and complain. I'm sure there's a law about sitting down.' It disarmed and yet annoyed him, June's helplessness in the face of authority. She never thought of doing

30

anything; he knew the majority of the human race was like this, shunted about wordlessly – well not wordlessly, complaining but complying. He felt, however, that his wife should demand more. He did not want her to be like the others.

'. . . so anyway, Steve, it was just one of those days. And a rude woman brought back her mascara because the wand had broken, and another one kicked up a fuss because I'd given her the wrong change, you know we've got these new tills in, all computerised, and then there were all those Arab ladies not knowing what they wanted and trying to bargain . . . you see, Steve, I'm not really hard enough. It was better before, when I was working on the general counter. Sometimes I just can't cope. They only gave me the job because I looked all right . . .'

'Poor Juney.' He could feel her slender shoulderblades, the ribs down her back. She was a bird trapped in the frailest wickerwork cage. He rubbed her, feeling the soft wool, the knob of her bra-strap. He thought: I can never get enough.

'. . . so I said to myself, I've had enough.'

Steve's hand paused. 'What?'

'I've had enough, I've given in my notice. I told Miss Finch I was packing it in. I never thought I'd do it.' She turned and gazed at him. 'Steve, do you mind? After all, you've always said that now we're married we don't really need the money.'

'So you're not getting another job?' Steve felt the faint stirrings of unease. Not just about money – though to tell the truth it was useful.

'I mean, I've been working ever since I left school.' She paused. 'I'm married now.'

Steve relinquished her and walked over to his aquarium. His neon tetra remained in its bag, suspended in the water to equalise the temperatures. 'But June – I mean, you can't spend all day alone in the flat. You'll be so bored.' He

31

gazed at the fish; it swam round and round its little plastic bag. 'June, what will you do?' Sometimes it bumped against the sides, thinking it could swim clear.

'Care for you.' She came up behind him and put her soft woolly arms around his neck. She had changed out of her regulation blue suit into a sweater and skirt. 'Keep everything as it should be. I've never really got this flat into shape. It's no good, just doing it the Saturdays.' Her hair tickled his neck. 'Cook your dinner. Steve, I've never really given us a proper home.'

Steve was quiet for a moment. He should feel pleased, shouldn't he? A lovely loving wife to welcome him home, a meal on the table.

He looked at her, at the red lips parted enquiringly. He had wanted her to model for *Liberesse*, they had needed a new face. She had refused; she would have none of that unbuttoning. Also the ugly men's clothes.

He did not reply to the red lips; he leant towards them instead, for that was simpler.

It was not just June's child-like translucence that made Steve feel protective in the months before their marriage. It was also Arnford Crescent, Orpington, where she was born and raised along with her three large, untranslucent brothers. Arnford Crescent was part of a council estate built in the thirties to serve the surrounding factories; the stucco semis were greyish now, with dark stains below the windows. Upon the flattened grass outside number twelve stood the dismembered motorbike belonging to Clive, the eldest brother, a muscle-bound greaser who would nod wordlessly when Steve parked his car and walked up to the front door, feeling over-spruce in his weekend clothes (suede jacket, Hush Puppies).

Inside, the house was cluttered; there were too many men for the small rooms. In front of the huge, veneered TV set June's father would be slumped. He drew a disability pension; wreathed in smoke he gazed at the screen, where at Kempton paddock the colts were circling skittishly. The brothers were always in and out of work, they were always at home propping up the doorways, playing their trannies, leaving their dinner plates on the sideboard, smears of brown sauce and pallid worms of bacon rind for June to tut-tut over when she came downstairs. June's mother, a pinched woman, toiled five days a week at the Sunlight Laundry, returning from the dirty clothes of the unknown to those of the only-too-familiar, stooping to lay newspapers over the kitchen floor and pause, humbly, while the men passed in their great boots. Steve, hovering downstairs waiting for June, would remember for ever the sounds – the quickening monotone of the racing commentator to his left, the Capital jingles to his right (*Barratts, Barratts, come to Barratts, Barratts Liquor Ma-a-art*), and upstairs the faint clunk of the iron as June pressed her dress, doggedly. June was always particular about her grooming. In her slip of a bedroom with its snowy net curtains she strived for gentility.

This masculine chaos with which she was surrounded lent her beauty an ethereal, princess quality. In such unlikely surroundings she seemed rare; she was his slender Venus rising not from a fluted shell but from a jumbled heap of Guinness empties and broken carburettors.

When Steve returned home the first day that June, herself, had stopped working, it was the muffled clunk of the iron that again greeted him. She was pressing her apron.

'Your *apron*. You can't.' He laughed, picking her up and swirling her round, causing her hastily to set down the iron. 'We're going to the pictures.' He kissed her face, flushed from its toils. 'I'll treat you to a Chinese Take-Away. Lovely leaky chop suey.'

To his horror her eyes filled with tears. 'Steve, how could you? Don't you remember? I said I'd make a special meal.'

33

'Sweetheart, I'm sorry. Hey, don't cry, you'll lose your contacts.' June refused to wear glasses. Half Steve's life was spent grubbing around on the carpet, a patterned Axminster, all black and orange swirls and scrolls which did not make it any easier.

'I've cooked Pork Paprika.'

'Mmm, my favourite.' Steve felt fond and stagey, sniffing appreciatively. He looked around the tidy lounge. 'Say, you've been busy.'

June had always been neat. When they met, he had been living in a bedsit. The first time he had brought her back there, she had stiffened against his bare chest. His eyes, following hers, had rested on the gas fire. Its cement surround was littered with fag ends, his vestigial reflex from the days of burning logs. As a fox might rub its scent around what were now safe suburban gardens, so he flung his butts into what remained, through some dark ancient prompting, an open grate. He was shamed by his loutish habits. No, not loutish – untended. He needed a girl like June. 'Tend me,' he had said, rolling her over on the rug. '*Steve.*' She had drawn back, alarmed that he was suggesting something nasty.

Tonight Steve gazed around the spotless room. His desk had been tidied. On top of the metal filing cabinet where he kept his customer records was a neat stack of magazines, gathered up from around the flat and from the lavatory where he liked to peruse them at his leisure. (*Motor Sport, Amateur Photographer, Aquarist and Pondkeeper*.)

'I've polished your swimming cups,' June said, 'and sorted out your bits and pieces.'

Steve's eyes darted around. Before today, when they had both been out at work, tidying up had been a shared Saturday occupation (well, he had fiddled around with his papers, admiring the way that June's apron, as she hoovered, nipped in her waist). Now she had all day to do it.

He paused. 'Junekins, where's my schooner?'

'Your model thing? I put it up there, and all the little bits I've put it in that box.'

Steve opened his mouth and closed it again. His schooner, an Airfix 8-master, was at a particularly delicate stage of its construction.

'Let's see the kitchen then,' he said. Perhaps she'd polished the vegetables in the rack. He wouldn't put it past her.

'Steve, why're you smiling?'

'Nothing.' There were some jokes he could not share with June. No, many jokes.

FIVE

Claudia slapped on the emulsion. It was Saturday and she was painting the bedroom. Behind her the furniture was jammed against the wall, the large bed shrouded. Its dust sheet was spattered, expressionistically, with paint from past redecorations; amongst the streaks she could recognize Forget-Me-Not, which for seven years had covered these walls and which was now being engulfed by her flicking brush. (Forget-Me-Not; together they had smiled at the blue Mix'n'Match colour card, dismissing Fathom and Bluebell.)

One wall was finished. She stood back. This shade was called, non-commitally, Tempo. It was oh so subtle – mushroomy, greyish, so tasteful it was hardly a colour at all. It changed according to the light and the time of day; this room could become anything. She could become anything.

And what, once married, had Adrian become? He had become less. That was the trouble really. Gradually as a husband he had changed from the Adrian of those ardent, uncertain months. He remained just as kind and just as sensible, but he settled into his armchair, he grew a little paunch. He became too comfortable to stir himself and poke the embers; the sweet, bitter, questioning days were over. Had marriage simply changed him into a middle-aged man?

Claudia lifted her brush; she hesitated. No, that was too simple. Marriage to him was an end rather than a beginning. She had not realized this at the time. During his wooing days he had blossomed; frustration gave him a voice. He bought books, he took her to the theatre and argued afterwards in smoky pubs, he questioned things in a way he seldom appeared to question them again. As a male bird in the mating season develops ruffs and colourful plumage, as it struts and bows and behaves in a generally uncharacteristic manner, so Adrian swivelled with verve at discos (places it turned out he loathed), drove too fast (normally he was a cautious man), made love to her in Greenwich Park (before their marriage, he did not notice how muddy his trousers became). She had thought: this is Adrian. It was sometime later that she realized this was not Adrian himself; it was an Adrian who was concentrating upon her – stimulated both by her and for her. Somewhere she felt a vague mixture of disappointment and claustrophobia.

Well, that was how she liked to see it all. Simpler to put the blame on him.

'Call that a colour?'

Mr Gunter came into the room. He stood in his overalls, scratching his sparse hair. 'Suppose you want me to start in here.'

'Kitchen's finished?'

'Some people might call it finished. All that plasterwork needs re-doing. Like to meet whoever botched that up.'

'My husband, actually.'

'Ever looked behind your cooker? All crumbling away.' He spoke with relish. 'Horrible mess.'

36

'Oh dear, I'm sorry.' Why was she apologising? 'Well, anyway, could you possibly start on that other wall there? You can have the nice brush.'

She waited, poised, for him to move. Mr Gunter was the local odd-job man; she had thought it would be more companionable, as well as quicker, to get in someone to help. In the past Mr Gunter and herself had got along all right; with Adrian somewhere in the flat she had parried Mr Gunter's caustic comments and greeted his rude remarks with ruder ones. Today, with no Adrian, she felt uneasy with this bald, overall'd man in her bedroom; she could not find her old tone.

'A left-handed lady, I see.'

Claudia concentrated on drawing the brush carefully along the junction between wall and ceiling. At least she could do this properly. She could paint a wall; she could go to the office and actually manage to work. But even then the ground had shifted just slightly under her feet. Nothing quite fitted; the sudden jolting end to her marriage had altered her memories of it, she could not trust them any more. If anyone had an affair, she had presumed it would be herself. It was not. For well over two years her husband – seemingly so mild, loving, dogged and faithful – had in fact been performing a painstaking and for him most painful series of subterfuges and lies about working late. Adrian of all people. If she could not trust him, whom could she trust?

Claudia, balanced upon her ladder, gazed around at her stripped and disrupted room. Its framed prints had been taken down and stacked in the corner; its shelves had been dismantled. There were clean, paler rectangles where things had hung, but already she could not remember which had been made by pictures and which by mirrors. And even her ladder was shaky.

'You're smudging it. Look, all along the edges. Should use a smaller brush up there.'

She paused, and went on painting. Mr Gunter's manner had been encouraged by his various employers who laughed at his jokes, indulged his fancies, and plied him with Guinness. The reason for this slavishness lay, of course, in the scarcity of good odd-job men – he was the last of a nearly extinct species – and the necessity for his retention. Plus a vaguer feeling of class guilt.

'Anyway, what's the old man doing not helping you?'

'Well . . . er, he's away,' she said.

'Leaving the missus to do all the work, eh? Someone's got the right idea.'

'It's my flat, anyway.' This was true; her husband had just arrived and left.

'Where's he gone?'

'Oh, Muswell H – I mean, up north, I think. Business.'

Why did she not tell him the truth? There were many people she had not told – Mr Gunter, the local shops, distant business acquaintances. She kept putting it off, partly out of dread for the mutual embarrassment such news would cause and the subsequent change in manner on both sides. Partly because circumstances might alter. (How? Adrian might return?)

'Suppose they call that king-size.'

'What?' She twisted round, balancing on her ladder. 'Oh, the bed.'

'Plenty of room, eh? Plenty of scope.'

'Oh by the way, could you possibly paint the radiators the same colour?'

'What, with this stuff? Supposed to have special paint. Won't last a week, emulsion won't.'

'I never have these radiators on anyway.'

'Ah.' He paused. '*Body heat*, eh?'

Claudia blushed. She had let herself in for that one. She heard a rattle of paint pots. At last, and thank goodness, Mr Gunter had given up and was thinking of starting some work.

Pushed against the wall lay the bed. Claudia gazed at its spattered shroud. In bed with Adrian, sometime during the week following her promotion. Production Manager of *Yours*. It was a great surprise; she had only been working at the magazine for a year. She was the youngest person, man or woman, ever to get that job.

A certain amount of twisting and turning under the sheets . . . then, nothing. 'Sorry,' he whispered, face buried in her hair. 'Don't know what's the matter with me.'

Her own voice, rather brisk. 'Never mind, darling.'

'I do mind.' His muffled voice.

'We're tired, we'll be lustful tomorrow.'

He had raised his head. 'Is that how you'll talk to your new subordinates? The tactful "we"?'

She should have realized then. But what could she have done, refused promotion, made herself less as her mother had? Besides, the trouble could not have been as simple as that.

At times she had tried. In the earlier years, anyway. After they had had – well, not a row, Adrian did not blaze and shout – but a talk along the lines of *You make me feel so redundant*. Such remarks had chastened her; humbled by this troubled man, she would for a few days care for him, scrub the kitchen floor, defer her problems and wait, mutely, for him to take longer over solving them than she would do herself. Overcome with fondness she would be disturbed at her inability to become a housewife, a wife.

'Pardon me for saying so, but you've forgotten that little bit in the corner.'

She tensed, paused for a moment and went on painting.

'Independent type, aren't we.' Mr Gunter moved away, coughing noisily. She heard a mutter, the clank of his paint pot as he put it on the radiator. He coughed again and spat, presumably into his handkerchief but she did not care to turn and verify this.

Rebuffed silence; some more nose-blowing.

Adrian, chatting to her as they painted this room; giving her the one new brush, beautiful in its cellophane hood, and using the caked old one himself.

She slapped on the paint; slap, slap, spreading beige.

SIX

It was sunny on deck. In fact, it was a remarkably hot day for October. Above Steve's head the rigging criss-crossed against a blue sky; when he ran his hand along the stern of the ship the wood felt warm. It was Saturday; Saturday made the sky a deeper blue, the far sounds further away and more echoing.

'*I must down to the seas again, to the lonely sea and the sky,*
And all I ask is a tall ship and a star to steer her by. . .'

He remembered little from school but he remembered this, warbling it now with his terrible singing voice:

'*I must down to the seas again, to the vagrant gypsy life,*
To the gull's way and the whale's way where the wind's like a whetted knife. . .'

'Wetted?' said June. 'That's a funny way of putting things. Even I know it's *wet*.' She paused. 'Steve, why are you squatting?'

Steve squinted up at her. 'From here, if you look over the sides you can pretend you're at sea.'

'Do get up.'

It was true. Though the *Cutty Sark* was embedded in concrete, surrounded by buildings, an empty bandstand, iron railings and mums and dads pushing pushchairs, from this angle he had a glimpse of the glittering waters of the Thames against the sides of the ship, with nothing in between.

He straightened up. 'Imagine, June. They were months away, years even.' He threw out his arms. 'All the way to Australia, all the way across the Pacific. She's a clipper ship, see. First she took tea, then later she took wool.'

'Steve, can we see where they went to bed?'

She followed him along the wooden deck; tap-tap went her white high-heels. He loved teaching her, showing her things. She did not know much, she was young, she was his. Sometimes at the weekend they went to museums, June clinging to his arm in the Ethnographical Section, squealing at the shrunken heads. He pointed them out to her; he was her lover, her teacher. She listened – sometimes she listened. More often, in fact, he felt her just looking at him as he spoke. Of course he was flattered by this. 'Steve, you're so clever – Winkie, how do you know it all?' Couldn't complain, could he? No man in his right mind could complain.

Today the ship was crowded; the autumn sun had brought people out of their homes. They strolled the decks and gazed up at the rigging. So tall, the three giant columns of the mast; it was like walking through a great cathedral with its vaulted, netted sky.

Steve when younger, and his mother reading the psalms. *'They that go down to the sea in ships, and occupy their business in great waters; these men see the works of the Lord, and his wonders in the deep.'*

'Ooh, it makes me dizzy,' said June, 'looking up.'

'Nimble lads, those. There's ten miles of rope up there. *Ten miles*, June. And with a gale blowing.'

But the ship no longer tossed, embedded in her final berth convenient to Greenwich High Street and available bus routes.

'This way, sweetheart. Hold the rail.'

They went down the steps.

'Steve, they're ever so steep.'

'Shouldn't wear those shoes.'

'Whoops.'

'Here, hold my hand.'

Steve bent his head as they entered the dark little cabin. 'Just feel this wood, June. Isn't it lovely?'

Everything was solid and polished – polished brass portholes, polished mahogany shelves. Everything fitted together, nice and secure.

'Hey June, makes a change from our little place, doesn't it. No tacky plywood here, no plastic toadstools. Just look at that solid little table.'

'Steve, you like them, don't you?'

'I love it. Love it.'

'Stevie, I'm so glad. They look so nice in the kitchen. When you made those rude remarks in the shop – you know – about plastic toadstools –'

'Ah.' Steve paused. 'I don't mean our banquette seats.' He had purchased these, under a certain pressure, the previous Saturday. 'I mean the cabin. I love this cabin.'

'*Steve.*'

'Look at it, June. Just take a butcher's.'

At the table sat a plaster seaman with a pipe in his mouth. Beside him sat his plaster dog; in front of him sat his mug. It looked satisfactory. Pipe, dog, mug – what else did the man need? What else did anyone need?

'It's a bit pokey, Steve. Such a tiny little window.'

'Porthole. I think it looks snug.'

'It's so dark.'

It was dark; everything brown, heavy, seasoned, gleaming. A man's room. Within its solid walls June appeared flimsy. She was wearing her yellow dress and her Easter Bunny cardigan – white and fluffy with a row of fancy buttons.

'What a tiny little bed, Steve.'

'Bunk. They were shorter then. I couldn't fit in it.'

'It looks so hard.'

'It was a hard life. They called the mattresses donkey's

42

breakfasts. Straw, you see.'

'Ever so narrow, too.'

'Couldn't fit you in, gorgeous. Though I bet they'd try.'

Dog, pipe, mug – what else did a man need? Outside a storm was blowing, rain lashing the decks. Scrape, scrape, an upturned bucket sliding to and fro on the boards above. In their bunks lay the men – short, leathery, yearning. Just then, a tip-tap, a stumble as she negotiated the steps in her spikey heels; a scent, not of salt air but of *Liberesse*, and there she would be: June in her Angora cardi.

'Steve, what's the matter? Open your eyes.'

They made their way out of the cabin and down to the 'tween-deck, where an exhibition was laid out in glass cases. This was the upper cargo hold. Where once small, tanned men strained and pushed the bales, there now strolled larger, paler husbands, accompanied by children and wives. At the approach of June the husbands grew alert; they moved nearer and interested themselves in the cases close to the one she was inspecting.

'Here's a diagram,' said Steve. 'Look, it shows you where they climbed down to the lower hold.'

'I've got a ladder.'

'What?'

'I've got a ladder. Steve, I only bought these tights yesterday.'

'We'll go down to the lower hold and I'll show you. It's empty now, of course.'

'Right up my leg. It must have been one of those nasty iron things. Look, Steve.'

The neighbouring, studious men shifted their position.

'Poor old Juney.' Steve led her past the sales desk. On display was a large box containing a do-it-yourself kit. *The Cutty Sark – Build a Legend In A Weekend*. Steve passed it by. Another three hundred plywood fragments to litter the carpet?

Indeed the lower hold, once packed with cargo, was

empty now. It was vast, a cavern roofed with curved beams as if one had been swallowed by a whale and were wandering down its ribbed interior. There was a sense of great peace down here. June and himself were alone, except, that was, for the row of painted wooden figureheads on either side, leaning out as if about to launch themselves into space.

'One woman,' said Steve. 'I was in love with her all through my youth.'

'Who?' June looked alarmed.

'Come here, I'll show you. When I was a lad I was always biking over here clutching my ps, but it was ds then. After I'd looked at everything I'd end up just gazing at her.'

'Steve, what do you mean?'

He led her along the row of figureheads. All of them were dressed – buxom, crinolined ladies or naval captains in full uniform. Only one was bare; simply painted white, her only colour was the green vegetation clinging to her hips.

'Amphitrite, goddess of the sea. Isn't she lovely?' White wooden breasts, white wooden eyes forever gazing out at something Steve could not see. Never would she spoil anything by speaking. Never would she fail to get the joke.

'Just for a moment, Steve, I thought you meant somebody real. The girl who took the money or something.' June gazed at the figure. 'She's a bit pudgy, isn't she?'

Steve gazed at the goddess. Upon her plump arms the paint was flaking; he could see the grain of the wood underneath. He paused. 'You're right.'

'Know something, Steve?'

'What?'

'I'd really fancy a Booster.'

'A what?'

'I saw the van outside. I mean, I don't usually have them, you know that, especially in winter, but it's so warm. . .'

'What's a Booster?'

'It's the red one. Sort of like a rocket, with ice-cream inside.'

Five minutes later she was licking it, carefully, thoroughly, with the absorption of a child. She removed it from her mouth.

'Sure you don't want one?'

Steve shook his head. She bent to lick, delicate yet greedy. A drop fell on her hand; with her tongue she licked it off. Though her fingernails were painted they were also bitten, she had never grown out of that. Child's hands, woman's hands. The afternoon was drawing to a close; long shadows slanted across the concrete; behind the *Cutty Sark* car doors slammed as people started for home.

'Looks nice though' he said.

She paused, her crimson lips parted. Her mouth was so dewy; into it she slid her long red lolly. Steve felt weak.

They were closing the ship. Within it was his white goddess, forever poised forward, forever gazing out with her blank wooden eyes.

'Did you like it?' he asked.

'Like what?'

'The ship.'

'Oh. . .' Her eyes, too, were blank. 'Oh yes.'

Already she had forgotten it.

Later, dusk, on the grass of Greenwich Hill.

'Steve, what are you doing?'

'Just checking your respiration.'

'*Steve*. Go on, do it up.'

'Hmm, all in order. Breathing nicely.'

'Steve, not *here*.'

'Any discomfort when I do this? No? Good.'

'*Steve*.'

'Just check your heart rate, shall we? Take a deep breath – one – two. . .'

'Steve, I said do it up.'

'Ah June, June. You're so soft here.'

'Steve, somebody might be looking.'

'Hey, it's pitch dark. Don't you like all those little lights down there? That's the Thames.'

'Anyway, it's ever so chilly.'

'*Look*. A shooting star.'

'Where? *Oh*, that's not fair.'

'June, you're so lovely. Know what's not fair?'

'What?'

'You being so prim. With a body like yours, it's immoral.'

'Steve, I said don't do that. You're sex mad.'

'I want to lick you all over like a lolly. Every inch.'

'Steve, you're getting grass stains on your trousers. They're your best ones.'

Steve sat up. 'Hey June, you weren't like this, once.'

'I'll soak them when we get home.' She paused. 'We're married now.'

'What's the difference? We used to do this all the time.'

'We had to, then. Now we can go home.'

'That's not the point. Where's your spirit, woman?'

'Don't you like our lovely bed?'

It was beautiful, and nearly the most expensive. They had tried them out in Selfridges, Steve flinging himself down on one after another, grinning up at June who hovered, pink-faced. Impassive, the salesman who watched them, accustomed to all of this, to bridegrooms larking about and going on about practical demonstrations; accustomed to the embarrassed ones easing themselves down on to the mattresses, shy couples lying rigid, clothed and parallel under the gaze of passing browsers and the fluorescent light. 'Come on June,' Steve had urged, turning to the salesman: 'Always a challenge, getting a bird like this into bed.' At last June had consented, unstrapping her shoes, taking his hand, lying on bed after bed obedient as a doll. They could afford a good one, Steve's yearly bonus just having come through and June getting her Christmas sales commissions. Wide and springy, their Slumberdown – wider and springier, for sure, than those hard little bunks down there in the darkened *Cutty Sark*.

'Oh dear, Steve. Now you're angry.'

'I'm not angry.'

'Yes you are.'

'I'm not. Just bleeding frustrated.'

'Oh all right, Steve. If you want to. . .'

'My God, June.' He lowered his voice, throbbingly. 'June my darling, have we come to this?'

Despite the B-movie voice, they had indeed come to this. June did up all the little fancy buttons and they walked across the grass – June was right, it was on the chilly side – back to the waiting car.

'*At the approach of spawning, there will be noticed amongst both males and females a heightened colour and general state of agitation. The females present a more distended appearance, owing to the bulk of the roses. Also to be noticed* – hey Juney, listen to this – *also to be noticed amongst the females is a more tense demeanor.*'

'What's that? It's terylene, you see, so I don't know if this soaking will help really. Look at the water, Steve, I put in that new stuff they show on the telly. Biological.'

'*The spawning itself is accompanied by vigorous pushing and nuzzling of the plants and gravel, with occasional halts. This may go on for some time. The mating pair remain side by side, vibrating. . .*'

'I was thinking, Steve, perhaps I shouldn't have soaked them at all. Perhaps I should've sent them to the dry cleaners. You just can't tell with synthetics. Shouldn't touch water, some of them.'

'*. . .and with a certain quivering of the bodies, a group of eggs are extruded and fertilised.*'

47

'Ugh.' Arms in the washbasin, June stopped. 'How disgusting.'

'Hey, listen to this bit about the purple-headed barb.'

'I don't want to hear. I'm going to hang these up. I mean, they're very pretty but I don't want to know about their nasty habits.'

'The story of our life,' he murmured.

She lifted the wet trousers out of the washbasin.

'Here, let me help.' He closed the book and jumped up from the edge of the bath. He scrubbed the basin with a sponge. 'Give them to me, I'll squeeze them out.' He touched her cheek. 'I don't like to see you doing it all.'

'Steve, you're being very nice.'

'I'm a nice guy.'

'Then we hang them in the airing cupboard.'

Clutching the damp bundle, he followed her out into the passage. In fact, though he preferred to think that this eager helpfulness, this need to put June into a good mood, stemmed simply from his being such a nice guy, he had to admit that a certain part of it stemmed from his longing, as it were, to spawn. Indeed, there was a whole range of behavioural characteristics peculiar to his pre-spawning state. Not only could be noted his heightened agitation, his nuzzling of the female with occasional halts; there was also, beyond this, an unusual readiness to wash the dishes, to fetch June's cardigan, to notice and admire the way she had laundered the cushion covers, to listen, with sympathetic attention, to her telling him for the second time how Mr Mayhew downstairs kept moving his dustbin in front of theirs, how her food mixer was making a funny rattly noise and was it worth taking it down to Bensons Electricals when they were always so dear?

It was not put on, this. No no. He genuinely felt it, for the simple reason that June herself altered – in his eyes she altered, his desire altered her. Longing for her body, he found it charming, the way she had washed the lounge

48

curtains; thought-provoking, her views on the Kenwood Chefette. The way she bent over, ostensibly to pick a piece of his modelling putty off the carpet, yet seemed full of grace and suggestion, an echo in advance of the way that later that night she would move with him.

He opened the airing cupboard door. He pressed his face into June's clean, silky hair. He embraced her, leaning against the shelves of folded sheets. On the air was the chaste scent of laundered linen, fragrant as this slender girl – no girl, his wife – who must be stroked and coaxed.

'Close your eyes,' he murmured, moved by her, maddened by her. Close your eyes, my beautiful, sightless one . . .

Later, and June lying beside him, dozing on the disordered Slumberdown. So dozy, that although she had pulled up the sheet she had failed to cover one leg. It lay beside his spent, hairier body. Beside her slender limb his own appeared coarse; beside her white, manicured foot his own toes seemed yellow and horny.

And the bedroom; it looked so lacy. Frills everywhere. When had she patiently stitched – this last couple of housewifely weeks when she had been home all day? Perhaps she had been doing it for months and only now was he noticing. Yards and yards of broderie anglaise were creeping up on him; it was like nestling in a drawer full of underwear. He was sure he should have remarked on it; she got hurt when he didn't. She had trimmed the lampshade; Jesus, she had trimmed the Kleenex box cover. She had trimmed the dressing table, that lace altar to the June she so diligently wanted to give him. The window was looped and swathed in layers of nylon; across space she hung this multitude of veils, but who was to see them, up here on the fourth floor?

A week earlier he had asked June if she regretted leaving work. 'The shop? Oh no. You see, Steve, I wasn't very

49

good at it. I'm not like you, I'm not so good at selling. Better at buying really.' She had paused, her finger on the cookery tips page of her magazine. Gazing up, she had surprised him with her blush. 'I wanted to do something else. You see, Steve, I've never had a chance of that. I want to make a proper home. I *know* I'm good at that. They can sneer if they like.'

He had seldom heard her so eloquent. He had been moved by her words. And she was right, of course; she did do it well.

Steve felt swaddled; the central heating must be switched on high. He gazed at her smooth leg, at her smooth shoulder. It pleased him, that he could cause her to become dewy and disarranged, oblivious for a while that her mascara had smudged, forgetful – this was a mixed blessing – that she should be cooking his supper. She stirred and sighed. He felt so nearly happy, so nearly satisfied, that he did not care to notice the difference. Had it in fact been different once, those early days?

Early days in his bedsit; outside, the rumble of buses down in Ladbroke Grove. Beside the gas fire, June brushing her hair. She was wearing his enormous brown pullover. Her hair was so fine, so sparkling as she bent to brush. He had sat beside her on the rug; he had wanted nothing more.

June stirred. He rubbed her leg with his yellow toe. 'Remember Notting Hill?'

'How you stood that place,' a muffled murmur, 'I'll never know.'

June coping with chaos; hanging the damp dish-cloth out of the window, storing the Weetabix in the chest of drawers, sharing the clumsy and intimate mechanics of his life. June, creeping downstairs past the other rented rooms, down to the bathroom to insert her diaphragm. Out in the street the pubs closing, men shouting, cars revving up to drive to other destinations. He had wanted nowhere but that narrow bed and the creak of the lini'd stairs as June returned to him.

Nowadays of course the diaphragm was secreted, a few carpeted steps away, in the bathroom cabinet. He was not supposed to show that he knew. In a sense he knew her better then, their little awkwardnesses exposed.

His draughty bedsit, his universe. Here it was so stuffy; Steve shifted his shoulders. 'Hey June, what number did you put the central heating?'

She mumbled and turned on to her stomach, burying her face in the pillow.

'Remember your folks' house?' He spoke to the white ceiling. It had been good there, too. 'Remember having it off to *Match of the Day*?' They could hear it through the floorboards. Throwing off the blankets, scrambling out of bed when they heard the signature tune because then her brothers would be stomping upstairs.

June gave an annoyed grunt, either because she wanted to sleep or because such memories were not nice – the clutched sheet, the bald bottoms like a French farce.

'Hey June, it was nice.'

Snatched love had brought them together, what with their risky devices, their ruses to be left alone, their lawless lovemaking to the rhythmic soccer downstairs, their rigid clinging when, in Greenwich Park, a dog barked too close.

Steve gazed at the ceiling. Now he looked back on the erotic plots, he could see that June had actually been the blushing, passive partner – squirming, giggling, lustfully led. Still, she had been a partner; they had been in it together.

'Remember when they came back early from Spain and I had to squeeze out the bathroom window?'

No answer. June slept.

7.30 on a Saturday night; Steve felt wrong in bed, restless and disorientated. Hungry too. He got up, went into the kitchen and made himself, in a bachelor haze of burn-

51

ing fat, three fried eggs. He shook on the brown sauce, sandwiched them between hunks of bread, extracted from the fridge a can of beer and took it all back into the bedroom.

In his absence June had shifted. The blankets were pulled up around her head; she slept curled, nothing visible but tangled skeins of hair. His side of the bed was straightened; she had returned to herself, folding herself up like the laundered sheets in the airing-cupboard. Often she seemed like this; again a virgin, could she be reached by him – had he, in fact, ever reached her?

Steve sat in the upholstered armchair and balanced the plate on his knee. Silence in the room. He opened the McEwan's, *psst*. At least she could not see him drinking it out of the can.

What was she dreaming? Was it of places unknown to him, beyond this small and finite territory; landscapes far from the four walls of this loved and polished flat? Or was it of one long shopping list, painstakingly written in her round, childish hand?

She had known other places, chinks in the narrow alley of her past. The ticket to these countries was her slender body, the passport her lovely face. Men from all walks of life had taken her out. Approaching her counter for a Max Factor Gift Set, husbands would linger, fiddling with their Access card; finally bundling it into their wallet they would glance up with much throat-clearing and please-don't-think-I'm-in-the-habit-of-this. Arab playboys with white teeth and well-pressed slacks would be more direct, describing to her the charms of their Mayfair pad, suggesting an hour when their Audi could pick her up. Though choosy, and indeed prim rather than promiscuous, she had accompanied a variety of men to a variety of places; a minor TV personality had been infatuated with her, so had the drummer of a rock group. Where others must enter through graft, hard work, talent and long apprenticeships,

52

she had no trouble. Walls melted simply through the arrangement nature had given to her face.

She had learned a little, or tried to learn once or twice. She knew she was uneducated. When her current escort was a professor of history, she attended evening classes on the Crusades. This did not last. She did not have the concentration. But she had tried. Steve had been touched by her room at home with its two or three large books; she used them to prop up her paperback romances. *The Thinker's Treasury of World History*. 'I only got to page ten,' she told him.

June turned over, mumbling, and buried herself in the blankets. Steve bit into his sandwich – leathery, greasy egg, just right. June flinched at brown sauce, considering it coarse. Steve gazed at the humped blanket; by now, just a wisp of her hair showed at the top. Once, of course, he had been hotly jealous about her past boyfriends, probing her with questions, agonized, hypnotized. Sometimes he heard Dead Gristle on the car radio. His ears took in nothing but the throbbing beat of the drums; their suggestive and quickening tempo was intended for June, legs crossed in the passenger seat. Likewise with the TV announcer. Once a household name, he had recently been demoted to an off-peak-hours holiday programme. Steve had watched him on the box – a thickening, family man stationed in front of a lurid Yugoslavian coastline cliffed with high-rises. '*The accommodation is aboove average*,' he was informing the screen in his flat northern voice; '*included in the package is shower and bidet in all the, er, bedrooms, single and dooble*.' His jowelled face gazed beyond the million viewers; it gazed at June who had entered the lounge with the tea tray. These hygienic and intimate details were being spoken, with emphasis, for her alone.

June grunted; she pulled up the blanket still further. Nothing of her now remained. From the bedclothes came a faint, rhythmic snore – she would have died if she had known. Steve finished his second sandwich and bit into the third. In fact, though mainly concerned with the June aspect of these males, he had also been intrigued by the men themselves. Questioning her upon this had been disappointing. One had preferred her hair up, another down; one had disliked painted nails and another had said she looked just like Britt Ekland. None of them, she added, were as nice as him. So flattered had he been at this last remark that it had been a while before he thought; was she boring, finding out so little? Preferring not to explore this he had replaced the question: in her company, in fact, were they themselves boring? This seemed likely. Knowing, from sources close to home, how the most subtle, witty, many-faceted men were rendered – well, *simple* by lust (simple but scheming), Steve decided to change this subject. He gazed at the bedclothes. Their pink, satin-edged blanket rose and fell to the gentle rasps beneath. Dream on, June. There's girls who must envy you. Steve took out his cigarettes. And there's some who must pity you too.

Steve finished the McEwan's; he put down the can on the dressing-table. It looked out of place, as did his greasy dish, in this woman's room. Dainty pots stood on the dressing-table, amongst them several from Pintaubaum; the air was fragrant with the scents that he and his like had created for her. He put his cigarette back into the packet; he did not like to smoke in here. Seated sailor; your mug, dog and pipe. Seated Steven; can of McEwan's and packet of fags. *Oh I must to the seas again.*

So stuffy; he could do with a breath of air. He took away his supper things and went downstairs. It was a clear starry night; fresh, with a hint of frost.

He breathed deeply. He looked up at the block of flats; on the fourth floor the bedroom was the faintest, muffled glow. His lace-trimmed, Ideal Home. Behind the curtains, swaddled in pink blankets, possessed yet unpossessed, lay his Sleeping Beauty.

SEVEN

'I think I shall get a lodger,' said Claudia.

'Simpler than a husband,' said Verity.

'I've redecorated the spare room.'

'Ah, that room.'

'Your room. And I've cleared out the kitchen cupboard. Adrian was the one who did things like that. I'm having to learn them all over again.'

'The dull things,' said Verity.

'No, the necessary things. Keeping up the *status quo*.'

'A great one for the *status quo*, our Adrian. I always thought he was dull. I can tell you now.'

Actually, could she? Claudia shifted in her seat.

'He was an unexamining, colourless man. He was never up to you.'

'I don't know,' said Claudia. 'I think I got too bossy. I reduced him.'

'Let's face it, he wasn't much to begin with. God, it's such a relief to admit it.'

Chin resting in hands, Verity gazed at Claudia. She had shiny white skin and searching eyes; Adrian had always feared her, with her probing questions and frizzed hair. Though it was a relief that Claudia could now come down to Kent and see Verity more often, it was also a let-down that when she returned she had no one to tell it to.

In the past Adrian had made the odd, diffident criticism of Verity; Claudia had risen to Verity's defence. Verity was beyond judgement; she dated from too far back in Claudia's life. They had shared the same trim Kentish hedgerows, the pavement walks to school, the decade of Saturday mornings. She was part of Claudia's childhood and of the years when she had considered herself, perhaps mistakenly, a mature woman. They loved each other, though they sometimes did not meet for months.

Verity leant forward. 'You see, he was basically a passive person, a non-achiever. Physically strong but weak inside. You being so much cleverer and more efficient made him feel terribly inadequate. *Ben*.'

She lunged after her son. Claudia gazed at the kitchen wall. She would like to say, when Verity returned: I seem to have got a good deal less clever and less efficient since he left. The wall was hung with withered bundles of herbs and photos of someone else's Victorian ancestors ('Aren't they amazing? £1 the lot.') A severe, whiskery face glared down at her. No, it made her uneasy to talk like this about Adrian. Partly because he was not here to defend himself – her husband, *in absentia*, had more of her loyalty; partly because it unnerved her, that all these years Verity had been thinking this.

Verity returned with a struggling infant. 'Little bugger. Hooked on chicken mash.' There was a brown paper sack slumped in the corner. 'Hold him a moment, can you?'

'His nappy's wet.' In Claudia's arms Ben, as usual, started to struggle. Meanwhile he took small softened pellets out of his mouth. 'Shouldn't we do something?'

Verity returned with a pestle and mortar. 'How long's he been with that dreary girl?'

'About a month.' Claudia paused. 'Actually, five weeks today.'

'And not a word? Daisy, stop pulling at his nappy.'

56

'A couple of phone calls – you know, about arrangements. He says he'll write when he's more sorted out.'

'She probably gazes at him with enormous round eyes and agrees with everything he says. She'll pluck at his sleeve and make him feel manly. You see, you were always so terribly self-sufficient.'

'I'm not any more. I –'

'Daisy, for God's sake. Look, go and eat a carrot or something.'

'Don't want a carrot. Want a Smartie.'

'Darling, we don't have Smarties. If you're hungry, there's some lovely dried figs in –'

'That lady's got Smarties.'

'It's Claudia, Daisy.'

'That lady's got Smarties in her bag.'

'Sorry,' said Claudia, half because of the Smarties and half because Verity's children had never liked her enough to know her name.

'Want Smarties,' Daisy chanted. 'Don't want figs, don't want raisins.'

'Shut up.' Verity turned to Claudia. 'What do you feel about her?'

Claudia paused. 'Not what I expected. I've only spoken to her on the phone but she sounds rather nice. Shy. A bit hesitant, but then I don't blame her. She's only nineteen, you know.'

'Amazing.' Verity sighed. 'Who would've thought it of Adrian? He's such a dogged type. So doggedly –'

'Unfaithful?'

There was a silence. There had always been a silence when Adrian was the topic. Claudia gazed around the kitchen. It was a large, low room. Verity and Wil had gutted it, ripping out the formica put in by the ethnic old couple who had previously lived there; in its place they had installed stripped, rustic pine purchased at considerable expense. Bookshelves had been built containing glossy volumes on *Whole Grain Husbandry* and *Organic Living on Planet Earth*.

'He's a coward. Why won't he see you?'

'I wish he would. I feel in a sort of limbo at the moment, Verry. I long to talk to him. I think he feels I'm going to shriek and scream and blame him, but really I'd just like to chat. There are so many unfinished things I want to catch up on, like whether he's getting his teeth fixed and whether he got the insurance for his lost watch. And things at work, and two or three people who're his friends rather than mine, what's happening to them. You can't suddenly just stop. I want us to be friends. We always were, before.' Yes, when they were married, but could they be now? It sounded so simple and civilized, sitting in this wood-panelled kitchen in the country, miles from it all. 'It seems such a waste of all those years. Seven years, Verry, the same as you and Wil. It sort of shuts the door on them, rather bitterly. I'm sure we could be friends now, honestly.' She fiddled with a thread dangling from Ben's tights, twisting it around her finger. 'It should be –'

'*Ben*. You pig.'

'Sorry,' said Claudia. Unnoticed in her arms, Ben had pulled apart a garlic bulb. Over the table were scattered papery skins and segments narrow as nail parings – their modest size proclaiming their origins in Wil and Verity's vegetable patch rather than the greengrocers.

'Peel us a few, could you, Claudia? I'm making *pesto*.'

Claudia got to work. Ben struggled damply. He had now found the thread and started pulling it. 'You see, I feel so vague and undefined. There's nobody to do things for so I don't know what to do. Or I can't be bothered. I always thought I didn't need somebody to look after, to make breakfast for. Adrian always said I didn't. But without them –'

'Hell.' Verity got up. 'Forgotten the pine nuts.' She opened the larder door and foraged amongst the shelves.

She was an angular figure in layers of knits and a long corduroy skirt. Both she and Claudia were tall – as tall, in fact, as their husbands. Though Verity wore scuffed espadrilles that kept her down on a level with Wil, Claudia had never compromised with her footwear.

Verity cursed, dislodging oozing kilner jars of chutney. Claudia, annoyed with Verity's preoccupations, thought: Why does she make so many jars of chutney and so few of jam?

She asked politely: 'What's *pesto*?'

'We're having it for lunch. Pine nuts, olive oil, basil, garlic all pounded together. It's our own basil, you know. Had a marvellous crop this summer, Wil planted it, grew bush basil and sweet basil. . .' Her voice grew muffled as she hunted deeper into the larder.

Claudia gazed at the cluttered kitchen. Verity had always been artistic; it was one of the things about her that Claudia most admired. She herself had been considered cleverer at school, but this had been in the more boring, mathematical subjects. The admiration was mutual, Verity saying she envied Claudia her knitted suits and credit cards and the way she lunched strangers. She herself had been a fabric designer when they had shared the flat; since her marriage and removal to the country, this talent had been reduced to sewing up the holes in her babies' dungarees.

Thuds and scrapes from the larder. The kitchen was in a constant state of flux, things simmering, children shouting. By contrast Claudia's flat seemed barren with its smooth redecorated walls (she had finished this last week) and its objects that were never moved.

Claudia readjusted Ben and shifted herself on the wooden pew. Dwindling flocks had necessitated its removal from some defunct Welsh chapel to arrive, via the King's Road Pine Shop, at this Kentish kitchen, to seat the increasing congregation of Verity's offspring. Adrian had never remembered the names of these infants: 'Parsley and

Sprouts? Cabbage and Sage?'

Verity emerged. '. . . some of it I've been storing for the winter in this marvellous olive oil we brought back from Tuscany – first pressing, really thick and green, simply can't buy the stuff in England.'

'Fancy that.'

'Next year we're planning to make our own – not olive of course, sunflower.' Verity sat down and started pounding the pestle. Lumps flattened, juicily. 'But Claudia, do you want him back?'

Above the orange halo of Verity's hair the Victorian patriarch glowered. Though the photo was faded the chin still jutted, the eyebrows were still lowered. Black and white, he said, right and wrong, he said. Queen and country, Britain rules the waves, I know what God intends, he said, and I know how to get it.

Claudia sighed. 'I don't know,' she said.

'That's very unlike you.'

'I don't think I do, but it's all so much more confusing than I expected. My reactions, I mean. The fact, for instance, that in some ways I'm sort of *pleased* for him –'

'Christ, the bread.' Verity jumped up, tripping over her skirt, and hurried across to the Aga. With a clank she opened the door and pulled out a tray; she sniffed at the dark, humped tins. 'Just in time. Lucky I remembered. It's this new flour – we're grinding it ourselves now, did I tell you? Marvellous old thing, found it at an auction, all levers and knobs. 50p. *50p*. Wil adores grinding – you know, when you've been working with your brain all day. *Daisy* will you take that thing outside? This minute.'

'Is Wil working in London today?' Claudia had taken the day off to come down; she was owed some holiday.

'No, upstairs. Some ICI campaign. Some big account anyway – he'll be down in a moment. Claudia, he's very worried about you – what, Daisy? Oh all right – *bye-bye worm*. Now piss off.'

60

Claudia gazed at the children's drawings pinned to the larder door. They were crayon explosions explained in spidery capitals below – MY HOUS, MY TEDY, MY MUMMY. In her lap Ben twisted around, squirming for his mother. Verity pushed back her hair, harassed, fecund, needed. Claudia felt annoyed with Ben, that he did not want her and yet at the same time left a spreading patch of damp on her pale and just-cleaned trousers. And irked with Verity, that she had no time to listen, too busy with the *pesto* that needed pounding and the pot that needed stirring and the children clinging to her bottle-green corduroy skirt. And all this healthy food took such ages to assemble. Claudia herself would prefer fish fingers if only that would give Verity more listening time.

Verity straightened up. 'Be an angel and dig up a couple of leeks, could you? It must be ages since you've seen a proper leek.'

Outside it was grey and drizzly, a chill October day. Mud underfoot, and planks. Verity and Wil were always knocking down and building up; planks lay everywhere, laborious props to their own laborious preoccupations. In her thin urban shoes Claudia picked her way around the puddles. She felt irked and ill-fitting; it must be Verity's fault. What happened to people who went rural, that they became so convinced of their superiority? She resented Verity's last remark. For the life of her she could not see what was so intrinsically superior about spending half the day cleaning out the slugs and grit from a couple of leeks when she herself could buy far better ones at the greengrocers, clean and white and a fraction of the cost if one took time into account, and have all the rest of the day to do more interesting things like reading books and listening to her friends and giving them a gin and tonic (it was well past drinks time, in fact well past lunch time). Verity and Wil considered themselves so aware but there seemed precious little time for this, what with all that cleaning and scraping and bottling and kneading . . . perhaps she was just feeling disaffected and bereft.

'Claudia.'

Her name was stated rather than spoken. She turned round. In fact, she had heard the squelching footsteps but she had chosen not to acknowledge this.

'Claudia, it's so good to see you.'

Wil's tone was low and sincere. He stood very close, as if needing to keep her warm.

'Hello Wil. What awful weather.'

Wil was silent. Eyes lowered, Claudia could see the hem of his pre-bleached Levis and, below, his Roots boots frilled with mud.

'This is really heavy,' he said.

'Yes.' She gazed at the Kentish clay, at the knobbled stalks of the sprouts rising from it.

'Like, you and Adrian.'

By the end of October the Fosters' vegetable patch was acquiring its usual First World War look; scattered regiments still stood but tattered and yellowing now, some bowed towards the mud. The wind whistling through the telegraph wires added to the period desolation.

'Still hung up on you, is he?'

She shook her head. 'No, I think he's truly fallen in love.'

'Wow, you can say that?'

'I think Beth's restoring him. I whittled him away.'

'You know, you give off this aura. Really strong and, like, together. I guess some guys just can't cope with that.'

'Wil, have you got a fork?'

'Come again?'

'I told Verity I'd dig up some leeks.'

'Ah. Yes.' He hesitated, then he went to the shed and returned with a fork. He was a small man with a brooding face and sparse, reddish beard, a D.H. Lawrence in co-ordinated denim. He dug up a leek and returned to stand beside her.

'Really beautiful, my leeks,' he murmured. He handed it to her. She had to admit it was not bad, stout and white, though streaked with soil.

'Yes,' he said, 'I guess he just couldn't cope.' He touched the leek's smooth side.

There was a moment of silence as Claudia listened to the whistling wires. Then thudding, breathless footsteps.

'Mum says,' Daisy caught her breath, 'Mum says, where are her leeks?'

While Wil dug up the second one Claudia looked out at the fields. Faint, the murmur of the motorway that led back to London. In the distance elms had been chopped down and saplings planted. Beyond them she glimpsed a low, modern building.

'Some guys can't –'

'I've never been here in winter,' she said quickly. 'I never realized there was a motorway service place.'

Wil's voice changed. 'Christ, we were furious. Knocked fifteen thou off – I mean, it's the rape of the countryside, isn't it. Hideous place, terrible design, no attempt to blend in –'

'Please can't we go there,' whined Daisy. '*Please*. We can have chips.'

'Daisy sweetie, I've told you a thousand times –'

'And tomato sauce and sausages and –'

'Terrible place, plastic food.' Wil pulled up the second leek.

Claudia pictured it. Central heating, sizzling bacon, hot sausages . . . she gazed at the far building, hazy through the thin trees and the thin rain. A warm, busy, city cube, marvellously un-self-sufficient. She felt a longing – for that? Could she actually yearn for a motorway cafe?

She rallied. 'I'm looking forward to that *pesto*,' she said, shivering. At least they were not going to have lentils.

When, after lunch, Wil asked her if she could give him a lift back to London (he had to take some clients out to dinner), Claudia's heart sank. He changed into a beautiful grey velvet suit and climbed into the passenger seat of her car – also grey, a Peugeot saloon.

'You match,' she observed.

'I know.' His voice was low. 'I've noticed.'

They pulled away from the brick cottage, within whose walls Verity would be scraping their plates into her stockpot. She had a religious belief in left-overs. The rain had ceased. Past the runner bean poles, knotted with lifeless stalks, Daisy was pulling a headless Dingalong Doggie.

They drove through the village with its rows of little labourers' cottages and its rows of parked cars: Citröen, BMW, Audi, Rover.

'Christ,' Wil muttered.

Claudia chose not to hear this. 'This way?' she asked.

They passed the church. *St. Marks Restoration Appeal*, said the sign. A giant thermometer was quarter filled with blood. £4,500, the red paint had reached.

'You know Verity's pregnant again?'

'She told me,' said Claudia. 'Isn't it lovely.'

'Great.' He paused. 'Just great. She told me at breakfast.'

'Daisy and Saffron are sweet. And I adore Ben.'

'Four kids, Claudia. That'll be four kids.'

'Verity's a marvellous mother. The way she copes, what with the nappies and the chickens and all that super bread –'

'Remember her breasts?'

Claudia swerved. 'Sorry. Pothole.'

'They were beautiful once. Now they're, like, shrivelled up.' Fields flashed by, grey ploughed earth. 'Claudia, we used to be great together in bed. Sex was important to us. Now there's always some kid screaming or creeping in under the damned duvet.'

Ahead the motorway sign loomed. *London 25*. With any luck they would be there in half an hour.

'Claudia, it's amazing how I can talk to you.' A pause. 'See, she doesn't reckon me as *me* any more, as a human being. I'm some guy who writes out the cheques and digs the goddam potatoes. Like me, Wil Foster, I'm redundant.'

'My husband used to say that.'

'What did you say?'

'Nothing.' She cleared her throat. 'Hey ho, motorway ahead.'

'You know, you've got this fantastic empathy. Anyone told you that?'

'No. Ah.'

Roadworks. The traffic slowed down; two lanes of the motorway were closed, barricaded in by a row of red-and-white cones. Some had fallen over like skittles. The cars and lorries formed themselves into a crawling line.

Wil cleared his throat. 'Claudia, can I ask you a personal question? How's it like – well, with other guys now? Husbands and suchlike.'

'Oh, battering down my door. Ravishing me on the hearthrug while their wives load the dishwasher.' She giggled. Nerves had made her silly. 'Must be my *Liberesse*. Drives them wild.'

There was a silence. Wil fingered his beard.

She said: 'Actually, nothing.' To tell the truth, this had surprised her. Marital folklore and scores of novels had led her to expect the odd phone call at work, the hesitant invitation to lunch, the ready volunterring to pop round and fix her broken stereo. If not that, at least the chance, wistful glance over the wifely head. She need not have worried. 'Perhaps I don't look very helpless.'

'I find that amazing,' said Wil softly. 'Truly amazing.'

The cars crawled along in single file. Claudia was trapped behind a large lorry. Some witty finger had written upon it I AM DIRTY.

Wil said: 'It'll come, Claudia. I hate to tell you, but it'll come. You should see the guys at work – you know, really happily-married ones, always going on about the little woman at home ... there they are, phoning up to say they'll be working late ... *working late*. Believe me, Claudia, the double standards nowadays, it's worse than Victorian times. It's pathetic. Sad really.'

Claudia was silent. She gazed at the looming lorry, its underparts furred with dust.

Wil said: 'There's what's called the mezzanine room, for client entertaining. It's got a booze cupboard, a sofa, a lock on the door ... Claudia, these are pillars of the community, these guys; two offices away they've got photos of their kids on their desks. If it wasn't so terrible it would be funny – you know, the way they see women as objects, something to be screwed, the way they fall into the crazy pattern of deceiving and deceived, the way they can't relate as *human beings*...'

The lorry changed into first gear; grey fumes belched from its exhaust. Claudia glanced at her speedometer. 15 m.p.h. She was trapped by the lorry; by the row of clownish, two-tone cones. She could think of nothing to say; she seemed to have lost the words for this situation.

'... they tell the chicks their wives don't understand them. Claudia, it's so dishonest.'

The cones finished. All clear. Claudia put down her foot. She could at least drive; she had always been competent at that. Motors were so simple; however labyrinthine their engines, they were made from solid metal. Not grey and human, blurred and contradictory.

Wil muttered: 'Like if I were to say to you – well, like I don't have to meet these people till eight – which, frankly, is true, I needn't get to the hotel till then – so why don't we have a drink together at your place ... you'd know that I was meaning *you*, Claudia, the whole person. That it would be great to have a quiet drink, to relate a little, without distractions – kids and everything . . .'

60 . . . 70 . . . 80 . . . the thin red rod reached 85. It quivered there, reprovingly, Beside her, Wil stirred. Perhaps she was trying to impress him. 90 . . . she was half-thrilled, half-alarmed. Who was she trying to frighten, Wil or herself? This was so silly.

It was six o'clock when they reached the flat. It was dark, of course, as always. Upstairs the Monsons' flat was light, of course, as always. She invited Wil in.

They went down the long, dark, shared hallway and into her flat. She put on the light. Wil leant against the wall in the passage and she fetched some ice from the kitchen. She returned with the ice-container under her arm; it was a black plastic object with a knob on the top. He did not move; for some reason they were both reluctant to make a move, to go along to the living-room, switch on its lamps and draw the curtains.

Wil stepped closed to her. 'It's been really bad, hasn't it.'

'No, no, of course not.' She laughed shrilly.

'You put on this amazing front, Claudia. Even with Verity I've seen you really trying. When we came to supper last week and you were being witty about the decorating man, she was so pleased. But I could see the pain underneath, Claudia.' There was a moment's silence. 'It's bloody lonely, isn't it.'

Claudia paused.

'Yes,' she said at last, simply. Even Verity had not quite realized this. Or not had time. She still felt irked with her, and disappointed. It was rare that they had a day together; Verity had been as nice as ever but preoccupied, distant, pulled from all sides.

'You take it for granted there's someone there,' said Wil. 'And suddenly there's nobody. Right?'

'Just your friends, but you can't always be ringing them up. They've got their own lives. And you know you're not such good company, because you're sad, and that they're

67

making allowances for you. And they can't make allowances for ever.' She spoke rapidly. 'And you hate yourself for noticing how happy and fulfilled they are.'

'By *noticing*, Claudia, you mean resenting, don't you.'

'Dear God, yes.' She felt breathless; her eyes were moist with self-pity and relief. There was something mesmerising about Wil, with his intense, sombre face. 'And then you start clinging to your solitary friends, the ones who've been living alone, and that's just as depressing in another way—'

'Claudia —'

'We must go into the living-room.' She started to move. Wil put his hands on her shoulders. There was a moment's silence. He lifted her chin with his finger. 'You're such a beautiful woman, Claudia. I've wanted to tell you that for a long time.' He was wearing a silken, striped tie; above it his eyes were sincere and lustrous. 'So beautiful. Jesus.'

'Wil, please.' She did not move. When had a man last talked to her like this?

To herself she repeated: I don't much like you. In fact, I despise you. I tried to stop Verity marrying you, remember? Verity is my greatest friend. Your real name is Wilfred. She is worth ten of you, Wilfred.

His arms were around her. She leant against the wall, pressed against the warm grooves of the radiator. His body against hers was thin and hard. With one hand she wedged the ice bucket against her hip, with the other she touched his beard. For seven years Verity had embraced this body.

Wil held her tightly, needing her. 'Claudia,' he murmured. He was trembling. He kissed her, his mouth soft in his damp beard. She put her spare arm around him. She did not know who she was; she was in limbo, here in the passage.

He was edging her to the left. With her arm around his velvet shoulder, she felt them moving along the ridges of the radiator, then sliding along the wall and coming to rest against the panels of the bedroom door. The handle jutted to her side; he moved his hand to grasp it. He eased it down to open the door. Stealthy. Furtive. A husband on the loose. She stiffened.

'*Wil*. Stop.'

She twisted from him. The ice bucket knocked against the door surround, slipped from under her arm and fell to the floor. Ice cubes spilled over the carpet.

Claudia gathered her scattered wits. She pulled the door shut behind her. 'I'm sorry, Wil.' She held the handle. She paused. 'You see, I've got a lodger.'

Wil drew away, frowning. There was a silence as he fingered his beard.

She said quickly: 'He's in there, asleep.'

'Come again?'

'He's in there. That's the spare room.' This, in fact, was the truth; her bedroom was the adjacent door. 'He's just moved in and he's very tired.'

Wil gazed at her, his eyes dark above his hollow cheekbones. He must know she was lying. Claudia tried to behave sensibly; after all, she was a grown woman of thirty. During her marriage certain episodes with Wil had veered towards this; she had fended them off sensibly enough. Why could she not cope now, instead of gibbering with lies like a sixteen-year-old?

Claudia remained in the hall for some time after Wil had left. At the foot of the radiator the ice cubes were already shiny; soon they would be melting in pools on the carpet. The central heating, her ghostly, automatic lodger, had switched itself on as it did every evening.

She tried to justify herself. Of course, she was not entirely lying. Had she not mentioned her intentions to Verity? A lodger would be useful, not just to fend off the type of meaningful dialogue like the one proposed by Wil, but to help with expenses. Not just to help with expenses but to be there day in and day out. A radio playing in the bathroom. Someone for whom she could bother to tidy the flat. (And *she* was thinking this, Claudia, who had thought she despised homemaking, who found housework dull and demeaning. . .)

The next evening she opened the Rooms Wanted pages of *Time Out*, also their sister page in the *New Statesman*. Perusing them, she found that *homo sapiens* offered up two distinct sub-species for her inspection: in the *New Statesman* clean, professional gentlemen and ladies, in *Time Out* gays and bi's, most of them aware, into cats, sounds and EST, and all of them unable to rise above £9 a week.

Pages of them . . . rooms wanted, lonely hearts. Lonely, lonely heart. Claudia sat down in an armchair; she sagged with the weight of herself, with the weight of them out there. In the *New Statesman*, her would-be lodgers were preceded by pages of closely-printed articles on Chilean elections and *Collected Letters Vol VI of Arnold Bennett*; in *Time Out* by pub-rock venues, lesbian women's workshops and photographs of fuzzy-haired youths giving the finger to helmetless policemen. The question was: where was she? Neither of these magazines interested or fitted her; no longer did she find them speaking to her in a familiar voice. This was something she had noticed since living alone. Even *Yours*, to which she had always been loyal, appeared to her new eyes strident yet lightweight. She was finding it difficult to choose something to read; everything seemed either too trivial or too gloomy, with nothing in between.

So where, and who, was she now? She gazed down at the print. Should she contact *accountant, non-smoker, references given* or *together Piscean musician, into growth*?

EIGHT

Steve enjoyed motorway meals, piles of greasy chips and little foil-sealed sauces. He was a man alone with his plastic tray.

He finished his coffee; he walked across the motorway bridge towards his car. It was a glass corridor; beside him rose and fell his reflection – tall, thin, dark-haired, it walked with springing strides. Below him flashed the traffic; past him, people hurried; musak murmured. Much of his day was spent in places like these; echoing, impersonal transit spaces where people stopped for ten minutes, half an hour, leaving behind nothing but a little heap of scrumpled packets, a curled receipt. His job left him so free. Amongst the giant struts of multi-storied car parks he was the lone male, the hunter, the seller. His prairie was this windy concrete wilderness, his mount this polished Cortina.

This stretch of the motorway had been carved through a wood; clinging to their raw, sliced banks, the old oaks faced each other across a sliding stream of cars. Around the car park, however, saplings had been planted upon landscaped lawns, well-groomed children of the countryside beyond. At this point the woods were thin, the fence low – still it was unthinkable to penetrate that rural world. Through the mist of wintry branches he could see the roofs of some

71

Kentish village which lay in the distance, unreachable.

In most respects Steve was an untidy man. His car, however, was spotless; he even had a vacuum cleaner, a midget version of the one June used so thoroughly in the flat, to suck up the ash from its carpeted crevices. He cared for it, he felt loyal to this capsule that sped him through time and space, sealing him into warmth and the music from his assorted cassettes.

Steve swung into the motorway. He roared past the rows of lorries, past a coachload of old dears dozing after their lunch, windows of lolling grey heads. No, nothing would make him take that promotion.

Roadworks ahead. *800 yds.* He slowed down. *600 yds.* No, whatever June said.

A line of cones narrowed him in. He changed down into third and eased himself into a procession of cars, his foot itching on the pedal.

'Think of it, June, sitting behind a blooming desk all day.'

'Steve, you can't *like* sitting in the car, going round to all those grubby shops.'

'Hey, it was only three weeks ago you were working in one, remember?'

It was curious, how quickly she forgot. For two whole years she had stood under the little lit sign: MAX FAC-TOR. For two years she had been boxed into her counter of cosmetics, her silky hair looped back, around her throat a chiffon scarf. Upon the counter stood a fringed table lamp; its glow gave her a radiant intimacy. She looked so efficient, so peachy. Her surname, then, had been Jenkins. One day when she was fetching her coat he had shuffled through her order forms. Between them was a piece of paper. JUNE MULLEN, she had written, experimentally, with eyebrow pencil, JUNE AVRIL MULLEN, J.A. MULLEN.

Soon afterwards they had indeed married. Their shared

work bound them together. In the evenings they would chat about new lines; upon each other's wrists they would spray their respective scents. They had been so tender together. He knew her skin as a lover did; he knew her skin as a salesman did, discussing what she used to cleanse, powder, scent and tint it. They were ardent colleagues, they were sisters at their mother's dressing-table.

But she hardly remembered it now, dismissing it with a sigh, turning back to what she must have been waiting for in her little lamplit booth – the tending of husband and home. June lived in the present, simply; that she neither drew from the past nor adjusted for the future had come as a surprise. Each day she avidly read her *Daily Express* horoscope; beyond its print she saw nothing.

It was a shame she even knew about that promotion. He believed in telling her everything but he usually grew to regret it.

'Saw a lovely fitment in Tempson's today, Steve. Wall cupboard to match our stools. The man said they do it in yellow too.'

'Let's go. Let's get it. We'll go Saturday.'

She had looked up, her nail brush poised. Upon it trembled a scarlet drop. 'But we can't afford it. I mean, there's the fridge to fix, and then we're saving for the bedroom carpet.' She bent to her outstretched finger. She bit her lip, painting it with slow, careful strokes.

'You mean, we could get it if I took that job.'

She had not replied. She was closed off again, dipping the brush in the pot, returning to her nail, concentrating on getting it right.

Steve revved the engine. The cones stretched for miles, closing him in. By now he was feeling an old acquaintanship with the car in front, so long had he been following it. A silver-grey Peugeot, rather nice. Two heads were framed in its rear window. In traffic jams he would make up lives for the people in front, based on the available evidence –

make of car, chance window-ledge objects, occupants' hairstyles, the animation of their conversation, the frequency with which they gazed out of the window. Sometimes along some crafty lesser route he would find himself trailing a car for miles, his feelings of cameraderie growing with the knowledge of the shared short-cut; when they put out their winker and disappeared he felt it as a personal snub.

In this Peugeot the woman drove. He admired this; he had been pestering June for months but she would not learn, she was scared. The pair of heads was deep in conversation, the man turning to the woman, head tilting. How long had they been married, that they still had so much to say on such a long and boring stretch of motorway? On the back ledge lay a woman's magazine, *Yours*. It was not, however, like the usual ones. He knew it through its Pintaubaum ads; it actually contained news and current affairs and what was going on in the experimental theatre, plus some fashion pictures more suitable, he thought, for *Playboy*. Its presence upon the windowledge spoke of joint cultural outings, of opinions passed, alive and provocative, from woman to man, man to woman. How long could they have been together?

The cones finished; the cars shot forward, he lost sight of the Peugeot.

'*My love for you*,' warbled his cassette, '*is deeper than the sea...*'

At one point on the motorway he could see the Channel, when he was driving further south. Today the clouds were down.

'*Wider than the o-o-ocean...*'

Since he was a boy Steve had loved the water. At school he had been a champion swimmer; first thing Sunday morning he would emerge from the curtained maisonette wherein his parents still slumbered, and run down to Catford Baths to catch it as it opened. Ah that first heady whiff of chlorine; cool tiles underfoot; echoing down the corridor, the solitary clang of his cubicle door. *Walk Don't Run* said the notices. *No Towels Beyond This Point. Smoking Strictly Forbidden*. Then, stepping through the shower, that long stretch of blue water, empty, waiting. On the bottom the black lines rippling. Nobody in sight but the old man on the far side mopping the floor.

He was keen on all sports – he was restless, active, his school desk cramped him – but it was swimming he loved the best.

'When I'm old and past it,' he told June, 'I'll get a one-way ticket to Brighton. I'll just strike out into those great grey waves.'

'Ugh, Steve, you're horrible.' June hated talk like this.

'No, it'll be lovely. All that empty water. See all your childhood speeded up. Anyway, you like the seaside, don't you?'

'Tarragona was lovely. Steve, can we go back next year? I got such a gorgeous tan.'

When he left school he wanted to join the Merchant Navy. His parents had been alarmed. 'Our only son,' said his mother. But he could not settle down; he had tried various jobs – driving a lorry, chopping down trees – and had ended up at Pintaubaum, footloose not upon the open sea but the open road, his contact with ships being confined to Airfix models. *Aged 12 Years* said the cardboard boxes *And Upwards*.

Steve left the motorway. He had a couple of calls to make and then he was through, driving back towards London along arterial roads blurred in the dusk, white foggy lights, factories looming up on either side. The houses closed in, the factories dwindled to small industrial premises, he drove past a row of lit shops. The traffic slowed down.

At first he thought it was an accident. Ahead, a crowd stood on the pavement; he saw the glint of a policeman's

75

helmet. The cars crawled along; they crawled slower, at walking pace.

No accident. He saw a placard or two, a limp banner. SAVE THE WHALE. In fact it was only a small demonstration – a knot of people, crowded in by passers-by. Against the glass someone pressed a leaflet; he wound down the window, took the paper and parked further along the pavement. He could never resist a demo.

Steve switched on the light. *12,522 Sperm Wales were killed last year. The population is dwindling at an alarming rate. Unless we do something to halt this butchery, in 30 years the population will be virtually extinct.*

Steve glanced at the dashboard. Beside his dangling ingnition keys hung a plastic bag. Within it circled his black mollie, purchased in Tunbridge Wells. The aquarium was full; soon he would have a population problem on his hands. How many fish was it to a cubic foot? He should never have bought the mollie but he was weak to her charm. She flowed rather than swam, liquid black velvet.

'We'll just have to fit you in, won't we?' He leant forward. 'You beauty you.'

The products we take from these unique creatures are easily replaced by synthetics. Boycott the following companies.

No, she did not flow, she rippled. Dense, inky black, rippling fins. Little, rippling, midnight mollie. He would just have to buy another tank, wouldn't he.

Gloves, said the list, followed by a column of names. *Cutting and Gear Oils* headed another column. *Cosmetics and Perfumes.* Steve tilted the paper against the light; originally typed, it had been muzzily cyclostyled.

Pintaubaum was there. There, fourth down. *Pintaubaum International.* There were several others of course, but still . . . Steve felt the flush he remembered from school, when the headmaster had announced that someone had been stealing from the cloakrooms. He had stolen nothing, but

76

still he had blushed.

Beside him on the passenger seat lay his dispatch case and a pile of papers; in the back an empty display stand. His guilty apparatus. He hesitated; he climbed out of the car and strolled towards the crowd.

It had begun to drizzle. Most of the passers-by had dispersed. The demonstrators themselves appeared to be packing up. 'Bloody perishing,' said one. 'Taking the tube, Di?' Steve brightened when he saw that the majority were women, young ones at that, their damp hair gleaming under the street light. There could only be about twenty of them.

The nearest girl had dark hair pulled back in a rubber band. She was stuffing leaflets back into a bag. When she saw him she straightened up.

'I've got one,' he said.

'Ah.' She bent down and continued bundling them into the bag. She wore jeans, boots and a khaki jacket similar to the one in the *Liberesse* ad, but on her it did not look chic at all, just something to keep off the rain. Not too effectively either.

He said: 'I've read it too.'

'That makes a change. Nobody else does.' She glanced up. She had sad, enormous brown eyes in a thin face. Hmm, not bad, thought Steve; could do with a bit of make-up.

'Here, let me help.'

'I can manage, thanks.'

'Why doesn't anyone read them?'

'They take them to please us, because they're weak and polite. They don't even read the banner. We might be the National Front for all they know.' She slung the bag over her shoulder. Under the jacket she wore a tee shirt; under that, nothing else.

'Hey,' she said, looking at him, 'I think you're really interested.'

'Right. Right. What's it all about?'

77

She pointed behind her. It was an old brick building, flourescent-lit from within. Outside a wooden sign; Steve could make out the words *Leather Goods*.

'We picket these places, we send them letters. We put the pressure on them but it's an old industry, they're old-fashioned firms, they can't bear the idea of change. So sodding conservative.'

She scratched her head like a man, yet her hand was slender. Some of her hair had escaped from its rubber band.

'You must be frozen,' said Steve.

'Sperm oil.'

'What?'

'Sperm oil. We've told them, they *know* they can get alternatives and still they go on using it.'

The drizzle was changing to rain.

'Here, take my coat,' said Steve.

'Why? Then you'd get cold.'

'Look, there's a pub there, why don't we –'

'They say it's for the run and feel.'

'What?'

'The run and feel – when leather stretches but returns to its former shape. That's why it's so important for gloves. But they don't *need* sperm oil, they can use synthetics. Hey, its raining.'

'That's right. I was just thinking – well, if you'd like a drink. Just a quick one. There's a pub across the road.'

'Wow, I didn't realize I was so cold. No, I don't drink. I wouldn't mind a cup of tea.'

She spoke a few words to the last of the demonstrators, some of whom, Steve noticed with a pang, were disappearing into the pub.

They crossed the road to a café. It was empty, but for two youths who sat by the window. They did not glance at Steve and his companion. Steve, accustomed to escorting June, felt invisible and strangely private with this slight, bedraggled girl. Though proud of June, in pubs and cafés his conversation with her always seemed theatrical, with its audience of shifting eyes. When men came through the door, their hesitation rekindled for him June's beauty, but he could never be alone with her.

'Hey, I'm paying.'

'I've done it now.' She carried the cups from the counter.

'You can't – I mean –'

'Here.' She passed him his cup and sat down.

Steve felt put out by this. He looked at her in her frayed, revolutionary's jacket. Liberated she certainly was, but she could do with an item or two from the *Liberesse* range – lipstick certainly, a touch of blusher on those pale, unblushing cheeks.

She took one of his cigarettes, which made him feel better, and blew out the smoke.

'No,' she said, 'we campaign all those firms on that list but they tell lies, they don't answer, they prevaricate, they put their smoothie PR men on the phone.'

'Sounds fishy to me. Geddit? Fishes – whales.'

She looked at him coolly. 'Whales are mammals.'

'Heck, I know. I keep fish. I just meant –'

'It's the cosmetics firms that are the most obscene.'

Steve's cup paused halfway to his lips. 'Oh yes?'

'It's all so ironic. They use whale products to keep up the price. People actually *like* paying more for all that muck they put on their faces.'

'That's right. It's a prestige market. Nobody buys cheap scent.'

A good deal of her hair had escaped, now, from its rubber band and hung down one side of her face, damp and crinkly. It looked nice like that; she looked appealing, spaniel-like, with those large solemn eyes.

She pushed back the hair and blew out smoke. 'Ambergris, they use, to fix the scent. They get it from the intestines.'

'The intestines?'

'Of the sperm whale.' The hair fell forward again. Around her neck hung a chain bearing a delicate golden M. It seemed touching and personal against the washed-out tee-shirt. Madeleine? Mary?

She said: 'And then they use the spermacetti wax.'

'What for? Moisturisers, foundations, that sort of thing?'

For the first time she looked at him with interest. 'Hey, you know a lot.'

Steve shifted in his seat. 'No, no, not really . . .'

'Yes, really.' Spaniel-like, this should be said admiringly, those enormous eyes gazing deep into his soul. But her voice was cool. 'Yeah, we could do with more people like you. See, I get so pissed off with dilettantes. Just for a moment they get all weepy and soft about the poor old whales, but they can't relate, not really. You see, whales aren't as pretty as kittens or baby seals, you can't put a ribbon around their neck. That's one sort. The other sort are just trying to lay you. Either way they don't care a fuck about actually doing anything.'

Steve shifted. He wished she hadn't put it like that. Besides, he disliked women who swore. He felt a pang for June, who knew how to make herself pretty, who listened to him with devotion in her eyes, who was not aggressive. Still, he felt an itch to know this girl's name. Marsha?

She went on: 'Then some people get all excited, you think they're committed, and the next day they've forgotten all about it. And the whales go on being butchered.'

Steve suddenly thought: Mollie.

'Find that funny, do you? Strange sense of humour.'

'Sorry. Your name's not Mollie, by any chance?'

'Ah, so it's that scene is it?' She sighed. 'I should have known.'

'No, no, it's just that there's this fish in the car – hell, it sounds silly.'

Her face changed. She pushed back her chair. 'Christ,

80

wrong again, you're a crackpot.' She fumbled for her bag. 'Nutters. We get people like you, too.'

'Hell, sorry – actually, it wasn't very funny at all. I just felt guilty.'

She stopped. 'Guilty?'

I'm guilty about my dispatch case, my pots and tubes of pressed whale. Piles of order forms for dozens, hundreds, thousands more.

She was standing up, puzzled, clutching her large canvas bag. She could not make him out; for the first time she looked human. She hesitated. 'Well, if you really want to know. . . .' She turned to leave. 'It's Marge.'

He stood up. 'Hey Marge, I really am interested. About the whales.'

She looked at him. 'OK then. I'll mail you. What's your address?'

Steve and June lived in south London. Their neighbourhood was one of large Edwardian mansions set in gardens dank with rhododendrons. There was grandeur there in the huge trees, in the buildings with their attics and their stable buildings, now containing cobwebs, gardening tools and rusting Morris Minors. Maids no longer flitted from window to window. Gone, the pinafore'd girls who skipped scrunch-scrunch down gravel drives, past stables stirring with horses.

Now the buildings were divided into flats or else converted into preparatory schools, veterinary surgeries and Hindu meditation centres. Through french windows the sun shone on to parallel gymnastic bars or the stiff-backed, mis-matched chairs of empty waiting-rooms. Different people's curtains in separate windows; in the porches no longer a single brass bell but a row of plastic buzzers.

Where Steve and June lived even the building had gone. The family house had been replaced by a purpose-built block of flats. Shulman Properties Ltd. described them as

Executive on account of the Georgian-style front door. It was a small block, just four storeys high, with a tarmac forecourt for the cars and a stretch of lawn, maintained by a landscape contractor for a yearly fee. A few relics remained – an overgrown rose arch, a potting shed roofed with sagging corrugated iron. Steve had a soft spot for these, but Shulman Properties had plans to demolish them.

'That rose thing's ever so dangerous,' said June. 'It's just about to fall down. You're only making a fuss because you wanted a flat in one of those hideous big houses. This one's much better.'

'June, take a look at this door. Everything's made of bleeding plywood.'

Tonight he jumped from brick to brick of the half-hearted attempt Shulman had made to edge the car park. He usually did this. Up on the fourth floor he saw June's silhouette at the window; he leapt up the stairs, two at a time.

'Steve, I was so worried. You're late.'

She put her arms around him; mingled aromas of perfume and roasting chicken.

'Hey Juney, you know I can't say when I'll be back. You can't predict, with calls.' When she worked she had understood this; after all, they were in the same business. Now she was home all day it was not the same; she fretted, glancing at the electric kitchen clock.

'Anyway,' he said, 'I got caught in a demo.' He told her about the placards and about the spaniel girl, the whale girl, Ms Marge. 'She was tattily dressed,' he said, forbearing to mention the nipply tee shirt. 'Know something? She made me think.'

'What about?'

'About my motives.' (Several sorts of these.) 'About my job.'

She stared at him. 'Your job?'

'No, no.' He had forgotten that he could not alarm her

about this. 'She told me about these whale products, see.' He paused.

'Your coat's wet, Steve. You'll catch your death.' She reached up. 'Here, let me take it.'

He stopped her. He wanted her to want to know. He explained to her about the whales. Warming to his theme he put down his briefcase so that he could move his arms; he stretched them out to show the great oceans, the huge shapes rising to the surface to blow, their bulk, their gentleness, the terrible romance of the whaling ships he had read about in his childhood, the hard whalers, their harpoons poised, yet their rhythms were the rhythms of the sea, they hunted but they shared the grey waves with the hunted, they shared the sleet and the storms.

'Steve, know something?'

'What?'

'You look ever so handsome when you're excited. Your voice sort of falls over itself and your eyebrows wiggle up and down.'

Steve paused. 'You're not listening.'

'Oh I am. Steve, those poor fish.'

'Whales are mammals.'

'Oh look.' June noticed something. She moved away; over the door handle, where Steve had hooked it, hung the plastic bag. 'Steve, you didn't tell me. I've never seen a black one before. What is it?'

'A mollie.' He felt pleased that she was so interested, sharing his pleasure in this velvety little fish.

She said: 'It'll look so pretty with the other ones – sort of set them off. A touch of black.'

'That's just what I thought.' Steve smiled. What had Marge said – something about small and pretty with a ribbon around its neck? Whales were not as pretty as mollies, protestors not as charming as June.

'Winkie, why don't you sit down? Here, let me get you your beer.'

At times June chose to call him by her own diminutive of his middle name. When they were alone Steve did not object to this. He sat down, he let her tend him fussily, lovingly. On the table, all ready for his glass, lay a small circular mat. They had a whole set depicting, from old prints, scenes of Brighton – the Pier, the Pavilion. This one showed the sea front; laminated houses, laminated waves beneath.

'I wish you'd join me,' he said as she set the glass down. He did not want her to be like her mother, serving the seated male.

She wrinkled her nose. 'You know I don't like beer. Anyway, I'm halfway through the sauce.'

On the other hand, he had no intention of getting up and helping her in the kitchen. It was comfortable here; he had earned this soft cushion, soft as her arms, this soft warm nest to which he had returned.

A gust of rain rattled against the window. Outside the windy concrete spaces, the windy sea.

NINE

It was the third of November and drizzling. June felt awed, walking up the steps between the grimy stone pillars. She had not visited the British Museum since school. Then they had sat in a coach singing saucy songs. She pushed through the swing doors, allowed an elderly man to rummage in her handbag, and hesitated in the entrance hall.

She had forgotten what it was like. She had vaguely expected brainy types, professors with leather patches on their elbows, and dusty glass cases. She was reassured; the place was full of people who looked as lost as she was – blonde types in blue anoraks, clutching maps; small foreigners in hats. She should have remembered the tourists.

Upper Egyptian Galleries. June mounted the stairs. She was wearing a damp raincoat and brown woolly hat; she felt dowdy and anonymous with her freshly-washed hair tucked out of sight. This was fine. She did not want to be interrupted. As a rule she could not forget herself, people coming up to ask the time when she could see they were wearing a perfectly good watch themselves. She was bad enough at concentrating as it was.

She reached the first gallery. *Funerary Offerings. Middle Kingdom Deities*. Behind glass stood tiers of lopsided stone jars and little metal cats. Other wierdies – dogs, snakes and crocodiles with men's bodies – watched her as she passed. She bent forward to read the cards but they only told her incomprehensible names and dates. A keeper winked, alarmingly alive. She turned back to the display. A bird-headed man carried food on a platter. It's early closing, she thought, and I've missed the butchers.

She moved towards the next room where the mummies were. She stopped in her tracks and gazed around. She was surrounded by empty wooden boxes. They were worn with age and covered with paintings. The gallery was large and silent. Huge figures stood against the walls gazing out with their beautiful tinted masks. Some were made up with paint – red lips, thick black lines around their eyes – and some were just gold.

She knew about mummies, of course. She had seen them in pictures and in one of Steve's books but she had not expected them to be so big and to make her feel so unimportant. Laid out horizontally she could see some tattered shapes wrapped in brown bandages. She was not frightened – not now she was alone. In fact she felt drawn to these ancient human parcels. With no arm to cling to, she did not feel like clinging; with no suede jacket to shudder against, she forgot about shuddering. The painted beauty was like that lady on the *Cutty Sark* but these had once been real. She took a step.

'I think you're thinking the same as me.'

She stopped and turned.

'That death seems so poignant, when their faces are painted for it.'

It was a man. June stiffened, half-resentful, half-flattered. Is my nose red from the rain? Has my mascara been washed off? But she relaxed; the man's voice was low, his face sincere. He was obviously as surprised by these figures as she.

'They're dressed for the ball,' he said, 'they've outlined their eyes with such care, but the dance is the dance of death.'

That sounded like poetry. 'They've put on so much make-up,' said June. Her hand went to her own powdered cheek. 'It sort of makes them seem more dead.'

'Because they thought they were defeating it. That makes them seem rather brave and human, doesn't it.'

June shivered. 'That's just what I was thinking.'

'I could tell.'

'Why?'

'You have a very sensitive face. Hasn't anyone told you that?'

She looked at him. His face, too, was sensitive: delicately modelled, with sad blue eyes that gazed into her very soul. Not your coarse type. Though bearded, this was a short, light affair, well under control. Her preoccupations seemed trivial when faced with his pale compassion. Around them the masks gazed timelessly.

They walked around the gallery and he explained the captions. It was a relief, having somebody to inform her at last. His name was Wil somebody and he worked in advertising. An art director, he said. He had come to the museum to think of some ideas for a new campaign. She did not catch the name of the product but it was a sort of colour retainer for fabrics. '*Some Things Never Fade.*'

He glanced at his watch and then laid his hand on her shoulder. 'Listen June – may I call you June? It's twelve o'clock. Why don't we have a quiet drink somewhere? There's a nice pub opposite. You look as if you could sit down for a while.'

Her shoes did pinch. They went outside. He rearranged a parcel under his arm and opened his umbrella. In the car park stood a coach, its windows steamed up. Raincoated Japanese men trotted towards it. She was shielded by this man's brolly which was large, black and confiding.

Snug in her seat, a Martini and lemonade in front of her, she had an urge to talk. It would be such a relief; she hated not telling Steve.

'It's because I don't know things,' she said. 'I didn't know that whales were mammals – he had to show me a book after tea – and porpoises and dolphins. I didn't know what devolution was, or sanctions when it came up on the News.' In truth she did not really care for the News at all, except the end bits about missing children and things that really mattered. 'I don't like to ask him about everything, he'll think I'm silly. Or he might laugh at me. He does sometimes. Sometimes he reads out a bit from the newspaper and nearly kills himself over it and I can't see what he's getting at. I really can't.'

'Who's "he"?'

'Steve, my husband. He's so clever and quick. He's always leaping from one thing to another.'

The man gazed at her thoughtfully. 'Perhaps he's afraid to sit still. Have you thought of that?'

'And then in the pub. I don't want them to think I'm ignorant so I just sit there trying not to put my foot in it.'

'Just like a decorative feature. Not a human being at all.'

She nodded, sipping her drink. How well he understood. 'When I stopped my job last month I had a bit of time to myself. I could think about it then. Before, I'd always had to work.'

Why it was so liberating for a woman to work she could not understand. Her mother was not liberated by it and nor was she. There was no time to think at work, and then you got home and there was to time to think there either. Now she had time. No Clive and Vince and John clamouring and messing up the house and not noticing they'd done it; no Mum to worry about; no Dad to fetch and carry for, though she knew he could have done half the things himself. She looked up. 'Anyway, I'd got a bit tired and I was going to the doctor about my migraines when I read this magazine in his waiting room. *Yours*, it was called.' It was not really her cup of tea, *Yours*; it did not have interesting recipes and how the stars really lived, what their bathrooms were like, things like that. In fact there was not a lot to read in it at all. 'Then I saw this article. There was a picture of a girl looking out of her kitchen window and the fridge behind her was just like mine. Electrolux. It was called "Use Your Resources" and I thought it was about how to get the most out of your freezer so I started reading it. But it was all about using the local library and museum and swimming baths and whatever, to widen your interests. "Don't be imprisoned in your home", it said.'

June sipped her drink. She herself hardly thought of her home as a prison – her little consultancy booth had more fitted that description. She looked up. He did not seem bored. Across the small pub table he nodded understandingly; his moderate half-pint rested in front of him, barely sipped.

'But that night one of Stevie's friends came round and they were talking about something and they didn't even bother to explain it. They knew I wouldn't understand. I knew I wouldn't as well. I can't even remember what it was now, either.' She laughed. The man's pensive look wandered over her, searching the answers. 'So I thought I'd do what it said. The magazine.'

'Great idea, June.'

'So I went down to the library and looked at some books in the reference place, and got a library ticket so I can take books home.'

There was a pause. 'Know something, June? When you're excited you get this amazing blush – rather delicate, like a petal.'

June stopped. She looked at him. Then another, uneasy thought crossed her mind. The words sounded familiar. Had she not spoken them, or words to that effect, last night when Steve was telling her about the whales?

She went on hastily: 'Anyway, I've been there four times. I look things up – ships, Egypt – he's mad about all those gods and mummies – and trains and trad jazz and things. I try to keep a notebook too because I'm so bad at remembering. I write down things I hear on the radio. And I take books home to read while he's at work. At least I try to read them. I keep them in the airing cupboard because it's the only place he doesn't go. At least he did the other day when he was putting away his trousers but I'd hidden them under the sheets. The books, I mean.'

He did not seem to mind her rattling on. She took another sip. 'If it wasn't for Mr Poultney I don't think I would have kept it up, but he's been ever such a help finding me things to read and not laughing when I ask stupid questions. There was once a teacher like that at school, only he left. It was Mr Poultney who told me to come to the British Museum. The Egyptian Room's the finest in the world, he said. Very – what did he say – comprehensive. He told me how to get the room plan and find my way about. Next week he's going to tell me about the Greeks if there's nobody bothering him.'

'Er, who's Mr Poultney?'

'The man at the library. The librarian. The head librarian, actually, but he's not at all high and mighty. He's a bit shy. That helps because I don't feel so silly. It shouldn't be silly, should it? You see, I want to better my education. I

89

don't want to get like my Mum got.'

He leant forward. 'That's great, June, really great. Seems like you're starting to do something on your own terms. Work at it, June, keep at it. But remember one thing.' His eyes were bright blue in his face, blue and sincere. 'You're not doing it just for Steve, you know. You're doing it for yourself, June. That's why I think you should keep it to yourself. It's a part of *you* that's growing, a separate part. Keep it yours, June, just for a little longer.'

There was a silence. How well he understood; she herself had never put it into words like that. But she felt uneasy, talking about Steve to an almost complete stranger. With her finger she pushed a Harp coaster back and forth; its cardboard edges were stained with someone else's beer.

'I've got no complaints about Steve. Please don't get me wrong.'

He raised his eyes to hers. 'But it's a little sad, isn't it, June, that you can't communicate about this together. Just what kind of a man would make a wife like you feel inadequate?'

'That's not right,' she said hotly. 'He doesn't: *I* do.'

To change the subject she turned to the brown paper bag on the floor. Its contents jutted out – *Brock Fireworks Bumper Family Pack*. 'I love Guy Fawkes,' she said. 'Are you going to let them off with your family? Do you have lots of children?'

The man lowered his gaze. 'Well, you know. . . .' He shifted his poppy-printed tie, as if his collar were too tight.

'I love children. Are they boys or girls?'

There was a little silence. 'Both. June, let's get back to *you*. I feel you've told me some important things today. Check?' He drank a little beer and paused. 'June, shall we make it *our* secret? I wonder if I'm being presumptuous. I hope I'm not. I just feel we're starting to get to know each other. Perhaps I could help you a little – there's the V and A, we could make a trip there some lunchtime. . . .'

June put down her glass. The whole conversation fell into place. She was right; she really was very stupid. She had thought the subject to be different. A familiar feeling began, one of constriction and disappointment.

She gathered up her handbag, making polite excuses about having to get to the shops and it's being early closing. She felt a wave of longing, not just for Steve but for the calm impersonal library and the calm impersonal Mr Poultney. This man spoilt it all.

She did not feel upset, just let down. She pulled on her hat, buttoned her coat and tap-tapped along the pavement. After their brief respite her feet ached again in their pinched and strappy shoes. She felt trapped inside her cream polo-neck and her raincoat, trapped inside her powdered face. Her looks were her mask, like those mummy cases were masks.

No, the British Museum was one of the educational centres she would not revisit. He haunted it, with his floral tie and his creepy sympathy. Him or someone else. And she was just beginning to get interested in the Egyptian bit, too.

TEN

Guy Fawkes night. Outside in the damp sky a rocket shattered. Claudia sat in the armchair, a book propped on her knee, trying to read.

Not, now she thought of it, that Adrian and herself had ever done much about Guy Fawkes. Only once or twice, in fact, had they gone to Greenwich Park to watch the fireworks from the hill. But hindsight made of these occasional trips something regular; it settled them into a ritual whose absence she could now feel, wistfully. Loss organ-

ized her memories and made them neater, sometimes mis-
leadingly so. Still, even their own non-participation made
of those firework evenings something special; the popping
gas fire seemed more conspiratorial when all over London
the bonfires were crackling.

Was this happening with Beth? Were they snuggling
down while over Muswell Hill the sky exploded? Or was he
inaugurating a new trip, to Alexandra Palace perhaps or
Hampstead Heath – starting a lifetime of them, in Beth
territory? A whole new pattern emerging, Adrian and
Beth, cemented by the steady punctuation of national and
family celebrations. No longer a love affair; a shared life.

Of this shared life, so far she knew but little. For six
weeks now she had not seen Adrian. *Will write when I am
clearer*, he added as a postscript to the short notes that
arrived, mainly about arrangements. He was buying a new
camera; this she learnt from a request for some forgotten
insurance form. They were planning to visit his cousins in
Derbyshire; this she learnt from a request for some book
he had promised his cousins the last time that they (Adrian
and herself) had gone there. The tone of these notes was
apologetic. *Terribly sorry, but rather vital,* or *Could you just
possibly stick it in an envelope?* She would, of course, prefer
to be bothered more. His tact frustrated and pained her;
the lack of meat between these chance bones caused her
hours of speculation.

There were so few props for the little theatre whose show
ran concurrent with her own. There was Adrian, of course,
but was he now playing a new part – more passionate
perhaps, and fulfilled? There was the handful of objects he
had taken, now rearranged inside those unspecified windows. And Beth? A hesitant voice on the telephone and
one muzzy snapshot. It showed Beth bending over some
roses, her face turned, smiling, up at the camera. Beth like
this, stooped and summery, had to be shifted here and
there like a cardboard cut-out, her sleeveless dress unsuit-

able for these autumn days, her blurred face tantalisingly indistinct.

This gardening girl, what was she now discovering about Adrian? Though at time she ached with jealousy, at others Claudia surprised herself with a motherly interest in this plump, timid young female. How is she managing? Has Beth discovered yet how he clicks his teeth against his biro as he ponders his paperwork; what an age he takes when he does the washing-up? Nowadays she, Claudia, clung to these trivial irritations; they eased her loss. At times she could commiserate with Beth, until the thought struck her: perhaps he no longer does these things.

A rocket cracked and the doorbell rang, almost simultaneously. 8 o'clock. She darted to the mantelpiece mirror; swiftly she took out her lipstick – *Come Closer*, a new shade. The *quiet gentleman* was certainly punctual. Or was this the *non-smoking accountant?* She had forgotten which one was coming at eight.

She opened the door of the flat; in the long, shared hallway she hesitated. Through the frosted glass stood a smudge. Still she hesitated – she, who had given countless interviews at work. But work was so easy. Like a bride, like a landlady, she smoothed down her hair and walked to the door.

He said: 'I've come about. . . .' he coughed, 'I believe you have. . . .'

'Do come in.'

'Er, after you.'

'Whoops. Narrow, isn't it.'

'Sorry. Up the stairs?'

'No, here, ground floor. Through here.'

'Sorry.'

'Sorry.' She squeezed past the long, raincoated figure and emerged into the living-room.

'Do sit down. You're right on time.'

'I waited until eight.'

'You arrived earlier?'

'I waited in the street. I waited until eight.'

'Heavens, you should have come in.'

'Oh no,' he said, 'no, I couldn't do that.'

Her first impression had been of great age and of great length, of a long, emptyish beige mackintosh. Glancing at him now, she saw that she had been wrong about the age. He was very thin; he stooped; the skin on his pale, bony face had the yellowish, stretched sheen of an old man. So smooth and waxy, that skin. Yet in fact he must be quite young, probably in his twenties. He sat down on the edge of the sofa.

She smiled at him. 'You must be *quiet gentleman requires bedsitter*.'

'Indeed, it was my humble little announcement. . . .'

'Would you like a drink?'

'Thank you, but. . . .' he twisted his long, pale hands, 'no, no thank you.'

She hid her glass with her foot. 'Have you come far?'

'Kilburn. A swift journey, courtesy of London Transport.'

'Ah.'

He was a librarian, he told her, Alistair Poultney by name, and had been living in Kilburn for some time. This was far from his library, which was in south London, nearer Claudia's flat. 'Besides, Mammon has reared his ugly head.'

'How?'

'In the form of a notice to quit. A new landlord – you can imagine, redecorating the rooms, knocking down walls, putting up the price. Where one falls, the other rises.' He coughed again. Was he apologetic or just unwell? 'Beyond my means, I'm afraid.'

'Would you like to see the room?'

She led him there, going first this time. 'I've just painted it.' She pointed to the walls; Tempo in here too, in colour as

94

non-committal as his raincoat. 'There's a wardrobe, and a wash-basin over there.'

'It appears to have all the necessary, the necessary –'

His voice was drowned in a battery of bangers. Gunfire from all sides. Through the window the sky burst into silver glitter. The whoosh of a rocket, a shower of sparks. 'They're having a party next door,' she said. All London seemed to be sending up fireworks. Uninvited, the two of them stood in the small, dun-coloured room.

'In cases such as these, I believe. . .' he was fumbling in his pocket, 'references are called for. . . .'

He bent over his pocket, standing beside the chaste, candlewick-covered bed that had held Verity, and had held the slumbering bodies of her friends. From his pocket fell a ball of fluff, a creased bus ticket, a scrap of paper on which was written her own address. She turned her eyes from this private collection.

'Aha.' He passed her a piece of notepaper. '*Most particular in his habits,*' she read in a wavery scrawl, '*a clean gentleman . . . Mr Poultney has resided here for six years . . . no complaints. . . .*'

'There's a razor socket here,' she said, 'and an electric kettle.'

They hovered for a moment, formal and yet domestic, gazing at the china tooth-mug and the small, waiting rack for shoes.

'Rather small, isn't it.' The woman, whose name Claudia had failed to catch, gazed around the room. 'Of course it's only temporary, I need hardly say. Just a stop-gap.' She fiddled with the toggles on her overcoat. 'I've got a large number of friends here, very good friends, many a home I'd be welcome in, believe me. . . .' She twisted a toggle. 'But just at this point in time . . . you know how it is. . . .'

Of uncertain years, she had a startling appearance. Her thick hair was dyed black; its ends, however, were singed and reddish. Make-up had been carefully applied; on her forehead were pencilled two curved eyebrows. Below them, bright eyes darted to Claudia. 'Yes, I'm really blessed in that respect. I can tell you this, I can see you're a woman of intelligence, that's why one relies on the *New Statesman* .... Of course they were horrified when I told them I was looking for a room. *Joyce*, they said, *you're not the type* ...'

Swiftly she was opening the wardrobe door; she checked the number of hangers on the rail; she opened drawers and closed them. Pencilled brows raised, her eyes darted around the room. So many times she must have done this. Again Claudia turned her eyes away.

'Central heating, I see.'

'We put it in a year ago. My husb –'

'An electric ring, good. What about kitchen arrangements?'

'Snacks you could do in here. Other meals you could use the kitchen.'

'I mean, we just like to know where we stand, don't we? Best to get these things settled now – avoids misunder –'

A bang.

'Just a firework. They're having a party.'

'Noisy neighbours?'

The party seemed to be in full swing. In the sudden, staccato silences of this conversation Claudia could hear the murmur of voices, a shrill giggle. Through the window there spread a rosy glow. Leaping sparks gave the room an unreal, theatrical air. She looked at the woman's painted face. Why was her hair scorched – from always being the onlooker at other people's fires?

'It's nice and large,' said the *Retired Accountant*. He appeared more optimistic than Pencilled Eyebrows but then this room, it seemed, could become anything. An elderly, gallant man, he followed Claudia around the flat, complimenting her on the pleasant, residential nature of the neighbourhood, he had always been fond of Wandsworth, on the convenience of the bus routes, on the way a young lady like herself had managed to make it all so – well – nice, what with the plants and the books. His better half had passed away this August; how fond she, too, had been of books, you couldn't tear Amy away from a good biography; how fond, indeed, she had been of plants, passers-by stopping and staring at her window boxes, she always put on a fine display, first bulbs and then the summer bedding.

Next door the bonfire had died down and the garden was dark. Claudia drew the curtains. Eleven o'clock; she was full of other people's ghosts, of their ten-minutes occupation of her blank room, a small room, a large room, with its ready bed. The accountant had gone. Who would she choose, whose Corn Flakes would join hers on the table, a little breakfast marriage?

She closed the front door and went outside. The road was empty, its terraces stretching down to the far, lit high street (this in fact was Battersea rather than Wandsworth but she did not like to correct the accountant). A bus passed, reappeared briefly between the buildings and was gone. Whence had they come, tonight's visitors? Via some printed lines they had stepped into her warm flat. The fireworks were finished. On the pavement lay a cardboard cylinder, a husk, its gay lettering burnt. Briefly it had soared; now it lay forgotten, tomorrow's hurrying feet would tread on it as they passed. Where had they gone, those and the countless others? Back into the dark, back into their rented rooms where they were clean and gentlemanly, never noisy, never giving cause for complaint, oh no Mr Poultney is most particular in his habits.

A fireworks party when she was younger. She had been in the garden with the grown-ups watching the rockets; after a while she went indoors. There she found a circle of girls, ones of her own age who were frightened of the bangs. They had sparklers instead. The living-room was dark; no one spoke. They were waving their sparklers around and around, in the blackness the liquid white lines swooped, looped and circled, a weave of dreams. Every now and then some shadowy adult leant forward to light a new sparkler; for an instant a girl's face was lit up, rapt. Then the match and the face were extinguished. Where had they gone, those girls who had sat on the rug, tense and radiant? Were they still dreaming? Perhaps they were out in the dark alone, where she, Claudia, had joined them.

ELEVEN

It was the day after Guy Fawkes' and already dusky, this dark month, by four. Steve walked down the Battersea shopping street. Under a fluorescent glare, moist meats were displayed in the butchers. In the hair salon ladies sat under the hoods, their heads hotting up.

Denton Drugstore was crowded and the manager occupied. Steve waited beside the pharmaceutical counter. He was thinking about June.

Ease the pain, said a bottle. *Sooth the itching*.

He felt so guilty. Did not everyone consider him lucky? Should he not consider himself so? He had everything anyone could want – beautiful wife, clean home, warm dinner waiting.

For minor wounds, rub in thoroughly.

Was it something small and nagging or was it a deeper void?

Mr McClure the manager cocked his head, attentive to a lady customer. Steve shifted on to the other foot. His whole life seemed to be spent pressed against display racks, waiting. Once he had thought this job to be so free, but that was an illusion. No roads were really open.

Lamps lit, warm flat, warm woolly arms around him.

Feeling stuffy and congested?

June jumping up, frowning, to wipe his spilt drop of beer. June, her lovely mascara'd eyes following his every move.

Himself when still unmarried, gazing at her. What had he expected? Sometimes nowadays he glimpsed what he had thought his marriage might be, as when, driving in a car along a motorway one glimpses here and there the winding leafy lane that the motorway has replaced.

'I want it frosted,' said the woman.

'Sorry madam. We only have it in a glossy.'

'I don't like glossies.'

'We have *Dream Come True* in a frosted. This one.'

'It's not the same. It's a dirtier pink.'

The harsh fluorescent light exposed the surrounding faces. Those who wore make-up appeared orange and powdery; the pencilled lines showed around their eyes, the crimson smears around their lips.

'*Dream Come True*, madam, is almost exactly the same shade.'

'Let me have another look.' A pause. 'I still say it's a dirtier pink.'

Once he had thought June was ill, so pink were her cheeks. He had rushed up, all anxious. In fact she had just put on too much *Liberesse* Blusher.

'What about those ones over there?' said the woman. 'The ones in the nice gold tubes.'

Ladies and gentlemen, do not put your trust in packages. Steve shifted on to the other foot.

The woman purchased the gold one. The transaction completed, Mr McClure turned to Steve. They went through the usual lists.

'Anything new to show us?'

'Just a replacement Pochette holder. Yours looked as if

99

it had been a bit knocked about. Oh, and some advance stuff about our new skin preparation . . .'

Steve rummaged in his dispatch case. Leafing through the papers he uncovered the photo of a scalped rabbit.

He snapped shut the case. 'Nothing new.' He paused, then made a gesture that included all the neighbouring display stands. 'Anyway, it's all the same rubbish.'

Mr McClure did not hear this; a customer interrupted and he turned away. Steve picked up his case. Within it, bundled away amongst the Christmas promotion stickers and printed order forms, lay the anti-vivisection leaflet, yellow and flimsy as his conscience. *This Must Be Stopped*, it said. *Cosmetics Testing, Let Us Put The Evidence Before Your Eyes*. A series of snapshots showed hands holding up rabbits and cats; their mutilations were mercifully blurred by the bad photography. When he had given his address and phone number to Marge he had half expected a murmured assignation. Instead she had sent him this.

He squeezed past the wobbly, plastic cosmetics stands and rummaged for his car keys. Outside on the pavement he hesitated. He would salve his conscience about Marge, likewise about the cats and rabbits and whales. He might not quiet his deeper doubts but it was better than nothing.

By an odd coincidence, it was situated in the next street to his old bedsit. Steve lingered on the pavement. Beside him rose the peeling Notting Hill terrace. It contained the kind of shops which seem neither entirely open nor entirely closed – a sewing-machine wholesalers; a hearing-aids supplier; a sleazy-looking *Sayeed Bros. Import/Export*. When he had lived in this area he must have passed, countless times, the small hand-painted sign: *First Floor: Green Earth*. But that was over a year ago; perhaps it had not existed, then.

Steve climbed the stairs and stood on the threshold. The room was filled with smoke and the clatter of typewriters.

It was crowded and shabby, its walls peeling with posters. He stood there, wishing he had come in his weekend gear.

However, nobody noticed his entrance. Nearby, a man sat at a typewriter. Leaning forward, he read what he had typed, scratched his beard and continued. There were many other people in the room; over in the corner a figure of unidentifiable sex fiddled with a duplicating machine. Thick brown hair fell over its face. Could it be Marge? He had never seen her with dry hair. Steve coughed. Still no one noticed.

'Just ringing Saltdene Phosphates . . .'

'Got the proposed route . . ?'

'Phone for you, Dave. *Time Out* . . .'

'Who's making coffee today . . ?'

'Got the elm figures here . . .'

'Fixed it yet, Marge . . ?'

So it was her. She shook her head and went on fiddling. Steve looked around. Who was the boss? Apparently no one. There was no partitioned-off desk; no preened secretary sat attentive, pad on stockinged knee. Men and women worked side by side. A thin, hairy man walked from table to table dispensing mugs.

Where's the talent then? Bruce would have said. Steve approached a girl, passing with a sheaf of papers. She had a shiny face, innocent of make-up. Instinctively Steve glanced down. *Two aspirins*, Bruce would have said, *on a blooming ironing-board*. Steve smiled at her.

'I wonder if I could speak to Marge?'

'Over there.'

Steve made his way around the tables, stepping over the scrumpled paper. *What a mess*, June would have said, nose wrinkling. One of the windows was broken and patched with cardboard.

'Hello.'

Marge looked up. 'Oh, it's you.'

She wore a tartan man's shirt, the sleeves rolled up. It

101

was too large for her; she looked frail. In her thin hand she held a screwdriver.

'Can I help?' he asked.

'You don't know how it works.'

'I can try.'

'The inking's too heavy. It's fixed now.' She bent over and twisted in the last screw. With surprisingly strong hands she rammed down a metal bar. 'That's it. Sodding thing's always playing up.' She straightened up and pushed back her hair. 'Anyway, you'd have messed up your rising-executive suit.'

She put the tools away into a box. Above her head was a poster. It depicted an industrial canal frothing with suds. *Care To Come Fishing*? it said.

Steve gestured around the room. 'Bit crummy, isn't it?'

'It's the best we can do. We don't have much money.'

Steve paused. 'That's what I've come about.'

She looked at him for the first time. Above her head, transfixed in monochrome, lay the grey water with its floating foam. Pintaubaum had used a river for its *Youth Dream* campaign. Soft-focus greens and blues; amongst the grass daffodils in discreet plastic pots, imported for the occasion since they were out of season; a leggy model with her skirt hitched up, her feet dabbling.

'Money?' asked Marge.

'You were right about my job.'

'I never knew what it was.'

'It doesn't matter now.' Steve took out his cheque book. He wrote a figure. Marge stepped closer – simply, he realized, to look at the amount. He smelt her not unpleasant scent of hot young body and unwashed shirt.

'£250,' she said.

'It's all I can manage.' He had saved it up for the new bedroom carpet. Kossett deep-pile shag, in cream; the film star touch. 'Who shall I make it out to?'

'Green Earth,' she said. 'Thanks.'

That was all. No amazement; no breathy, flushed gratitude; no hand on his arm. He felt hurt.

'I'll take it to Les,' she said. 'He's the treasurer.' What did she want, a couple more noughts?

What did he, Steve, want? Nothing more, surely, than what he had got. Marge was bending over that fellow Les's desk, talking to him.

Steve made his way across the room and down the stairs. She did not even wave goodbye. Anyway, she was not much to look at. Too thin, too sallow. Half-irked, half-laughing at himself, Steve stepped into the street.

TWELVE

'That's lovely! It's so clean, Adr – Alistair.'

Increasingly Claudia called her lodger by her husband's name. She stood in the spotless kitchen. 'You've done a marvellous job.'

Never had the kitchen looked so neat, never since the days of Adrian's diligence. Longer and paler than her husband, Alistair stood beside the sink, twisting the dish-cloth in his damp hands. Why did she turn men into house-wives?

'You've saved me so much bother.' Claudia smiled at him warmly. It would of course have been much simpler to do it herself. It took a good deal of time to explain, at the outset, exactly where things went without appearing bossy and condescending; to closet herself in the living-room for a loitering quarter-half – no, half-hour, he took so long – fiddling around and pretending to be busy, alert for the sound of breaking china or wire wool upon non-stick pan. Then, summoned by the gush of the outside drain, there was a good deal of exclaiming to be got through, enough to gratify Alistair but not enough to unsettle him further, to cause his eyes to lower and the dishcloth to be twisted into a tighter knot.

And then, of course, there were the stealthy re-arrangements afterwards. She dare not do much; he was just starting to share in the joint tasks and there was a certain *modus vivendi* which she must never, ever show, by her altering, that he had in fact disarranged. Forever must her house-plants upon the kitchen windowsill be placed to one side, while in the central position must rest the Fairy Liquid and mug of plastic brushes, catching the best of the afternoon sun. So complex, her ruses to prevent their mutual embarrassment; so cumbersome, her devices to make him feel essential.

It was a week, now, that he had been living with her. Why in fact had she chosen him? Partly because she had endured two nights of interviews and could not face a third session of indicating the razor point; of mutual, veiled inspection. Partly because Alistair was the youngest and therefore the most understandable. Partly simply because he was the first. At the time she had considered him odd, with his shabby mac and white, fidgeting hands; however, distinctly less odd than the subsequent painted lady, the sad accountant, the stubbly-chinned man who pressingly read her palm, and the woman who never sat on a lavatory seat without first laying down paper, a supply of which she carried in her handbag, and would Claudia like to see a photograph of dear Boris, such a lovely tabby cat, no one else would ever take his place and look, you'd think he was smiling wouldn't you.

That first Saturday lunchtime: the thumps of Alistair's unpacking, then silence. He must be eating his meal in his room. She had urged him to join her in the kitchen; it seemed wrong, him alone with his rustling paper bags.

He had two meat pies and a pint of pasteurised, its cardboard spout unfolded. They sat at the kitchen table.

She helped him to salami; to be friendly and relaxing, she had asked for some of his pie.

'Hey, it's still warm,' she said.

'I purchased it, so to speak, *en route*.'

'With all your suitcases? You must have been lumbered.'

'I haven't overmuch luggage.'

'Some bread?'

'Er, just a little slice. Thank you so much. I put it on the radiator.'

'What?'

'The pie. To keep warm.'

'I hope I remembered to switch it on.'

'Oh, no complaints. The room is very cosy. Very adequate.'

'It's rather small.'

'Heavens – please have some more.'

'No, I mean the room.'

'Sorry.'

'No, it's delicious, I'd love a bit more. Do you have any family?'

'No, no, I'm a carefree bachelor.'

'Brothers and sisters? More cider?'

'Thank you, just a drop. No, I am a solitary blessing.' He coughed. 'My mother lives in Malvern.'

He did seem solitary. There was something both dateless and ageless about him; unloved, he appeared unaltered by the fluctuating fashions as there was no one, it seemed, for whom he needed to change. His colourless hair remained cut into a short back-and-sides. Revealed, his thin neck when he stood at the sink with his breakfast plate. His painstaking care of his clothes, their small stitched darns, told of someone who has only himself to tend. Personally clean to the point of finickiness, he yet gave off the scentless aroma of neglect.

He had not changed his room. No reason that he should. Why then should she feel disappointed, one day when he

105

was absent and she peered around the door? Everything was exactly as she had left it. A few additions, of course – some journals (*Listener, New Statesman*, a rather surprising *Time Out*), his two cardboard suitcases, books on the shelves (something pushed behind them, wrapped in a handkerchief); unadored, beige walls. On the floor stood his carrier bag of washing. 'I make a Saturday trip,' he had said, 'to the local launderama, or cleanerette, or supawash.' He would always have the same amount of washing, no more, no less. There was something so lodger-like about that carrier bag.

(Her husband's clothes. It was usually herself who went to the launderette. Years of this, then suddenly his words about Beth and she felt shy to touch them. A private bundle, as if he were her lodger. *But Claudia, I've always felt like your lodger*.)

Like its occupant, Alistair's room appeared so untouched. Had he grown up solitary – as a child, had he held up the two pieces of Lego and had there been nobody to show him how they fitted? Finally had he ceased asking? This was difficult to imagine; she could not picture him as a child.

But he did have a mother. On the rare occasions that he talked personally, it was of his mother that he spoke. They exchanged letters once a week. On the envelope the writing was shaky, but this woman had been young once. Once, surely, she had helped him with his patient constructions; once she had sewed name-tags upon his socks, smaller versions of those now rolled up tightly in the laundry bag.

After a week Claudia knew his little routines: for breakfast, a vaguely eccentric combination of Ryvita, margarine and paste (salmon or crab, he varied this), for supper pork or lamb chop plus tinned tomatoes and Smash (he never varied this). Upon his arrival he had placed his small store on the designated kitchen shelf – almost scraped-out tub of Flora, half-finished jar of Shamphams, painstakingly folded-over packet of crispbread, all transported halfway across London with two changes of bus. *Mr Poultney is very clean and quiet*. No, she had no complaints. In a way she wished she had. *Mr Poultney is very gentlemanly in his habits*. Thumping stereo, dishevelled girls ... she could cope with that. Nobody had visited him and he had so far not gone out, except to work late at the library. He seemed to be always there, this lingering, elderly youth. Dog-like, he yearned to be of use. In his brown bedroom slippers he followed her creakingly, enquiringly; he hesitated and then he coughed. In her own sitting-room she could no longer lower her coffee cup.

'A little more?'

The rasp of his nylon shirt as he lunged forward, pot in hand.

Saturday night, and Claudia was sitting in the living-room. From the kitchen came the grinding squeak of the tin-opener and the scent of singeing chop. Tonight she had eaten earlier; she wondered if he would bring in his supper on a tray. She had suggested this to him, lightly, to give him the option. So far their meals had seldom coincided; he did not have to get to the library until ten and so their morning routines were spaced a little apart. This was a slight relief. Since Alistair's arrival she had become extremely conscious of the bodily functions; the knob turning on the lavatory door, the silence, the muffled *sorry* from within. And then there were the couple of meals they had so far shared – his noisy nose-blowings and apologetic little cough, the crack as his Ryvita broke when he was spreading the marge, the crunch of her toast.

(Meals with her husband, the two of them familiar enough to be reading their respective books. Familiar enough or bored enough? By now she could not tell. Certainly so accustomed to each other that they no longer heard the noises.)

The rattle of saucepan; the creak of the kitchen cupboard. Was he getting the tray? By now she – and no doubt Alistair too – had reached the stage of waiting poised in one room until the other had safely closed his door; of becoming alert to the exact position and probably movements of the other; of developing a sixth-sense, finely-tuned lodger ears.

'Ah, good!' she said. 'Do sit down.'

'Please don't turn it off.'

'It's only some ghastly American thing.' She reached towards the television.

'Please.' He hesitated with the tray. 'I would feel terrible.'

She, too, hesitated; she left it on.

'Know something? You're the best-looking broad ever walked in through that section door.'

'Hey, I'm a cop too.'

'With legs like yours, it's kinda hard to remember.'

'Shall I put the tray down here?'

As usual, Alistair was wearing his grey trousers and nylon shirt, with the evening addition of the fawn bedroom slippers. So solitary, he seemed, yet he was not exactly ugly – pale, sensitive face; pale, boiled blue eyes.

He took a sip of water. 'I see that you're partial to literature.'

'Yes, that's right.' Together their heads turned to the bookshelves.

'I, too, am an admirer of Miss Austen.'

'Which one's your favourite?'

'*Emma*, I think.'

'That's nice. I like her best. I think it's because I'm rather bossy. At least, my friend Verity tells me I am.'

'Of course, it's mostly the ladies she appeals to.'

'Who?'

He lowered his cup. 'Miss Austen.'

'If all cops looked like you, I could live with the lousy pay.'

'Hey, Lieutenant, should you –'

'Just a little inter-precinct collaboration. Jeez, you smell nice.'

'Mmm, kiss me again.'

She asked: 'do you do a lot of it?'

'I beg your pardon?'

'Reading? When you're surrounded by books all day?'

'Bit of a busman's holiday, isn't it.'

'What do you get asked for most, at the library?'

'Romances, romances. The strong-armed cavalier, the swooning female.'

End of Part One. The ads came on. *Are you ready for Monsieur Pintaubaum?* A low voice, almost hoarse. *'Because underneath you're man, all man.'*

She turned from the bronzed torso to the nearby shirt. 'I have special feelings, actually, about that product. . . .' She waited hopefully.

Alistair cleared his throat and put down his fork. 'I'm aware of why you've so very kindly asked me in to, so to speak, consume my humble repast here.'

'Oh Alistair, I'm so glad. Just so that I don't have to ask you in future.'

'You won't have to. I've been very remiss.'

'Oh good. You see, it seems silly, you in the kitchen, all cold –'

'If I may say so, it was a most tactful way of putting it.' He struggled up from his armchair and started feeling in his pockets. Upon each of his cheeks a pink spot was spreading. 'It's all here, I think.' He held out a bundle of notes.

'What's this?'

'My weekly rental. My means of remaining under this charming roof.'

'Oh God, is that what you thought when –?'

'Please, it's entirely my fault.'

There was a certain amount of confused explanation, while on the screen a blonde tossed her hair this way and

109

that to show how Evespray held, but so gently. Claudia cursed herself, that she had not made clear some system for rent-collecting, that she had caused, unwittingly, this large embarrassment when there were so many small ones anyway. She had only lived with people she had known.

'Do look at that.' To divert things she pointed to the screen. Jean-clad rumps were wriggling, the camera zooming in to the labels. The models bent from side to side, playing at flicking dusters and rubbing windows, turning round to smile at the screen. 'Honestly.'

'It certainly looks,' said Alistair, 'somewhat degrading.'

The girls jerked and swayed at their housework, the music thumping. Another close-up of buttock and label.

'Yes, somewhat degrading,' said Alistair, 'for the fair sex.'

'The housework or the bottoms?' She glanced at Alistair, who himself had cleaned the kitchen so much more thoroughly than she could, or would want, to do.

He paused. 'I cannot call myself an expert.' He coughed. 'With the exception of my mother, the female species has always been a mystery.'

He produced a battered packet of Turkish cigarettes.

'How very exotic.' She looked at him. He seemed a mystery too, with his pinched ways and his sensual smokes.

She tried to explain on the phone, a few days later, to Verity. It was after work but Alistair would not be back until nine as it was his late night at the library. It was a relief, being alone. She kicked off her shoes and lay on the rug, wriggling her toes in their grey tights.

'He seems so odd and solitary, Verry. Nobody's telephoned him. I feel sort of smothered and watched and relied on.'

'Claudia, it's terribly natural. I'd have expected it.'

'But it's not quite right. We're so awkward and embarrassed. Squeezing past each other in the corridor. The flat

110

seems so cramped now. Oh, I can't put my finger on it.'

'It's obviously the first relationship he's ever had, judging by what you've told me. Hence the clinging. No darling, it fits on the udder.'

'What?'

'Well, then that bit does, the tube bit. Then the pipe takes it to that big machine. Sorry Claudia.'

'He's so neat and tidy and he just sort of hovers around and hesitates.'

'I told you he would.'

'Would what?'

'Get like Adrian. You do that to people. They either veer away, terrified, or else they become weaker and more reliant. And more boring. Adrian became weaker, less of a person, just like your mother did with your father. By the end he had your taste in everything he said and thought; it wasn't good for either of you.'

'But Alistair has some odd tastes – you wouldn't think it to look at him. Like his Turkish cigarettes and his Lapsang Souchong tea. And he's always reading women writers.'

'Adrian became more of a woman.'

'But this is different. I don't know –'

'What? Then it all goes swoosh swoosh into that big thing and then they stick it in bottles and then we drink it. Do shut up.'

'What is it, a book?'

'I don't understand it, it's full of blasted machinery. Where the hell's Wil? He's never home.'

Claudia paused. She wished a crackling telephone did not separate them. Could she be false and bland? How much did Verity know? Lately she had been telling Claudia how pregnancy drew her and Wil closer, how he loved her swelling like a ripe fruit, how it turned him on. That was even more disturbing than Verity's current mood. Years ago when they had shared the flat Verity and herself had laughed, of course, at all the right taboos; *they* would be

111

different – they would be free, they would have lovers. They were; they did. Then they married and had both remained, in fact, remarkably faithful to their husbands. These husbands' present betrayals made Verity and herself closer than ever, close as sisters. Yet it was the one thing of which Claudia could not speak.

Verity said: 'I'm bored with my whining kids and this freezing house and all the mud.'

'Hey, I'm sorry. I thought you loved it.'

'Well today I don't.'

It could still surprise Claudia, Verity's bluntness in the midst of her usual modulated understanding. She preferred it, just as she preferred, secretly, Verity's brown roots to the henna'd frizz that sprang from them. 'Let's meet and talk,' she said. 'Can you come here?'

'It's so difficult with all the kids. Look, come down this weekend. No, next weekend.' She paused. 'Perhaps he's a murderer. Have you looked in his suitcases?'

'He's written some diaries.'

'One shouldn't look, of course.'

'Of course. I mean to say.'

'I mean to say.'

They both paused.

'On the other hand,' said Verity, 'perhaps you'll murder him. I can see the headlines. They'll come down and interview me. It sounds as if he irritates you terribly.'

'Funnily enough, in most of the ways Adrian did.'

'Not funnily enough,' said Verity. 'I'd expect that.'

'He's finicky. Like he flicks at a chair before he sits down on it. And the way he sort of squares up his mashed potato with his knife before he eats it, and pats it on the top. Of course with Adrian I couldn't admit these things, even to myself, because he was my husband . . .' Again she paused. 'Anyway, I'm sure Alistair's just as irritated by me. I'm getting awfully secretive, Verry, and embarrassed. I wash my knickers in my room because I can't bear the thought of

112

him soaking in the bath with them dangling up there above him. I hang them over my radiator, rows of them.'

Another time she had been called from the bathroom by the telephone. When she returned she heard splashes from inside; Alistair was having a bath. She, Claudia, strong and sensible, blushed for the little heap upon the floor – her brush tangled with hairs, her Tampax lying in the nest of her nightie.

'Talk about the odd couple!' Verity was laughing, the downright Verity she had known at school. 'Christ, I'm longing to see you two.' Suddenly she grew sombre. 'Sorry. No, I can see that when somebody's been, perhaps, unable to relate, when –'

'Cut it out,' said Claudia, refreshed by this conversation.

He's written some diaries.

Having replaced the receiver, Claudia remained on the hearthrug. She scratched her long, grey leg and interested herself in a hole near the toe. Scratching, she glanced at her watch. Eight o'clock. Alistair would not be home for an hour.

She knew they were diaries, being handwritten exercise books with dates on the covers. She had only glanced at them, of course; she had not opened them. But one had to just glance around ones lodger's room, didn't one; it was part of a landlady's duty. After all, it might have been a bomb.

By now she was standing in Alistair's room. That he was several miles across London and still at work meant there was no chance of his interrupting her; more than that, it somehow made him seem less involved. He was far away and busy.

They were wrapped in a handkerchief behind his leatherette Jane Austens. So carefully tucked in, she had known at first glance that they would be secret.

Claudia hesitated. She removed *Sense and Sensibility*,

113

lifted up the paisley shroud, and pulled out the lowest, and most frayed book. She opened it at random.

'*Frog's Spawn for Pudding. Eek Grr Horrors, Double Latin this afternoon.*'

School. Reassured, Claudia turned to another page. Eavesdropping into the distant, schoolboy past seemed scarcely eavesdropping at all.

'*Dorm 8 p.m. Cawf, Maguire and Box were playing I-Spy. Asked if I could join them (Note: never dared before). They said All Right. Bix did F for Photo. F! I ask you. Box is thick. They all laughed. Cawf did S for Sock. Maguire started another one. I said Is it my turn now? He said All Right Henface (from Poultney – Poultry. Larf Larf. I prefer Grey Matter, A.P. and that lot call me this when they are in the Mood. They are referring to my Brains.) The other things seemed obvious so I said F. (Top Secret: Fanlight.) Then they stopped guessing. Cawf started on about some rotten bat his father was bringing down next weekend. Bat begins with B. I said what about my F? Cawf and Co. went on about cricket in general, bat in particular. Then the bell rang. (Note: Will decline invitation to play again, even if they come on Bended Knee.)*'

Claudia gazed for a moment at the page. Since those days the cramped handwriting had scarcely changed. She closed the book, slid it back into the pile and tucked in the handkerchief, parcelling up the past.

She felt warm with guilt. She would be especially nice to Alistair when he returned, to make up for looking. Swiftly she left the tidy little room, with its tucked-in handkerchief and its tucked-in bed.

THIRTEEN

'*A short rushing sound leaped out of the boat – then all in one welded commotion came an invisible push from astern, while forward the boat seemed striking on a ledge; the sail collapsed and exploded; a gush of scalding vapour shot up near by; something rolled and tumbled like an earthquake beneath us. The whole crew were half suffocated as they were tossed helter-skelter into the white curdling cream of the squall. Squall, whale and harpoon had all blended together –*'

'Steve, just look at that!'

Steve put his finger upon page 56 of *Moby Dick*. He looked up. The TV screen showed an assortment of ice floes. No, on second glance they turned out to be large white objects constructed of moulded plastic. Somewhere a studio audience was chanting, the voices rising and falling.

'*Can he do it?*' the compère shouted. '*Come on, Stan, Evie's watching.*'

The picture cut to a luminous clock; above it, in winking letters THE BIG PLUNGE. The finger jerked.

'*Twenty seconds,*' cried the compère, his voice shrill. '*Nineteen seconds, Stan.*'

The picture cut to a man on hands and knees. A young man, he wore a baggy orange track-suit one size too large.

115

He shuffled along a raised white ramp. There was a tube in front of him; he disappeared into it, his orange rump wriggling.

'*We're all on tenterhooks here tonight,*' said the compère. '*Aren't we, Evie.*'

Beside him stood the wife. She was very young, her hair curled and lacquered for this TV appearance. Beneath the stiff crests her face was impassive. She was watching her husband.

The man emerged from the tube and scrambled to his feet. Ahead of him lay a rink of tiny white balls. He stepped on to it, stumbled and fell. From the crowd a moan of pleasure.

'*Fifteen seconds, Stan! On your feet or there'll be trouble back at home sweet home!*' The compère winked at Evie. She was neatly turned out; her crimson necklace matched her crimson shoes and the handbag that she clutched. She gazed at the flapping orange figure.

'*Thirteen seconds, Stan! Let's take another look at those mouth-watering prizes.*'

The picture cut to a large window. The camera drew in closer. Behind the glass stood objects that gleamed. '*One Colston Conquistator Mark III Twin-Tub Washing Machine,*' the compère's voice grew hushed, '*one Kenwood Electric Whip'n' Beat Blender –*' he turned to the audience – '*and I think I know who'll do the beating, Stan, if you don't get over that hoop – attaboy!*'

At the bottom of some steps the man halted. A hostess stepped out and with a flick blindfolded him with a scarf.

'*. . . one Queen of the Night Multi-Dial Thermal Hostess Platter and, oh Stan, I can see the gleam in the eye of your lovely better half – one Luxury Boudoir Set of Battery-Heated Hair Shapers With Styling Wand.*'

On hands and knees, the man was inching up the plastic rungs. He arrived on a platform and got to his feet.

The clock jerked. '*Ten seconds, Stan. How's his – ahem –*

performance, Evie?' He held the microphone to Evie but she said nothing.

The man groped around on his platform. To one side lay a slide leading down into a frothy tub. To the other side stood a plastic board with a keyhole near the top. On the floor lay a key. Fumbling blindly, the man bent down and felt for it. He picked it up.

Into the microphone Evie whispered: *'Get it in, Stan.'*

'That's how she puts it, eh Stan?' A titter from the crowd. *'You've got just three seconds.'*

The audience chanted. The man was holding the key, jerking and jabbing it at the surface of the board.

'One second.' A pause. *'Stan, your time is up.'*

The thud of a gong; it sounded far away, as if muffled by fog.

'No hard feelings, Stan.' The compère smiled; the crowd held its breath. *'It's The Big Plunge for you.'*

The platform tipped. The man, arms flailing, shot down the chute.

From the audience came a great sigh, as if the ocean were subsiding. There was too much froth to make a splash. The man emerged and clambered to his feet. He was piled with foam; it clung to him in white, weightless drifts.

Very slowly he climbed out of the tub. He pulled at his blindfold. Pieces of foam, shaken free, floated to the floor.

'Great try, Stan.' The compère approached, hand extended. The hostess appeared with a towel. The man took it; he turned away and bent his head. For a moment Steve thought he was weeping but he was just wiping his face.

Only the wife stayed back, on the raised plinth where she had stood throughout. She gazed at her husband but she did not move.

With a sigh, June settled back into the settee. Beside her Steve paused for a moment; then he opened his book.

'The wind increased to a howl; the waves dashed their

117

bucklers together; the whole squall roared, forked and crackled around us like a white fire upon which, unconsumed, we were burning, immortal in the jaws of death.'

'Steve, just look at that.' June had said this partly to get Steve's attention from his book. Once his eyes were raised, even to the TV screen, perhaps they could chat a little.

Not that she disliked *The Big Plunge*. She enjoyed it; she always had. But she could easily watch it while she was talking with Steve. She neither entirely watched nor entirely ignored TV; it was something flickering in the room, a coloured stir in the corner, and had been at home for as long as she could remember. It could seep in without anyone noticing, like cold cream into skin or that osmiris, osiris thing plants did. (Osiris? Had she seen that in the Egyptian Room?)

In two days, Friday, it would be Steve's sales conference. His boss would be there; the question of promotion was bound to come up. Steve was worried about this – in fact, she suspected that he was not actually reading at all, but using the open page as something to think against without being disturbed. She was not as stupid as people thought.

She would like to talk. She had not said quite what she meant, going on about the cupboard to match the banquette stools and that dress at Tempson's. What she really wanted them to talk about was something a bit more general – the future, perhaps babies. But she felt shy. Neither her Mum nor her Dad had been much good at discussing things like that. In fact, it took her wedding day and seven pints for her father to squeeze her arm and mutter that it wouldn't be the same without her.

Besides, there never seemed enough time. Steve was so restless, he was always jumping up to do something or else flinging himself on the settee, legs spreadeagled, reading with fixed concentration. What had that Wil man said in the pub about this? 'Afraid to sit still?' But he did sit still;

118

the trouble was, he seemed unreachable. If she talked he would pull her towards him and pat her like his pet dog, smiling but abstracted, listening but not really listening.

She would love to be able to concentrate like that when she was reading her library book. But there were so many things she could be doing – the kitchen shelves calling to be scrubbed, *Woman's Own* calling to be opened, its recipes calling to be tried. The small, printed words could not compete.

Here in the library it was different. Even if she had wished, she could hardly jump up and mop this lino floor. Far above her the ceiling was edged with moulded plasterwork; she could see, quite clearly, a cobweb. It dangled greyly, but not for her.

Thursday morning, and outside the High Street would be busy, housewives pulling tartan wheeled shopping bags bulging with buys. She knew every shop so well, the prices, the bargains. Her bus stop was situated outside the library steps; for a year she had stood there with her heavy carrier bags printed *Courtesy and Quality at Tempson's*. The library entrance was pillared. For a year those columns had shadowed her, and she had never turned to look.

Inside, the library had been modernised, with partitions between the bookshelves – Fiction D-H, I-M – and with wrought iron plant holders and a spiral staircase leading up to a *Staff Only* door. It was warm and surprisingly unforbidding. Her family had not been in the habit of visiting libraries. She imagined her mother when faced with those entrance pillars and the steel security bar – hesitating, humbled and wary. But she, June, had stepped up and pushed open the revolving doors.

She crossed her legs and pulled down her blue pleated skirt. Not that she was a great reader, even now. She preferred the *Pictorial Encyclopaedia* due to its illustrations. Even then her mind would wander. En route to

Nazism (a bemusing interest of Steve's) she had been waylaid in *Naples* and then halted, for some time, by *Nativity* – there was a lovely coloured picture of Mary with her baby, she had felt moved and broody. Or her eyes would travel over the notice panel with its posters for over 60's art clubs and family planning bureaux. More frequently she would gaze at her fellow scholars in the reference section, many of whom she was beginning to recognize. In the main these consisted of muttering old men and busty, plain schoolgirls who spread their exercise books over the glass-topped table.

She re-crossed her legs. Looking down, she saw the blur of her face reflected in the glass; today she had tied back her hair with a blue ribbon, the blur looked bare and serious. Sitting in her institutional chair she felt quite at home now. In its hushed way the library accepted her as it accepted everybody. Nobody glanced up at her – a relief, this, after the British Museum and worse still the National Gallery, few of whose paintings she had seen, so briskly had she been forced to move from one to the next by gentlemen only too anxious to explain them. This was her fifth visit. She would make this a habit; that man, Wil, had encouraged her in this respect. Already she knew her way around the shelves and stiffened if somebody else was occupying her seat at the reference table. With the others she queued at the desk with her chosen books, waiting for the electronic wand to touch the inner page, ping, and release it.

But today she could not concentrate. With Steve being away tonight, she could draw back a bit and look at what she had been doing. It was time to tell him; these last few weeks seemed silly, even bizarre now she thought about them. Wil was right about persevering, but wrong about persevering alone – besides, he had ulterior motives about that. She had nothing of which to be ashamed; the longer she delayed telling, the more awkward the telling would be

– and hurtful, too, for Steve, who was himself so open. By nature she was less so; she had brought herself up to be careful, in a family like hers you had to be careful, you kept things to yourself to stop them getting spoilt.

Tomorrow, when Steve returned, she would tell him. Besides, she felt irked that when he asked about her day she had nothing she could tell him. June gazed up from her chair; she was full of vague warm feelings towards Steve. Just behind the glassed-in children's section she could see Mr Poultney. He was standing on some steps, reaching up to a top shelf. He looked the same age as Steve, tall and thin too. But whereas Steve was lithe, Mr Poultney was stiff. Just now he was wiping his fingers fussily with his handkerchief. She was growing rather fond of him, and the talks they had together, but his awkwardness made her long for Steve, so loose and relaxed, so ready with his laughter.

June gathered up her things. At the bus stop she felt quite weak. She would ruffle Steve's brown hair and run her finger along his surprised brown eyebrows. She would lay her hot cheek on his chest. He had a lovely long lean body; at a selected moment she would tell him so. She blushed; this was not like her. She preferred him doing these things to her, by choice in the dark, and for everything to be back to normal in the morning.

I am very liberated, she thought, all of a sudden. When her bus came she did not take it. Instead she crossed the road and took a bus to Beckenham, a couple of miles away. She would buy Steve a present.

She passed the Boots window with its *Liberesse* display – talcs, colognes, a row of tiny glass bottles. Steve had put them there, or persuaded someone else to do so. She felt a glow, in passing.

She knew exactly where the aquarium shop should be because Steve had described its location. Dead opposite the place where he had rented their TV. June walked down from Boots and stood on the pavement. Across the road and visible through the queue of lorries stood *Rediffusion Rentals*. She turned around and inspected the shop fronts yet again. On her side there was a dry cleaner's, a sauna and a greengrocer's. The sauna was the central one, dead opposite the television place.

It looked brand new, with a curtained window, a discreet panelled door and a little bell. She was not naïve. *Nicolette Sauna and Massage* it said in red neon, lit up in broad daylight too.

June hesitated, undecided. She must have got it wrong. Or had she?

A conversation last Saturday morning. Steve was phoning his friend Dave with whom he had spent the previous evening at the King's Head. 'Blimey,' he had said, 'mouth's like an Arab's armpit.' The reply was unexpected, since Steve had in fact dialled his spinster auntie in Walthamstow. He knew both the numbers so well and had simply got them the wrong way round.

June, more thoughtfully, gazed at the plum velvet curtains behind the plate glass. She would prefer not to visualise what happened beyond those folds of cloth. At all hours of the morning and afternoon. Passing trade and regulars ... businessmen ... salesmen ... nudge-nudge say no more.

She was staring like an idiot. She moved over and stood next to the more wholesome fruit at the greengrocer's. She did not want herself to be thinking this. But how easy – aquarium shop and sauna, two places he might frequent, for rather different reasons. Steve was always quick and careless; how very easy to describe, quickly, carelessly, the one instead of the other. To get the exit views (as he blinked in the sunlight) mixed up, like those two phone numbers.

Only the other day had he not come home with his hair wet? 'Went down to Catford' he said. 'Saw the old man and

122

had a swim, for old times' sake.'

But *Steve*? Could she imagine him? And in the middle of the high street full of mothers and babies in pushchairs, not three miles from home?

But then he was always, well, eager for it. And quite a lot of times she was not quite as eager as he was, and him pretending that he didn't mind. . . . What was that serial last year – *Knock-Knock*. All about a door-to-door salesman with his suitcase full of oven-scourers, and the things he got up to. . .

She was being silly. It couldn't be true. But it was there, niggling away at the back of her mind. Small but gnawing as she stood gazing at the bunches of bananas hanging on their hooks. And she couldn't even buy him a present now, which was even more annoying in some ways. If only he had told her accurately . . .

On the way to the bus stop she passed, again, the Boots window. This time the *Liberesse* girl, muzzy in her hideous battledress, looked different. Her photo topped the stand; legs apart, challenging and suggestive, she now appeared to be leering. Steve was accompanied by this lady month after month, his portable cardboard whore. The girl looked horribly knowing.

FOURTEEN

Earlier that Thursday morning, and Claudia was having breakfast with Alistair. Lately he had been getting up in time to join her in this meal.

She viewed this with mixed feelings. Alistair's library did not open until ten; by and large, during the week she had eaten breakfast alone, thus free to read the newspaper, lick the marmalade spoon and twiddle with the radio knobs. By nature faithless to one station, she liked to switch to music if the *Today* programme became bogged down with sports reports or some long-winded trade unionist. Now it must mumble on, *'at this point in time, my colleagues and myself can only say, with respect, that because of the present policy adopted by management* . . , while Alistair passed her the milk jug. To an outsider they might have appeared married.

'*Oaty-Os*. Well well.' Alistair indicated the packet. 'That's a new one on me.'

'Thought I'd give them a whirl.' Claudia sat down. 'Got them at the late-night supermarket.'

Outside it was a blustery, grey day. Indoors it was snug. Between them on the table rested the Oaty-Os. Upon it was pictured, in cheerful colour, a smiling family with their spoons raised. Painted sunlight streamed through the painted window. There was a mum and a dad, a boy and a girl.

'Why,' Claudia demanded 'do they always make the girl the younger one?'

'The frailer sex. That, at least, is their perhaps mistaken impression.' He leant forward. '*Golden oaten rings,*' he read. '*Harvest goodness, enriched with the following essential minerals.*' He paused. 'By habit, as is no doubt observable, I am not a cereal man. My custom has been sought in vain by those who produce the Sugar Puff and the Bran Bud.' He cleared his throat. In common with her husband, the clue to his being intentionally rather than naturally ponderous lay in the length of the pauses. 'However, just this once . . . nothing ventured, as they say, nothing gained.'

'Alistair, how nice. I'll get you a –'

'No no, please. Let me.' With a scrape of the lino he pushed back his chair. From the cupboard he extracted a bowl.

'My husband was a Corn Flakes man,' she said, tearing

open the waxed inner paper. 'I've always flirted around a bit, played the field – Shreddies, Rice Krispies, you name it. My husband knew what he liked. Corn Flakes for him.'

Corn Flakes still? Does Beth bend over him tenderly, shaking the packet, filling his bowl with goodness? Daily fortified with vitamins and malt, do they sit side by side wordlessly, sunshine within and without? Brimming. My cup overfloweth.

Her husband and herself at breakfast. His lips pursed, womanish, as he sipped his tea. The cutting of the toast into two exact rectangles. She had made him a humble man, prim and unhappy.

She said aloud: 'He's probably eating Corn Flakes at this

Alistair cleared his throat. 'I think that's the post.' He scraped back his chair.

Impossible to have heard it down those two passages, but he disliked conversations when they got like this. Claudia gazed at the empty seat. She would like to tell him something of herself; it made her uneasy, that he edged away. They lived so closely, their tea canisters wedged together upon the shelf; they shared their mutual lack of phone calls, they shared the world's news flickering in the darkened room; one after the other they lay in the same bath, familiar with the same stained triangle beneath the taps, and yet he hardly knew her husband's name. Except, of course, when she called him by it.

'So there *were* some letters.' She smiled. He sat down and she passed him the milk jug.

'Largely for your good self, as per usual.' He passed them to her. She recognized Adrian's writing. She put a spoonful of Oaty-Os into her mouth and slit open the envelope.

'*I do not know quite how to write this letter. In fact, my dear, I have tried several versions and consigned them all to the rubbish bin.*'

'They don't meet with your approval?'

'What?'

'These oaten hoops. I thought I detected a grimace.'

He sounded so distant; when, before, had he called her *my dear*?

'Over the past few weeks I have been trying hard to organize my feelings. I owe it to both of us. I know, Claudia, that I have hurt you terribly, and behaved in a way which disturbs and shames me. That I had to, I hope that by now you can understand. Would you agree that though the actual impetus came from my side, this was, in fact, almost incidental? Sooner or later the crunch would come.'

Crunch, crunch, went Alistair. She paused, he presumed for conversation.

'I find them, though crisp enough, somewhat bland. But for their shape, they would be hardly recognizable from those puffy things.'

Without thinking, she spooned in some more. She had put in too much milk; the pale rings jostled on the surface.

'In fact . . .' Alistair cleared his throat. 'To devise these must have been a somewhat *otiose* exercise. Oaty-Os, otiose.'

'There has been another reason for my cowardly delay. I did not want to tell you until we were absolutely sure. It is a bit unexpected, but delightful all the same. Without more ado, I feel that you should be the first to hear the news. We are expecting a child.'

Claudia stopped. She sat very still, her eyes on her bowl.

O, O, O, floating in milk.

'In fact,' said Alistair, 'I wouldn't –'

Her bowl blurred, her lodger's face blurred. With a painful hiccup she started to cry. So loud, her wet, jolting sobs. And all these weeks she had not shed a tear. The drops spattered onto the sky-blue notepaper. *'As you can imagine . . .'* the handwriting swam . . . *'wheels in motion . . . divorce . . . Grossmith and Bingham . . .'*

Her lodger's head was bowed. Slowly, slowly, a blush

crept up his face.

'I'm sorry,' she said, hiccuping, 'I'm terribly sorry.'

Alistair sat, rigid and red.

'I can't think what. . .' she began.

Suddenly he closed his eyes. 'Yes' . . . he said.

'It was this letter.'

A pause. 'Yes,' he repeated. '. . . remarkably similar to those puffy ones. Their name escapes me.' Beetroot-faced, his mouth made the movements of munching. 'Just a specimen hoop, for testing purposes . . . for total non-bias, the eyes should be closed.'

'It's from my husband, you see . . .'

'. . . I think I shall return to the trusted Ryvita.'

Hopelessly she gazed at the blind, reddened face. Another pause. She blew her nose as a sign she had finished.

At once he opened his eyes, though keeping them directed at his bowl. As if nothing had happened, they finished their breakfast.

Ten minutes later and she was in the living-room, searching around for her bag, getting ready for work. Stupid to have been so shocked by that letter. Sooner or later it was inevitable, wasn't it? It had not helped, the way he had put it. Not *Beth is expecting*, but *we are expecting a child*. Blind with love, he had lost his accustomed tact.

She found the bag. A child. Soon Beth would be swelling. Adrian would be laying his head against Beth's rounded belly, his ear pressed against the small, beating pulse; against his cheek would be pressed something that grew, something that she, Claudia, had declined to give him.

'Excuse me intruding.'

'Of course you're not.'

'Actually . . .' A small cough. 'Actually, I was just venturing in for a peep at your *Shorter Oxford*. Terribly sorry.

127

Think I've seen it on the shelves.'

'Here, let me –'

'No, no, please. I've found it.'

A rustling as he thumbed through the pages. 'N,' he muttered, 'O . . . *obstruent, obstupefy* . . .' He said: 'I'm afraid us librarians, even off-duty, feel impelled to chase things up . . . *orohippus* . . . *orthognathic* . . . I had a sudden fear that my little joke might have misfired . . . ah, *otiose.*' Across his face spread a radiant smile. 'I was right. *Otiose – having no practical purpose, sterile.*'

FIFTEEN

'What's your poison?'

'Need you ask, Brucey-boy.' Steve leant against the bar. 'Pint of Worthington.'

'Pull a finger out, Doreen.' Bruce turned to the girl at the bar; for reasons best known to himself he called all such girls Doreen. 'Else I'll be lumbered with that lot. A round for those buggers'd bankrupt me.'

Across the carpet they straggled in from the dining-room, the entire Pintaubaum U.K. sales force, well-fed and ready for booze. Every two months they met in this hotel, a concrete edifice next to Heathrow airport, for the sales conference. This consisted of dinner plus a few bevvies on the Thursday evening, an overnight stay and a day-long meeting during Friday in the Empress Suite downstairs.

Steve glanced around. 'Last time, wasn't it all nautical – *The Jolly Roger*?'

'Changed it, haven't they. Gone rustic.'

The room had been redecorated throughout upon a cheery Farmer Giles theme. Though outside aeroplanes took off and landed, control towers winked and cars hummed along the motorway, here on the second floor the tranquil drinker found himself seated in a corner of Olde Englande, its bar roofed with plastic thatch. The walls glinted with horse brasses; tiny hens topped the cocktail sticks; the Price List was printed upon a circular card resembling a chicken's nest. *Harvest Highball*, it read in fancy script, *Somerset Special. Donkey Fizz – The Cocktail With The Kick*. The large bar room had been rearranged into booths suggesting stables. It was nearly empty. A few swarthy businessmen, blank with jet-lag, sat in their little wooden stalls.

Doreen passed them their glasses; she was dressed in frilly milkmaid style.

Bruce murmured: 'Fancy a roll in the hay?'

'If you knew how many jokers asked me that.'

Bruce turned to Steve. 'I like her, I like her.'

'Think you're all so original,' she said.

'This merrie Englande bit getting you down then?'

'It's this bonnet. Ever so tight.'

'So am I, darling. Least, I'm working on it.' He gazed down at her bulging, low-cut blouse. 'Don't get many of them to the kilo.'

'Give over, you.' Doreen moved off. The two of them took their drinks and sat down at a table. Music tinkled. Beside them stood a wooden cart; it contained a bale of straw against which was propped a placard with slots for the insertion of names. *Welcome To: Fisons Chemicals Ltd. Pontobam International Ltd.*

They drank. Bruce, who put it about, gazed at Doreen bending to the beer taps. Steve, who no longer put it about, gazed at her also. Some of the other reps joined them: Dennis Veedon, Reg Tilling, little Dai Morgan who covered Cardiff.

'Look, our Steven's got a purple cock.' Dennis, who was well away, passed Steve the appropriate cocktail stick. 'Mine,' he spoke carefully, drawing it out of his pocket.

129

'appears to be blue.'

Reg pulled up a chair. 'Do us nicely here, don't they. Good victuals.'

'Better than last time. That chicken, what was it called?'

'Kiev. Didn't have a bone in it.'

'As the actress said to the bishop.'

They paused.

'Well, where's the talent?'

They gazed around. At the next table an elderly Japanese gentleman, perfectly tailored, sat beneath the stuffed head of a cow. He gazed into the room; above him, glass eyes stared into the haze-hung space.

'Can't be any flights in.'

'Remember those two birds from British Caledonian?'

'Remember the dark one – Lesley? She was nicely built.'

'Sense of humour. Not stuck-up like those Air France madams.'

'Wonder where she is now. And her friend.'

'Thirty thousand feet above Caracas, doling out the vodka and limes . . .'

'Reclining beside the pool in the Honolulu Hilton . . .'

'. . . in her bikini . . .'

They tipped their glasses thoughtfully.

'Excuse me, boys.' Dai, who was newly-wed, stood up. He rubbed his nose shyly. 'Just going to make a little phone call.'

They watched him as he crossed the room. 'Lovebirds,' said Bruce, shaking his head.

Steve watched Dai, who missed his bride, propped in the perspex booth. He himself ought to phone June; she got so fretful when he was away.

Bruce said: 'I give him six months.'

'What, of married bliss?'

'Phoning, dum-dum.'

'Out of sight,' Reg looked wise, 'out of mind.'

Again they tipped their glasses thoughtfully.

Bruce said: 'Talking of talent, how's the lovely wife?'

'June?' With surprise Steve remembered that indeed June had once been talent – so pretty and unknown, with that long blonde hair. 'She's all right. She's given up her job.'

'No longer flogging the Factors?'

'Why did Elizabeth Harden?' murmured Dennis. 'Because Max Fact 'er.'

'Honest, Steve?' Bruce raised his eyebrows. 'Could you be expecting a happy event?'

Upon the table lay the price list. Steve lowered his eyes and gazed at the laminated nest, its sheeny clutch of eggs. 'No,' he said. 'No happy event.' It had startled him, that June feared becoming stretched and heavy, feared the pain. *Later, Steve*, she said. *There's plenty of time*. At present she cared to care, it seemed, only for him.

And for the flat. 'She keeps herself busy,' he said. 'The housewifely bit.'

'You lucky man.'

'You're right, there.' Of course he was lucky. Tonight, though, he had to admit that it was a slight relief being one of the boys. A boozy night ahead, a few jars with his mates, upstairs on the third floor his simple bachelor bed. No June sitting at the table inhibiting their jokes, making them polite and gallant, a bit foolish. Worse, raising her eyebrows after he's had a couple of pints. *You men*, she would say. *Winkie gets so silly when he's drunk*. She would prod his stomach: *Look, he's getting a little pot*. He was not getting a little pot.

Dai returned.

'You took a heck of a time.'

'As the actress said –'

'All right, all right, Dennis.'

Steve got to his feet. 'Just going to give June a tinkle.'

'Talking of tinkles,' Dennis struggled up. 'Must make a little visit. Give a helping hand to the unemployed.'

'Tie a knot in it,' said Bruce. 'I've got a good one. There was this Irishman –'

Dennis waved him aside and staggered off beside Steve. 'Quite right to phone, Stevie lad,' he muttered. 'I mean, with a looker like June.' He lowered his voice. 'I mean, while the cat's away . . .' He veered off in the direction of the Gents.

Steve reached the booth. In a sense he wished that Dennis were right. Not a bloke, of course, but he would be pleased if June were up to something. Up to anything.

'Oh, nothing much.' Her voice sounded faint and tinny.

'Did you do a bit of shopping?'

A pause. 'No. I mean, yes. Yes, I did, er, pop out, but I didn't go anywhere really. At least . . .'

Her voice trailed off. A pause. In the corner of his eye Steve saw Bruce rising for the next round. Would he remember him, Steve?

'Do you miss me, Steve? Do you wish I was there?'

'Of course, darling.'

'I thought you'd phone me earlier. You usually do. I get so worried, Steve.'

'Blimey Junekins, I'm only at London Airport.'

'Are you in the bar?' Her voice sounded thin and sharp. It must be the line. 'Who's there. Girls?'

'You should see them. There's Lola, she's doing a belly dance, and Crystal – she's draped over Reg at the moment but that's just because I'm on the phone –'

'*Steve.*'

'Hey June. Tell me what you've been doing.'

'I've told you. Nothing much. Went to Beckenham.'

'Was that fun? What did you do?'

'Oh, nothing much. Steve, I wish you weren't over there. I keep thinking things.'

'Darling . . .'

Steve shifted on to the other foot. He was too tall for the perspex hood; his head banged against the side. June's crackling voice sounded far away; the interference gave it a tinny whine. It must be that he hardly ever listened to June without being there and looking at her; silencing her with a hug.

'Tell me what you had for your dinner,' he said, noting that he had no more 2ps.

'Oh nothing much. I made myself a boiled egg but I wasn't hungry. Actually, I've got one of my headaches.'

'Poor Juney.' A burst of laughter from his table. Bruce returned with the tray of drinks. Five glasses.

'. . . so I lay down for a bit. You know, Steve, I haven't had a migraine for weeks . . .'

Pip-pip-pip. 'Juney, we must —'

'When will you be back?'

'Oh, about seven tomorrow . . . I'll phone —'

The phone went dead. Steve ducked under the hood. He felt hot and guilty — guilty that his heart sank when she mentioned her headache, guilty that he strode with such springing steps back to the table that awaited him; smoke-wreathed, masculine.

A week earlier, when Steve received the letter marked *Private and Confidential*, he had guessed its contents before opening it. Now in the Empress Suite he watched its sender addressing the ranks of motionless salesmen. His fellow reps were spruced-up this morning, all smart suits and mingling aftershaves, hung-over but attentive on their rows of spindly chairs.

A.R.E., Steve's boss, pointed to the graph. Mid-November and the pressure was on. '. . . a six percent improvement on the second quarter. Please note the sales figures — here — for our *Liberesse* Body Caress,' he indicated a rising, jagged line, 'and — here — the shaker talc. To the left, the target figures in red. We have every confidence . . .'

Outside it was sunny. Across the three windows, however, the blinds had been pulled down; radiant, blurred slats, as if daylight were too large and too natural. In this seasonless, carpeted space the suntan oil promotions were announced in winter, the Christmas gift sets displayed in June.

'. . . the right product at the right time. I think we can say, gentlemen, that we are putting our finger on the pulse of what the, ah, *today* woman wants – with the help, of course, of your good selves . . .'

The Empress Suite was spacious but overheated. In contrast to the thorough job they had done upstairs, its motif was confined to a plum carpet and a coronet plaque upon the wall. Steve sat in the back row. At school he had always sat in the back row so that he could read his comics.

'. . . and may I draw your attention to the lipstick range; we have two new shades, Plum Crazy and Ms Heartbreak, bringing the number of matts to eight and glossies to twelve. You'll find them, gentlemen, on your amended order forms . . .'

Another reason for this position was the avoidance of A.R.E.'s eye. Steve fingered the letter in his pocket. That, after this session, A.R.E. and himself were to have a little chat lent an air of intimacy, Steve-directed, to A.R.E.'s pleasant gaze. Sunlight pressed against the slats. At school he was always playing truant. He had gone to the swimming-baths, he had hung around the record shops, he had sat beside the cinder track fishing in the canal, the air around him burnt with the smell from the brewery.

'And now I'll pass you to Doug Henson. He has a few words about our new skin preparation.'

Henson rose. He was the overall marketing manager and in himself an almost faultless product, tall and slim in his smooth grey suit. Whereas A.R.E. called them gentlemen, Henson called them boys; lightly tanned even in November, he smiled down upon them all.

Steve gazed at the management men beneath their plastic crown. A.R.E., deputy sales manager, was shortish and solid, with a mild, obliging face; a bit of a nonentity, dedicated to his work. Henson – 2.5 children and three acres in Virginia Water – was faultless and bland. Yes men, desk men, company men. Steve's father had grown prize crysanthemums in his back garden. *Pinch out all side shoots*, said his *Gardening Weekly, to encourage a large main bloom*.

And me? thought Steve. All side shoots, that's me. He looked up at the table raised on its platform. Three years on the road; did he care to sit up there? He should, of course; June presumed he should. Beside him Reg lit a Panatella, shook the match and returned to attention. None of them were free. Even driving along the open road, the motorway bridges looming then flashing over their heads. Their cars were rented and they themselves were rented; it made little difference whether they sat behind a wheel or behind a desk. They were selling something in which he, Steve, no longer believed. Had he, in fact, ever believed in it? He had never really given it a thought. Marge had had more effect than she realized and so, in a different way, had June. Steve scratched the bridge of his nose with his biro. Did he mean what he had told Marge, so casually, in that shabby office?

Smiling confidingly, Henson was discussing the ins and outs of acne promotion. Pintaubaum had done one such campaign in the past with its teenage *Diana* range. In fact, though Doug did not mention this, most of the products had simply been repackaged for *Liberesse*, the smiling, pony-tailed adolescent being replaced by her sister of the eighties, in her unbuttoned khaki no longer grinning. The visual challenge, according to the advertising boys, was to suggest that the cool, together girl synonymous with *Liberesse* might yet possess, underneath it all, a problem skin. Or might have done, if she did not use *Vanish*.

'*Vanish*. Boys, I want you to put everything into this. There's a quarter of a million campaign coming up in May.

135

Overall theme – *Liberate Your Skin*.'

Bruce murmured: 'Overall theme – *It All Boils Down To This*.'

'Overall theme,' said Steve. '*It's Breaking Out All Over*.'

'Lights, sweetie.' Henson turned to his secretary, a newly-acquired redhead. There was a good deal of speculation on the subject of these two. Had he got his leg over? The general feeling was yes.

The curtains were drawn, the room plunged into darkness.

'Just a quickie, a little peek at the campaign stills. Frankly, boys, I'm over the moon on this one. The trade's going to love 'em. They're very up-market, very modern, very *us*. Go ahead, Bob.'

A whirr; a large white shape wobbled on the wall, blurred and sharpened. An enormous face gazed down at them. No, not at them; gazed at herself reflected in three angled mirrors. She was naked to the shoulders; her face was very beautiful and very blank. She resembled June, but then June resembled many models. There was a hygienic air about the photograph – a glimpse, through the mirrors, of bathroom tiles, a hint of the corrective nature of the product. However, there could also be glimpsed an expectant, male torso. *Now You've Liberated Yourself, Isn't It Time You Freed Your Skin*?

Oh June, flawless skin, flawless bathroom. Scrub, scrub the blemishes, rub away those all-too-human flaws; make yourself what you believe I wish you to be. Could I liberate you? Could anyone?

Bruce leant over. 'Looks like she's saying: Where did I leave my dyspepsia pills.'

I'll leave it to our expert here,' said Henson, 'to gen you up on the trial offers. We're coming up with a really great special launch pack with gratis masking gel. Meanwhile . . .'

She is saying: Who am I? In her mirrors she is looking

136

beyond herself. Who am I, bare in my bare bathroom?

Or isn't she? Perhaps, in fact, she is considering her profile from all angles, her lashes darkened with her thick'n'long mascara wand; considering the way she is about to make some poor bugger foolish and disappointed. Or perhaps she is not thinking about anything at all.

'Hey Steve you're not listening. I said – looks like she's saying –'

'I heard, Brucey-boy.'

At four-thirty the session broke up. With a certain amount of wrist-watch inspection and heads cocked ceilingwards the other reps trooped upstairs to the bar. Steve was sorry to see them go; after a quick one, or two, or three amongst the hay bales they would be dispersing to their different corners of England – Dennis to the Kashmiri takeaways and windy pavements of Birmingham, Reg to his Norfolk chicken farm and his plump wife, Bruce to his Home Counties bungalow with its dwarf conifers and small, waiting girls.

Steve slipped away and drove down the road a couple of miles. He pulled up at Pintaubaum head offices. They were situated in a reinforced concrete building; at its entrance were concrete tubs of bare earth. A.R.E. had already arrived. His Cortina 2000 GL (a step up the ladder from Steve's 1600L) was parked on the tarmac. There were few other cars. The works bus had left; on Fridays they knocked off at four.

It was a large car park. This was less through Pintaubaum's size than the impossibility of its being reached by any means other than motor. In this area nobody walked, nobody rode a bicycle; the surroundings were a landscape of transit, mile upon mile of motorway and flat market gardens punctuated by random blocks – the Heathrow Hotel, the Europa, the Trust House Forte Motor Lodge. They loomed out of the cabbage fields. In the distance the M4 with its far murmur; on the other side the airport buildings hazy in the sunset. Every thirty seconds jets took off into the molten clouds, leaving their own brown haze behind them.

Steve pocketed his car keys. In fact it was a marvellous sunset; in this eerie, vacant landscape the sky was huge and the horizons wide. Sometimes, dwarfed by girders, black dots could be spied picking the cabbages.

Entering the building, Steve mounted the stairs to A.R.E.'s office. To himself he called him A.R.E. This was something to do with the faceless nature of the man; also a habit that dated from the days of office memos. During his six-week's training stint Steve had been initiated into the mysterious, staccato world of the memo, where not only products and departments but also fully-fleshed men were reduced to a cryptic set of initials. Already bored at his cramped and temporary desk, he had constructed a fantasy life around the character from the wages office who had ended his memos B.A.M. This turned out to be one Barry Miller, a wan, stooping youth unsuited to his explosive abbreviation (*I wonder if I may draw your attention to this apparent anomaly in your PAYE form? BAM*). There was also the chummy, confiding PST from Personnel (*At your convenience, please drop by and discuss your proposed agenda. PST*). When eventually met, PST revealed herself as one Mrs Taseem, a formal, distant Asian lady of uncertain years. To complicate matters there was Reg, who trained concurrently and who penned gossipy notes to SWM, WPB. Though assured of his own initials, it took SWM some time to realize that the mysterious WPB (Wally Balls, Willoughby Bottomly?) was in fact none other than his old companion Waste Paper Basket.

These impersonal initials – yet intimate, with their hint of a second name known only to the family circle – assumed a life of their own until dispelled by contact with their inappropriate owner. With A.R.E., however, they

138

remained. *Enclosed, sales forecasts for Fresh'N'Dry, roll-on and spray. Any comments, ARE?* To the memo's conclusion the initials gave a query, a metaphysical doubt unconnected to deodorant comparisons. Acquaintance-ship with the man himself did not dispel this. Though competent enough at his job, there was a nebulous, unfinished air about A.R.E. He had, Steve knew, an unsatisfactory marriage – in fact, gossip had it that he and his wife had parted. A.R.E. himself never talked of such matters.

'I expect you know, Steve, why I've asked you to kindly drop by.'

Steve sat down. 'I know. You're kicking me upstairs.'

A.R.E.'s room was grey and tidy. The only spot of colour came from the Lakeland Scene on the calendar from LBB Computer Services. Through the window the landscape was flat; in the distance lay a garage, its SHELL sign already illuminated, out-glaring the rosy sky. Steve had been training here at the time of his mother's fiftieth birth-day. In his lunch hour he had driven out, seeking gifts. If only she had been a motor; the garage forecourts held stands burdened like Christmas trees – blister packs of fan belts and spark plugs.

A.R.E. smiled. 'That's not exactly the way I would put it. Let me fill you in.' He paused. 'You're aware, Steve, of the recent takeover. Hakim's a vast multi-national, they've interests in a wide spectrum – breweries, catering, ship-ping, newspapers ... the fact is, though Pintaubaum remains, of course, basically unchanged, there's been a certain amount of re-shuffling at management level. Cer-tain openings have appeared.' He paused again. 'Would you like a cup of tea? My secretary's gone home but there's a machine.'

'Can't tell 'em apart, really.'

'I beg your pardon?'

'Never mind. I'll get it. Sugar?'

The vendor stood in the corridor. A row of yellowing labels, some re-sellotaped, acquainted Steve with the options. Was it all inside stewing away, eternally on the bubble, ready for the summons of finger upon button? Not *Black Coffee With Sugar*, not *White Coffee Without Sugar*, not *Tomato Soup*, but *Tea*. Not Reg, not Bruce, not Dai, but Steve. Or did they wait unassembled, unsuspecting? Dry sachets, vacant polystyrene beakers. Ready for the one to be dropped into the other. Ah, he could do with a pint of Worthington's, cool and frothing; a few jokes.

'Oops, sorry. It's hot.'

A.R.E. dabbed his desk with a handkerchief. 'When you joined our team, Steve, we couldn't really see you in your present position for long.'

'Nor could I.'

'Oh yes?' A.R.E. looked up, eyebrows raised. 'How long has it been, Steve? Three years?'

'Getting on for that.'

'We're not complaining, of course. Just the opposite. You've got a fine record – excellent customer relations, really excellent. Good sales figures. Let me lay my cards on the table; as I've mentioned in the past, we have high hopes of you at Pintaubaum, Steve. In fact, I think you might be expecting better things of yourself.

'You're right, there.'

'Ah, good. I see we're on the same wavelength.'

Not quite, but his own wavelength was still confused and murky. He liked A.R.E.; he would like to explain but he diJ not have the words, even to explain to himself. Instead, he nodded. He hated to disappoint; he remembered Gloria with her tears. *You don't love me. When I'm with you, I do*.

'I'm with you.' Steve took a scalding sip and winced.

'In a nutshell, we'd like to create a post for you here in the department. We've hinted about this before, of course, but it's only recently we've been able to carve out an opening. Field Sales Executive. Basically you'll be responsible for the entire southern sales team – co-ordinating, re-allocating, trouble-shooting, attending to the day-by-day running but also re-thinking on a fundamental level. Re-shaping our strategy. In a sense you'll be my assistant, but with a large slice of the action to yourself.' He took a sip; he did not wince. 'And with very – erm, attractive rewards. A rather substantial increase. I'll mention the figure I've been negotiating . . .'

He mentioned it. Steve's eyebrows rose. He could put a deposit on a house for that.

Outside the fields had darkened. The sun, a red disk, was slipping down beyond the horizon. A flock of birds flew past. Somewhere the moon must be rising – a chill, hungry, hunter's moon.

A.R.E. drank from his beaker. His pleasant, unremarkable face had settled into the lines that would deepen with age. How old was he, forty?

'Did you know,' Steve asked suddenly, 'about the spermacetti wax?'

'Come again?'

'The whale products that we – that Pintaubaum uses?'

'In what context, precisely?'

'In our *Liberesse* Leave-It-On Night Lotion.'

A.R.E. placed his beaker on the desk, dead centre – pen to right, pencil to left. 'That's not exactly our province, is it Steve?'

'Ah. They've been mailing you. They've sent you leaflets, haven't they.'

A.R.E. sighed. He gazed down at his desk. 'So you'll think it over, Steve? Shall we leave it there, and you'll come back to me?'

Steve bade farewell and left before A.R.E. pulled down the blinds. Questions, questions. Up in the sky, circling, birds and planes.

And God created great whales, and every creature that moveth, which the waters brought forth abundantly, after

141

*their kind, and every winged fowl, after his kind, and God
saw that it was good. And God blessed them, saying, Be
fruitful, and multiply, and fill the waters in the seas and let
fowl multiply on the earth.*

The air was chill. Steve crossed the tarmac. The wind
whistled through the thin, high telegraph wires. In the west
a glow remained. Steve clicked shut the door of his Cortina.

*So God created man ... and God said unto him: Be
fruitful and multiply, and have dominion over the fish of the
sea, and over the fowl of the air, and over every living thing
that moveth upon the earth.*

SIXTEEN

The sun had slipped below the horizon. It was dark outside.
Claudia sat at her dressing-table surveying the row of pots.
It was some time now since she had been to a large party.

Make up a face. What did it mean? Fabricate one, but
from what beginnings? When she was younger she wore
thick black eye-liner to disturb her parents. Her mother
feared it, the way it made Claudia look bold and altered, a
woman of the streets. When Claudia moved away she
stopped using it, there being no longer the need. And her
mother had been right, of course; it had not suited her
anyway. Shame that her mother had never known this
before she had died.

Claudia gazed at her face; at her dry, freckled arms
resting on the dressing-table. Since the departure of
Adrian she had been invited to a number of suppers with
friends but these had always been small – usually, in fact,
consisting just of the friends themselves. She had attri-
buted to her hosts a number of reasons for this – a desire to
hear the intimate details of the break-up, which she would

142

be inhibited from telling in the presence of other guests; a desire to be helpful and sympathetic, which would likewise be inhibited when there were others to be entertained; a fear of embarrassing either Claudia or the assembled guests by some unwitting blunder on anyone's part; a lack of that perenially rare species, the unattached heterosexual male somewhere between the ages of eighteen and eighty, to whom she could be introduced; a fear that her unhappiness would render her dull. Also, perhaps, a difficulty in choosing guests who were neither so fondly wedded that she would feel wistful not yet so miserable that they would bring back unpleasant memories ... Whatever the reasons, at this early period in her separation, when things were still uncertain, Claudia found herself in some respects a social outcast. How long would this last – until she made herself again presentable with a mate?

In another respect, however, she found herself much sought-after: as the recipient of long, serious phone calls from women friends, as the sharer of long, serious lunches, where not only would her own problems be discussed (with varying degrees of helpfulness), but the hitherto unsuspected secrets of her friends revealed – this prompted, no doubt, by a desire to comfort her and also to gain the advice of someone who had seemed so capable but who, at a stroke, had joined another club. No longer in demand for the first sort of social intercourse, she found herself much in demand for this second category. All things considered, she preferred the former kind.

Claudia made up her face with care. She was looking forward to this party. She rubbed eyeshadow into her lids. The question was: what to wear? Something alluring but not blatantly so; she must look neither dowdy nor over-sexed. One could be so much bolder when accompanied by a man. She opened the cupboard and inspected her dresses. This way and that she pushed them along the rail, these garments that had partnered Adrian to a multitude of gatherings. The wire hangers rattled, skeletons in her cupboard. None of them looked quite right; none of her clothes did nowadays.

Finally she chose a beige dress the colour, or non-colour, of Tempo; it was silky and loose – sophisticated, she had considered it, the way it draped and suggested the body. 'Very nice,' Adrian had said, but then he called everything very nice when he could not be bothered to look at it properly. (I must remember Adrian like this, she thought, I must not build him up and make him better.)

She pulled the dress over her head and sat down again in front of the mirror. The front door opened; footsteps in the shared hall; her own front door opened and was gently closed. Alistair was home. She heard him creak past her room. Even his footfall sounded apologetic, as if he were walking on tiptoe.

She adjusted her dress; it had big billowy sleeves. She gazed at her shoulders. They were broad and square – too much so for a woman. She had not thought about this for years, there had been no need – Adrian was used to them, she was used to them. They had both grown so accustomed to each other's faults, just as they had both become dulled to each other's good points; it might have been tepid but it was comfortable.

So many things she was remembering: that she had square shoulders and small breasts, that she could not fasten this damn necklace without help. Alistair was shuffling around in his room; she hesitated, necklace in hand. She could not ask him. She could picture it, his long fumbling fingers, the husbandly nature of the task. She twisted her neck and struggled with it alone.

Getting off, they called it when she was adolescent. 'What happened at Barry's last night?' Huddles outside the science lab. 'Oh, I talked to you-know-who,' rolling eyes and wise nods, 'but I didn't *get off* with him.' Verity was always getting off with boys and, later, men; in the flat

144

these would appear pale and unshaven at breakfast time. This happened with Claudia, but with less frequency.

It was a heavy tribal choker. The clasp clicked. For nearly a decade she, Claudia, had got off with nobody but Adrian. She leant over and picked up the little bottle. *Liberesse – It's Not Just Yourself You'll Be Changing*. She sprayed it around her throat. At thirty, what did getting off entail? The same tense, exhilarating grapples but now in the front seat of a family saloon? A paunchier body pressed against hers; in some distant house the shadow not of parents but, perhaps, of a wife. The smaller, longer shadows of children. For this second-time-round she was but a novice. Claudia got up, smoothed the counterpane of her bed and left the room. Simultaneously, Alistair's door opened.

'Off to make your supper?' she said gaily, almost flirtatiously. Her clothes made her bold: painted lips, painted nails.

'Good heavens, you look very nice.' He clutched his paper bag. 'I mean, I don't mean to say that you usually don't, I mean . . .'

'Don't worry.' She laughed. 'I understand.' She took her coat and her car keys.

'And what kind of festivity,' he coughed, 'are you going to grace?'

'Oh, some party. A kind of business one. You going out?'

'Oh no. No, I shall eat my chop,' he said, 'in solitary splendour.'

It was, indeed, a kind of business party. *Yours* – upmarket and glossy, for *The Career Woman who's still a Woman* – carried a good deal of advertising. Wil's outfit dealt with the accounts of several of these clients – makers of a briefcase with built-in vanity mirror; of a Swedish casserole that switched itself off and on automatically; of hair sprays that lasted through a busy day and through, it was hinted, an even more energetic night. Claudia herself dealt only in the technical side of this but she had met the production man of this outfit – it was he who was giving the party – and she also knew that Verity and Wil would be there. In fact, it was through Verity and Wil that she had been invited. The question was, did her hosts know her circumstances? Was that the reason for inviting her?

They knew. This Claudia saw in a flash, also taking in a room hazy with smoke, many people, cream leather sofas and a lot of foliage. She could tell they knew by the way they both enfolded her in sincerity and searching looks.

'*Hello*. So glad you could come. Terribly glad.'

Victor (Victor what?) was greying youthfully, his shirt unbuttoned to reveal a tanned triangle of chest; his wife was also bronzed. They gazed at her, ignoring their other guests.

'I *do* hope you'll enjoy yourself.' They inspected her sombrely. She was getting used to this, the way that people felt obliged to lose their sparkle in her company, as if she were seated in a wheelchair. She had realized a good deal about disablement, this last couple of months. She would prefer them to be flippant and flirtatious, even rude. Ordinary. How soon before people got back to normal?

Scraps of conversation floated past ... 'marvellous, raunchy book' ... 'little corner shop, even grates it own Parmesan' ... 'in the Dordogne, of course it's just a *hovel* ...'

She recognised one or two faces, people she had seen in the *Yours* office. If she could remember their names she could approach them, and be safe, because she could talk about the magazine. She would be a woman who worked, who sat at a polished teak desk that belonged particularly to her, who spoke on two telephones at the same time.

'. . . a sort of *coitus interruptus* in the middle of the play . . .' 'married a Nigerian man, terribly nice chap of course, awfully intelligent . . .'

Her hosts disappeared to get her a drink. Claudia stood beside a rubber plant, fingering the polished leaves. Or she could launch off, be the lady who had painted her face with such care, be bold and anonymous, a scented woman alone in this Chelsea jungle. Years ago she had been able to do this.

Easier than either of these would be go to over beside the window where Verity stood. Verity's frizzy orange head was tilted up at a male face that Claudia vaguely recognized from the TV screen. She longed to go over and talk to her but it would be unfair to interrupt this, when for weeks all Verity saw were the juvenile features of her children, smeared with jam.

Claudia turned her head. At that moment her choker fell to the floor. She bent down and picked it up. Without a mirror she could not fix it herself.

She looked around. Her hosts had been waylaid by some new arrivals. Verity still had not seen her. There was no sign of Wil, even if she had cared for him to perform this intimate little task. Nobody else did she know well enough.

'. . . went greyhound racing on my birthday, marvellously camp . . .' 'nothing for it but a Range Rover – you know, to fit in dogs and the kids . . .'

Suddenly she had no energy to approach anyone. All those people she should get to know, all those names, those pasts. All of them married, anyway. All those startings from the beginning again, wearisomely. No one knew about herself, her choker, the place she had bought it, the flat in which it was kept, her thin, troubled sister in Leeds . . . if only Adrian were here. Even Alistair, who shared her corridor and her breakfasts – even he would almost do.

Claudia, wedged behind the rubber plant, fiddled with the orange label around its stalk. Once, in fact, she had enjoyed parties. Secure with her husband she had relished the flirtatious conversations with strangers, glances, the sharing of the flaring match. It had resembled shopping for shoes. Amusing, selecting different designs in turn, twisting the foot this way and that, watching how slim and elegant it became, how changed with each subsequent style. But there was always waiting the well-worn pair in which she had arrived – unexciting perhaps but comfortable and known, stretched in all the right places. Slip them on and go home. But what happened when she arrived with her feet bare?

Claudia left the room and crept upstairs to fix her choker in private. Gripping the banister, she glanced from left to right; she did not care to be ambushed by her hosts. When married it was fine to be caught alone; when no longer married, it was taboo.

She crossed the landing and went into the large bedroom where the coats were left in a heap upon the bed. On either side of the mountain of fur and tweed stood signs of marital contentment: two reading lamps, two paperbacks with their places marked. She bent down to the mirror, twisting her neck and fiddling with the clasp.

Voices at the bottom of the stairs; steps ascending. Claudia straightened up and looked around. She did not like to be caught alone, single and furtive. Swiftly she left the room before the people had come into sight around the banisters.

She was in the neighbouring room, where nobody would come. It was a children's bedroom; she could tell by the Snoopy transfers on the door and the breathing quiet within. It was dark. The noises from downstairs – the guffaws, the shrill laughs, the thump of music – were muffled up here, they came from a different world. Up above the cigarette smoke it was a slumbering, family house. She could discern bunk beds. On the floor lay two teddies, slumped lovingly together. On a shelf near the door, the landing light fell upon a beautiful, careful model ship, its rigging casting a tracery of shadows against the wall. Writ-

148

ing on its bows; she peered closer. *Cutty Sark*. She heard the ticking of a clock and gentle, rhythmic sighs. A room of dreaming boys.

Two years before and they were finishing the washing-up. Adrian rubbing the draining-board thoroughly, over-thoroughly, his head lowered. 'Any new thoughts, darling – you know, about starting a family?' Herself pausing, in one hand a drying-up cloth, in the other an empty bowl.

At first the murmurs were but the continuation of this conversation, one female voice and one male, both so faint as to be indistinguishable. Herself murmuring soon, soon, perhaps next year. His reply indistinct . . .

The voices came from the next bedroom. Claudia tilted her head and listened.

'I am fetching the glasses please.'

'Hey, Heidi –'

'Mr Monson say me to fetch the glasses from the kitchen –'

'Hey Heidi. You know, that's a really beautiful name.'

'Always peoples tell me Heidi is name of kiddie book. I think the Daddies reads it to their kiddies at bedtime. This is OK?'

'Yes, well . . . you see, Heidi, I just needed to talk to you for a moment. Like, alone. Without distractions. You see, each time I come to Vic's house I can't help noticing – well, this tremendous sort of warmth, this empathy. I think you've noticed it too.' A pause. 'It's such a special thing, rather fragile . . .'

'Mr Monson say he feel fragile thing also. I no know.'

'Listen Heidi. I was just wondering if you and I –'

'Please I go now. I have kitchen topfull of dirty plates and dirty glasses –'

'Hey Heidi –'

A flurry of footsteps, a muffled curse. The voice was familiar, for it belonged to Wil.

Claudia pressed herself into the shadows until both pairs

149

of footsteps had disappeared. She counted to three . . . one, two, three. Three masts on the *Cutty Sark*. It must have taken them months, that lovely ship. Or perhaps their Daddy helped them.

Silence. Claudia had given up with the necklace. She went slowly back into the bedroom. Slowly she burrowed for her coat. Brown leather, a tired skin.

After this little exchange she no longer felt like facing the party. The only person downstairs whom she wanted to be with was Verity, and now even talking to Verity was spoilt. Spoilt by Wil, who would make her constrained.

Nobody saw her as she crept downstairs and made a quiet exit. Outside it was very cold. She walked towards the car. It was a pretty terraced street, family houses on either side, their curtains closed. How alert she was becoming, nowadays, to the conversational clues. She despised herself for picking up the signs – mention of a freezer, a dog, schools, a wife. *Why must you be so independent*? Adrian had muttered. Ah yes, but that was when she was safe.

Claudia got into the car, drove down the street and turned into the King's Road. She would like to gossip to somebody about the party, about so many things that had happened in the past few weeks. Unvoiced, tonight's eavesdropped conversation remained bottled up, hotter and more embarrassing than it need be. Likewise with other misunderstandings and small encounters; with no one beside her to smile, eyebrows raised, at Wil's gingery nuzzling in her corridor, it remained furtive and unfunny, her solitary burden. To be silent did not suit her – to share a joke would be to disperse it.

The King's Road was busy. It was only nine; the pubs were still open and the windows lit. There were shops full of shiny new shoes, waiting to be tried. Couples strolled arm-in-arm along the pavement. Once accustomed to solitary living would she become more obsessive, like her lodger the door closed on to an airless bedroom, thoughts turning around and around, what he said to me at the office, what I said to him, is it to be pork chop or lamp chop tonight? Indeed, eventually would she become indistinguishable from Alistair, lonely and spinsterish, Ryvita packet folded over, talking to nobody, no longer having the words?

She would stop at The Anglers for a drink. She could not go home all made-up, ready, in her beige jersey dress. It was Friday night, after all.

The traffic lights turned red. Claudia stopped. Beside her was a man's boutique. In the window stood denim-clad dummies; posed casually, their plaster heads appeared to be tilted towards the man who stood on the pavement gazing at them.

He was dressed in a raincoat; something about him seemed familiar. He turned slightly. It was Alistair.

Are you going out? *Oh no, I shall eat my chop in solitary splendour.*

Alistair glanced about; he looked uneasy. Then, clasping his mackintosh more tightly around him, he turned and walked down the street.

What was he doing? In the driving-mirror Claudia watched him. Even here he was deferential; as in her own passage, he pressed himself against the wall to let others pass.

The lights changed. Thoughtfully Claudia turned left, down the road towards the pub. Before her marriage she used often to visit The Anglers; it was convenient for Adrian, being near the flat in which he lived at that time. Also convenient for herself, being in Pimlico and halfway between her office and home.

Just a quiet drink or two. She had never had one at that party. Besides, she could not get home before Alistair; he had obviously not wanted her to know he was going out. But why the secrecy, and what was he doing wandering down the King's Road? It did not seem his sort of place.

SEVENTEEN

Through his car window Steve watched the numbers revolving . . . 3 gallons . . . 3.1 . . . 3.5 . . . *flip* 4. The petrol pump was busy with numbers, it hummed with them. Steve sat with one hand upon his knee. So much time he spent in filling stations, watching the gallons ticking away. How much petrol did he burn, his tank emptying, his order forms filling?

Sitting silently he could hear the faint, discreet pulse. His dashboard dials were lit from within, a subdued glow, confidential as a nightclub. With the engine off all the fingers were stilled but for the clock; time jerked on, almost noiselessly. He always had a clock that worked because he always had a car that was new. Near enough; every two years they had them changed. *We like our motors*, Doug Henson's genuine smile, *like our sales team, to be in tip-top condition. Am I right, boys?*

Steve swung into the road. It was dark but one need not believe this; the A4 was bathed in an orange haze from its high arc lights. He passed the white glare of garage forecourts, the sudden folksy pubs and their neighbouring car parks, the cars matt with frost. Nearly seven o'clock. Tick, tick, life ticking away, ticking along illuminated dual carriageways, their strings of arc lights leading this way, leading that way. Talking to A.R.E. tonight he realized it was time for a decision. He felt light, poised. Poised for what?

Steve branched right at the roundabout. *We expect great things of you, Steven.* He pressed his foot on the accelerator. Not great things, perhaps, but better than this. The road was empty here, three lanes with their stippled white lines. Long, rippling black lines at the swimming baths; himself when younger, when anything was possible, standing in his dry blue trunks. Poised for what?

At the next roundabout he should go straight on. He did not. He indicated left and turned towards central London. He would not go home quite yet. June would only question him about his promotion. He would phone to say he would be late.

Something stirred at the back of his mind. It was to do with June, with the knowledge that whether he had been away for one hour or one week she would be found in the same position in which she had been left. That faint, whining voice down the telephone last night. *Oh, nothing . . .* More and more, it seemed recently, she had done nothing. She had gone to Tempson's, she had sat on a bus, her feet had crossed and re-crossed the shiny linoleum of the kitchen floor. Tap tap, to and fro. Yet she had done nothing; nothing could enlarge her. He had tried, but it was a failure. He had only realized this lately. None of her small preoccupations were his. She had tidied up from his departure and prepared for his homecoming.

Traffic was thicker now; people were pouring into London for their Friday night on the town. The city welcomed him with lights. Of course he longed for June – strictly speaking he longed to look at her and to feel her, to put his mouth against the scented, secret skin behind her ear. So many evenings he ran his hands over her shoulderblades, pressed against himself the soft pink wool, her slender body, the burden of her vacant days.

153

He should be going home. Icy-cold, the railings pressed against his chest. How long had he stood here gazing into the Thames with her shimmering lights? He was drawn to water, he was always seeking it out. Simple schooldays down by the canal, beside him his tin of bait. The pleasures of angling.

Perhaps he should open his dispatch case and scatter his papers upon the water. That would be a gesture. But his gestures were always a bit of a flop; he remembered Marge taking his cheque.

I could do with a drink, he thought. Just a quick one before I go home. A quiet pint. He turned from the railings and made his way up a side street. Usually jaunty, tonight he walked slowly. He felt aimless and full of doubts. Perhaps he was being foolish. Perhaps he should simply take that promotion and stop inspecting his feelings about June. After all, everyone makes compromises, large ones and small ones all the time.

It was a street of curtained houses. People had returned from work; wedded and conversational, they were sharing a drink. At the end of the road he could see a small, lit pub. He made his way to its door, and paused with his hand on the knob. The door had frosted glass panels, *The Angler's Arms* in fancy script.

Inside it was a fine old Edwardian pub, only discreetly altered. The bar was made of mahogany and backed by decorated mirrors. It was not full; there was a cluster of regulars at the counter, a leather-coated woman a couple of tables away and an oblivious couple, their heads bent together. Steve bought a pint and sat down. Beside the door hung a framed manufacturer's sample of fish-hooks arranged according to size. Steel curls, they resembled diminishing circles of question-marks. What shall you do? What? Round and round they revolved, the sharp, needling questions.

The door opened; a gust of cold air. A couple entered,

the woman small and brown-haired, the man familiar.

Steve stared at them. He half-rose to his feet. 'A.R.E.,' he said.

At the same moment the woman in the leather coat put down her glass. 'Adrian,' she said.

EIGHTEEN

Dolly is touching her pimple. She cannot pretend it has departed entirely but it is certainly on the way out. She twists her head in the rosy light. Yes, it is the merest bump; she has applied her make-up with care.

Of course it always helps, the lighting in The Anglers. It gives a girl confidence. In the mirror at home she looks pasty. Here, at work, with her lashes fixed and that new sparkling eye-shadow she feels a different person.

Rubbing a couple of glasses she continues her inspection, this time beyond her own face. Yes, quite a dish. She likes his dark ruffled hair, it looks the springy type but soft with it. It gives him a wayward, appealing air; sort of lost. He has given her the eye, she is sure of this. Taking his pint and his change, his *thanks* had been full of meaning. She would swear that sitting at his table he is watching her now. She would like to go over and press his face against her turquoise bust.

A change, anyway, from the usual geriatrics. She has been here three months; she is acquainted with them all. Each night she feels like screaming when old Jock hobbles in rubbing his hands. 'Port in a storm,' he says, baring his bald gums. Then, at closing time, his attempts to rise. 'Action stations, action stations!'

Dolly stops, cloth in hand. She gazes in the mirror; a couple has just entered. The fanciable man has got to his feet; so has the woman who ordered a gin and tonic. Some sort of introduction seems to be taking place; all of them are shaking hands.

A blind date. At the romance of it Dolly smiles fondly, her small fancy forgotten. She is soft really. And all the time those two sitting there not three yards apart. Dolly turns from the mirror; the second couple is approaching her counter.

'Beth, do keep your voice down.'

'I'm asking you, Adrian. Did you arrange this?'

'*Please*. Good evening. Er, scotch and ice for me, please. A large one, I think in this case. What about you, my dear?'

'I want to leave.'

'And a bitter lemon, I think.'

'Did you hear me? I want to go.'

'We couldn't possibly. No yet. It would look peculiar.'

'Damn what it would look like.'

'*Beth*.'

'I said damn. You heard me.'

'Beth, this isn't like you. Thanks so much. Sorry, I've only a fiver.'

Turning to the till, Dolly glances again in the mirror. Over by the door the man is lighting a cigarette for the woman; their two brown heads are bent together. They are both tall, she had noticed that when they came in. They appear to be deep in conversation.

This couple, by contrast, seem squarish and inconspicuous. The woman has flat mousy hair and is clutching the fur collar of her coat as if afraid something is going to get in.

'Adrian, this can't be a coincidence.'

'Believe me, Beth – oh, thank you – I know you won't believe this –'

'I thought we were just visiting your old haunts. Your local, you said.'

156

'It is. I mean, it was.'

'I didn't realize you came here with *her*.'

'I didn't. Well, once or twice.'

'And you thought you might see her again. You hoped you would. Oh God.'

'Please Beth, we can't stay here, we must go and join them.'

'You want to join them, don't you. You never told me she was so pretty. Stop looking at her.'

'I'm not looking at her.' A pause. 'She's cut her hair.'

'Adrian, I haven't even put on any make-up.'

'I don't know that I altogether approve ... It's a bit boyish.'

'What? Adrian, listen. If this is your way of arranging things then I don't find it at all funny. Why didn't you tell me?'

'What's that fellow Mullen doing here? I only saw him a couple of hours ago. I don't understand.'

'Adrian, for heaven's sake.'

'Good God she's gone.'

'What?'

'Claudia's gone. So's Mullen.'

After a moment's surprise, the man and woman have carried their glasses back across to the far side of the Saloon Bar. They sit down. Dolly lifts the hinged counter and saunters over in their direction, ostensibly to clear up the half-empty glasses left by the other couple's sudden flight. She rubs the neighbouring table thoroughly, bending closer for a more detailed examination.

'Adrian, why did you leave her?'

'I was in love with you.'

'Was?'

'Am, darling.'

'You said she never made you meals. She never got back in time. She was always independent and busy.'

157

'That's right.'

'She made you feel inadequate. Irrelevant, or something, you said. All these months, you know, you've never let us talk about her. Not properly, Adrian. What's been stopping you – loyalty to her?'

'Beth dear, I didn't know my feelings.'

'Do you know them now?'

A pause. 'I'm still confused.'

'Worse than before?'

'No, no. Of course not, darling.'

'It's seeing her, isn't it. You're still in love with her.'

'Let's have another. Oh hell, you don't drink now, do you.'

'You have one. Don't mind me. I can't help it if I feel queasy all the time.'

Dolly has finished the table. She straightens the stuffed trout that hangs on the wall. Within its glass case it is framed with dead moss; askew, it appears to be gazing at the two tense heads below. Dolly dislikes the fish in this place, they are so morbid. All in all she would prefer to be working round at the King's Head where it is nice and modern with its fruit-machines and fun-loving clientele. Saturdays they even have a Disco Strip. Bit of a giggle.

'. . . though it's worse in the mornings,' the woman is saying. 'Sometimes when you've left I just can't face the vacuuming.'

'Beth, you make me feel so guilty.'

'I'm only telling you, Adrian. You don't seem to understand – not since I've been home all day, not lately.'

'But darling, you didn't have to give up your job. Not yet, it's not due till May. You sound so resentful.'

'I thought you'd *like* me giving it up. You seemed pleased enough at the time. How wonderful, you said, to come home and find someone there. Perhaps you don't want this child either.'

'Beth, for goodness sake. How many times must I tell

you? I'm absolutely delighted.'

'Just because it was a mistake.'

'Beth, please don't nag.'

'Nag?'

'Well, I mean – go on about things so much. You never used to.'

'I'm sorry Adrian. It's just that I thought I was giving you something she couldn't – nice clean welcoming flat, nice hot dinner, baby coming soon. In my silly little way I thought this was what you wanted. But something tells me, Adrian, that it's not quite the same now. Take last night when you were at that hotel. Your sales conference. I mean, I'm not complaining but a phone call would have been awfully welcome and not a lot of trouble. And last Tuesday – you know, I'd been slaving all afternoon over that *quiche*. Why didn't you *tell* me you wouldn't get back till eight?'

'Darling, I said I was sorry. Anyway it tasted all right. Really Beth, I'd prefer to have bread and cheese – you know, like before – if it'd stop you fretting.'

'Before?'

'When I used to – well, visit. Remember our funny picnics? Remember that time we met in Regents Park and it was snowing?'

'So it's all changed now, has it?'

'Oh God I was only trying to cheer you up. Listen Beth, I'm getting another drink.'

Dolly scuttles back to the bar. The man follows at a slower pace.

'Same again?' she asked.

'Please. Large.' He smiles at her; he looks rather nice then, his face creasing. 'And we only dropped in for a quick one.'

She gestures at Jock and Paddy in their sagging serge suits. 'That's what they all say.'

'A quick one. Just a quiet drink.'

NINETEEN

The King's Head, in the next street, was noticeably larger and more electronic. Breathlessly, Claudia sat down in the nearest seat. Men were clustered around a telly game. Between their shoulders she could see the white dot float up and down. Ping, it went.

'Hey, this is unfair,' she said, smiling. 'I didn't even get a good look at Beth. We must go back.' But she did not move. Steve went to get the drinks. She gazed at the white spot rising and descending. Amidst all the noise it seemed alien and serene.

He put the glasses down on the table. 'I've always wanted to do this.'

'What?'

'Steal the boss's wife. Ex-boss's wife.'

'Ex-boss's ex-wife.'

He looked at her. 'What happened, by the way?'

'He left me. I had a letter yesterday. He wants a divorce.'

'He left you for *her*?'

'For Beth. That's right.'

'Blimey.' A pause. 'Well, chacun a son something.'

Claudia took off her leather coat.

'Why's he your ex-boss?' she asked.

'He might be. I think I'm leaving this business. I'm sort of ·

160

making up my mind now.' He frowned, working it out, gazing into his pint glass. He had straight, dark eyebrows; a nice, changeable face that broke easily into a smile. At school they would have sighed and called his voice 'dark brown.' His suit, though, was a bit sharp, a bit vulgar. Light grey with a pastel shirt.

'So you're trying to avoid him,' she said.

'That's right.' He grinned at her. 'I don't know what the hell I'm doing, to tell the truth.'

'But it's easier not to see him.'

He paused. 'Perhaps I just wanted to spirit you away.'

'Do you do this often?'

He paused again, gazing at her over his raised glass. 'Oh, every night. Try to average three or four a session. I'd up me total if it weren't for these criminal opening hours.'

She laughed. She was drinking gin and tonic; she moved the ice around with her finger. 'I feel we're playing truant.'

'At school I was always nipping off. I went fishing. Or I'd hitch into the countryside, but it was the suburbs really. I went swimming a lot.'

'Did you? I did, too. I felt all free and liberated.'

'Where did you go then?'

'Tunbridge Wells.'

'I went to Catford.'

She stirred the ice again. 'I grew up in Kent,' she said slowly. 'I used to feel the sea was just beyond the next green hill. It wasn't, quite.'

They both gazed into their glasses. Beside them a fruit-machine rattled, disgorging cash. She looked up. 'Adrian must have mentioned you. Mullen . . . Mullen. He was on the road once, long before you joined. He always said he was no good – not persuasive enough. I think he believed too much in what he was selling.'

'My mate Bruce says I'm good because I don't believe a word of it.'

'Is that why you're leaving?'

'Everything seemed to strike me at once. The rubbish I was selling. What I was doing selling it. Things seemed to change then.'

'It's Not Just Yourself You'll Be Changing. Adrian thought that was the greatest slogan ever. He'd bring home these samples and ask my opinion. I always felt a failure because I couldn't think of anything to say.'

'That's because it's all the same stuff.'

'It's all in the packaging and marketing, right? That slinky black box for the Leave It On Night Lotion.'

'And jerks like me carting the stuff around saying it's great, it's unique, it's got this special secret formula.'

'How deep is beauty?'

'Skin deep. Cardboard deep.'

She said: 'How disenchanted.'

'I was, earlier. Not quite so much now.' He paused. 'Must be all these Double Diamonds I'm putting back.'

'Ah.'

He leant forward and addressed a nearby jukebox. 'She'd believe anything, wouldn't she.'

'Tonight, it seems. I don't know what I believe.' The dot was still rising and falling, weightlessly. It left a little blurred trail. 'I think I'm just as confused as you. It's been a strange evening. I just crept out of a business party. Me. I used to be able to cope with things like that.'

'So you're a business lady,' he said.

'I work on a magazine, *Yours.* You probably wouldn't know it.'

'Course I do. We did a promotion for it once. Remember the free *Liberesse* foam sachet?'

'Soak Away The City. I've got about four hundred left in my bathroom cabinet. Still trying to get through them.'

They laughed and then paused. Perhaps he was picturing her in the suds. She said quickly: 'So tell me what you do. Or did. Besides wandering around picking up strange ladies in Saloon Bars.'

'I was joking about that.'

'I know.' With her wet finger she traced a circle on the table. 'Do you joke about most things?'

'Most. The things that matter.'

Someone rang a bell. 'Drink up, gentlemen.' The lights were flicked on and off. The room was thick with cigarette smoke, some people were making a move. 'Your glasses *please*.'

Steve looked at his watch, a heavy, flash digital job. 'Jesus.'

'What is it?'

'Said I'd be home at seven. And I didn't even phone.'

'Ah.' She paused, and put on her coat.

They walked down the road together, towards the embankment. Figures were leaving The Angler's. She scanned them as they passed; she did not know if she wanted to see Adrian and Beth.

They reached her car first. She would like to have seen his. 'Where did you park?' she asked. He indicated the direction of the river.

She opened her handbag and rummaged about for her keys. She found them but she went on rummaging. Above them, someone closed a window.

They stood together on the pavement for a moment. She must go round to the other side of the car to open the door.

She walked around and unlocked the door. There was a silence.

'Hey, that was nice,' he said.

She gazed at him over the shiny expanse of roof; he was smiling.

'Thanks for the drink.' She ducked her head and climbed into the driver's seat.

She sat there, her key in the ignition. He was walking down the street; his head appeared and disappeared beween the parked cars. A nice man going home to his wife. All over the city, nice men going home to their wives.

TWENTY

Sunday was always the worst day of the week. Monday to Friday Claudia had been working hard and staying late; this autumn she had virtually taken over as production manager to the hi-fi magazine that occupied the next office, its own manager being off sick. This was fine; the more work the better. On Saturdays she was busy shopping; Saturday mornings had a breezy promise. But on Sundays the whole of London seemed to consist of closed front doors wherein dwelt loving couples. The Steven Mullens were family men. So was Adrian. Since Friday he and Beth were believable.

Outside her flat the long brick terrace stretched down to the high street; nothing stirred there but last night's chip papers, shifting in the darkened doorway of Tesco. All was quiet; in the butcher's window a row of pressed, virgin carrier bags, in Maxine's Hair Salon a row of empty hoods. In the country she presumed it to be different. All tolling bells and clicking secateurs, Sundays there would have a feeling of purpose and worship, of one's own needs dispersed in the leafy largeness of nature. But in her own streets Sunday was a lack – a lack of bustle, traffic and open welcoming shops. A lack of somebody with whom she could remain indoors, drinking coffee, sharing the papers and bickering. Having Alistair around only made it worse, for she felt lonelier – when he entered the room her face must stiffen into a smile, she must hastily pretend to have been reading the Sunday supplements. Only with intimates could one look vacant.

All in all she looked forward to the next weekend at Verity's. Sunday would pass unnoticed amidst the clutter of the Fosters' kitchen. It would also be a relief to get away from Alistair. She had not, of course, brought up her sighting of him in the King's Road. But since Friday she had noticed more closely his behaviour. He did, indeed, seem to be watching her. Wherever she turned, there he was. When the ash lengthened on her cigarette, there was the ready ashtray held in front of her. Had he followed her to the King's Road? Could he possibly have done so?

On Thursday he was out. He did not return until 11.30. Claudia was in the corridor, dragging out the rubbish bag from the kitchen. Tomorrow was the dustmen's day.

'Sorry, did I shock you?' She stopped. He was poised on the doormat, staring at her. His eyes were bright, his skin flushed. Had he just been drinking?

He recovered himself. 'No, no. I'm awfully sorry. Here – let me, please.' He hid his face, bending down to the plastic bag; he gripped it, his long white wrists protruding from his raincoat.

The bag was heavy. He dragged it along the floor and pulled it, with a bump, down the steps. She imagined herself trussed up in black polythene. *Perhaps he's a murderer*. So pallid and shy, surely he could not be? But then, as Verity would be the first to point out, were not many murderers inadequate sort of people? Was not that partly their reason for it?

Alistair followed her indoors, wiping his fingers with his handkerchief. 'Sorry I was so late,' he said, 'without informing you.'

'Good grief, don't apologize, I don't own you.' She laughed hastily. 'I mean, it's no inconvenience.'

They stood for a moment in the living-room. Head lowered, he appeared to be rubbing, thoroughly, his fingers one by one. 'As a matter of fact,' he muttered, 'if that's all right by you, you won't be having the, er, dubious pleasure of my company tomorrow evening either. I shall be taking myself off for the night.' He glanced up.

'That's Friday, isn't it. Actually I'll be away too. At my friend Verity's, in Kent.'

'I shall be at my mother's,' he said quickly.

'That's nice. She will be pleased.'

'Er, just for the night.' He bunched up his handkerchief. 'It's quite a distance, of course, to Malvern, but – well – it's her birthday.' He paused, eyes flickering up. 'No doubt I shall return promptly, on Saturday, for our lunch.'

The next day, Friday, Verity phoned Claudia at work. Would Claudia mind terribly if they changed it to the next weekend? Wil had been called out – some rushed job, some client in Norwich – he had to stay away the weekend and so she was taking the children down to see her parents, who loathed him.

Leaning against her swivel chair, Claudia felt a pang for Verity. Also a twitch for herself, that Verity presumed her quite rightly to be free at a moment's notice for the following weekend. Also a tiny, shameful twitch concerning Wil, who no doubt would be experiencing, in Norwich, something both meaningful and fragile.

'That's fine.' Her eyes travelled along the fibreglass panels of her office. Sometimes she wished she could work twenty-four hours a day. Despite the mounds of artwork, the printers' deadlines, the faulty colour separations and ensuing frantic phone-calls, it was so simple.

She returned that night to a flat she knew would be empty. She kicked off her shoes, pulled off her clothes and

166

walked naked down the corridor. She got into a bath. She splashed around for as long as she liked. She could leave the door wide open.

After that she went to her dressing-table, opened the drawer and took out an item from her blitz at Boots six weeks back. A sachet: *Country Meadow Face Pac*. Why Pac, for goodness sake? Steven Mullen would have had something to say about that; he would have made her laugh. *Natural Herbs for Natural Beauty*. With some water she mixed it into a paste and applied it to her skin; she spread it over her cheeks, a tinted putty. Her eyes stared out from their green, stiffening mask. Logically she had nobody to do this for. Why then: just because of some chance meeting a week ago?

She scraped up her hair into rollers; wrapping her dressing-gown around her she went into the kitchen. She felt as if she had dipped her face into concrete; passing the mirror she glanced at the spikey, masked figure, a lost extra from some sci-fi movie. All this cement and all these pins, she thought, to make me look as if I had not done anything.

She was just opening the fridge when there was a click. It sounded like the outer front door. It must be the Monsons, who lived upstairs. She took out some eggs, then hesitated. No steps were ascending the stairs. She waited, then heard the knob turning in the door of her own flat, the rattle of a key.

She panicked. The only hiding-place was a small space between the fridge and the cooker. She moved to the left and wedged herself in, crouching. Where's my husband? She felt her mask cracking.

Footsteps were approaching along the passage. Tiny flakes had fallen from her face; they powdered the black squares of the lino. The steps came into the kitchen and stopped. A shadow fell in front of her; she saw it through her fingers.

'Heavens, I'm terribly sorry,' said a voice.

She removed her fingers. It was, of course, Alistair.

Alistair seemed as alarmed as herself at this mutual confrontation. Well he might be, given her appearance and position. This was reassuring. Less comforting was his jumbled explanation of his presence. He had missed his train, he stuttered. No – his mother had put it off. Yes – yes – she had a bit of a backache. She had, er, terrible backache, his mother. Amidst joint, staccato explanations they had retreated to their bedrooms.

And who was she, Claudia, to interrogate? It was none of her business. Probably some tryst that had failed; a night of passion that had been cancelled. It was stupid to be uneasy.

Claudia told herself this until Saturday night, when Alistair had taken himself off, supposedly, to a lecture on Mediaeval London. Upon various errands unconnected to him she passed and re-passed his bedroom door. She must have done this six times before she stopped and turned the knob.

There lay the paisley package, behind the books as usual. She had done this once already; in a sense her moral virginity was already broken. Still she hesitated. She lifted the cloth as if she were lifting a skirt.

This time she picked up the most recent volume. Just a skim, she told herself, a few lines here and there. After all, his behaviour had been growing so odd. It was only sensible to have a look. She would do nothing so guiltily exact as seeking last, or this, Friday's entries.

She opened the book somewhere near the beginning.

'Sex.' Claudia's eyes swung, magnet-like, down to the word. '. . . *tall, for a member of her sex. To wash up, her sleeves were pulled back to reveal firm, slender arms. C. is attractive on several points. She has a) white, nicely freckled skin, b) straight profile as upon Greek vase, c) height. Tallness is point in favour, for beauty.*

p.m. Determined to write letter to London Transport.

168

Four 19s in a row this morning . . .'

Claudia's eye hurried down the page, skimming; she turned over.

'9 p.m. Pretended to be watching TV. C. wearing dressing gown. Could not keep eye from lower leg i.e. shin, for once stockingless. Imagined it waxen to the touch. Watching TV best time for this, as person in question unaware. Main disadvantage: lack of illumination.'

Claudia's heart thumped. Her hand fumbled open the next page. Her eye swooped down to a C.

'Thurs. p.m. C. out. After some hesitation, entered room. Selection of undergarments over radiator. Item 1: Beige nylon tights, with reinforced toe and upper region. Item 2: Blue lace-trimmed "panties". Item 3: Ditto of same, with pink flowers. Urge to examine closer but urge restrained. Retreated swiftly. Should Not Do This.

Finished last chapter of "Rogue Herries". Disappointing . . .'

The flimsy book trembled. Claudia turned one page, two pages.

'Sure C. has noticed. Asked me tonight if anything the matter. Had I been staring? N.B. Must Take Care.'

At this point Claudia closed the book. She could not read any more – not yet. She rose from Alistair's bedside chair and replaced the exercise book with care, tucking in the edges of the handkerchief.

With a series of thuds everything fell into place. It all fitted. How stupid not to have noticed – at least, to have noticed but to have made the wrong interpretation. All those weeks and she had not realized. That lingering gaze, the way Alistair hovered close to her, the way he sprang up when she entered the room as if in her absence he had simply been waiting, his blushes, his growing eagerness to share, the way he seldom went out . . . what a fool she had been not to realize that it all sprang from the simplest answer of all – love.

She went into the kitchen; she gazed out at the black Saturday night. She should be pleased, of course. In a sense she was. The old mechanism, a bit rusty, stirred within her. She must brush her hair, outline her lips with care.

She pressed her face against the window. She could see nothing outside. Drawing back she saw her own reflection. Why did she still feel so unsettled?

She opened the cupboard. She gazed at Alistair's tins and packets, pushed humbly to one side in order to give her own more room. Was it his subservience? But the curious, lurking tone of the diary was hardly servile. Was it his secretiveness, the exact way he had itemised her, the thought of him creeping around gazing at her intimate garments? (She herself was not entirely guiltless of this, of course, but her objects were books. Besides, she had not subsequently documented it.) She paused, hand on the handle. In fact, had he returned last night simply because he knew she would be absent; had he planned upon a whole evening of opening drawers and fingering underwear?

Of course she should not have encouraged him. Unknowingly she had, what with her invitations to share supper, her patting of the neighbouring chair when she was watching TV, the unwitting crossing and re-crossing of those waxen shins. What could she do – swaddle herself more tightly, retreat, ask him to find another flat?

In an hour Alistair would return. How could she behave, not just tonight but during the time that lay ahead?

She felt claustrophobia closing in – hotter and more stifling than her feelings before she had opened the book, before she had known their true reason.

TWENTY ONE

'Did you remember my refill?' asked June. Monday, and Steve had just returned from work.

'What?'

'You said you'd get it at one of your Bootses. My mascara.'

'Ah.' Steve hesitated. 'It must have slipped my mind.'

This was a formal, un-Stevish way of putting it. June glanced at him. He looked the same as usual – smart business suit, pink shirt she had pressed this weekend. For how many months had she been ironing his shirts – cuffs, collar, front and back, paying particular attention to the buttonholes – only for them to be unbuttoned by another?

June felt herself colouring and turned away. He always used to remember things like her refills. She fiddled with the pile of drinks coasters on the sideboard, placing them dead centre between the two vases Aunty Loïs had given them for their wedding present. Ever since she had looked into his briefcase and found those things – ever since then she had been laying little traps for Steve. She was not too clever at this; once or twice he had glanced at her oddly. But misery made her dogged.

Who would have believed that those vague suspicions outside the sauna would turn out to be only too true? At

171

the time they had just passed through her mind. Probably she would have mentioned them to him, shyly snuggling against him, her voice girlish, when he came home that Friday night. But he had returned home too late for her to snuggle shyly and he had lied about his activities. Even she, supposedly so dumb, had seen that. What could be a less likely story than happening to meet his boss in a pub in the middle of London, and the boss's old wife happening to be there at the same time.

Hardly likely, in the light of what she had found next day. For the first time in their marriage she had searched his briefcase. Steve never locked things up – his largeness, his carelessness half-endeared her still and made it more painful, her rummaging about like that when he was out at the football on Saturday afternoon. Underneath some promotion leaflets she had found a letter marked *Private and Confidential*. It contained an appointment for Steve to see his boss, Mr Ensor, on Friday afternoon.

'Steve,' she had asked casually when he returned from soccer, 'did anything happen about your new job – you know, that promotion?'

Steve had stopped dead in the doorway.

'Oh, er, not actually. No.' He had scratched his ruffled hair. How she longed, begged for it to be all right so that she could fling herself against him and bury her face in his blue, soccer-spectator's anorak. 'No – er, he'd gone away on holiday. The Scillies. Perhaps next time – in six weeks, when we're meeting again.'

How could he have gone away, she would have liked – no, hated – to ask, when you met him later in a pub? She had said nothing.

Nor had she said anything about the scrumpled note at the bottom of everything else in his briefcase. Scrawled in brown felt-tip, it had simply said: 'Steve – care to look at some *really* dirty pictures? Marge.' The really dirty pictures, needless to say, were not to be found.

172

Round and round her head this little note had been circling, all Saturday and all Sunday and now all Monday. She could think of no way to bring this up. It just gnawed away inside her, hollowing out the pit of her stomach, eating away the place under her ribs where her heart lay.

Steve came in with a can of beer. To someone who knew, he looked haggard, there was no doubt of this, with a shadowiness about his eyes. Worn out, no doubt. She herself, of course, had not allowed him to touch her since his return on Friday.

She turned away and plumped up the fluffy white cushions on the settee. Then there was the question of the cheque. Sooner or later she must bring this up but she could think of no direction from which to approach it.

At first, seeing the stub for £250, her heart had thumped with pleasure. £250 was the exact price; he had bought the carpet secretly, as a surprise. At some future moment, carefully planned of course, it would be delivered in a large van and she would clatter down the stairs, gasping with surprise, while he looked on fondly. Perhaps, in fact, this explanation could cover the other mysteries; perhaps they were all in some obscure way part of some elaborate plan – a plan that involved Steve's boss and someone (perhaps a carpet saleswoman?) called Marge.

She did not care to work out how they could, indeed, be part of a larger plan. Even her soft brain could see some odd facts that could not quite be pushed into place. Behind her she heard the hiss as Steve opened his beer can, then the silence of concentration as he poured it into a glass. Last week she would have done this for him.

She kept her eyes and her hands on the cushion. 'Steve.' She started her bright, prepared speech. 'Steve, shall we go out next Saturday and buy that carpet for the bedroom? You said last month that we'd got just about enough now.'

A silence. She glanced around. He remained poised, glass in one hand, can in the other. She felt as if they were standing upon a stage.

'Or perhaps I was wrong,' she said quickly, turning back to the cushions.

'No. No darling. Listen June – well, we'll do it nice and quickly, soon . . . you know . . .'

She let his strained voice trail away. There was a hopeless kind of silence. The cushions blurred with tears; their pom-pom edges swam, the turquoise weave of the settee swam. She kept her face averted; she loathed him standing there clearing his throat, she loathed herself for her cold little ploy, so terribly unlike her usual way of speaking.'

'Just peeling the potatoes.' She hurried into the kitchen. G.E., the cheque stub had said. Who was this G.E.? Certainly not the carpet shop, which happened to be John Lewis. G.E. . . . knowing, no doubt, the whole name he had only bothered with the initials. To what girl had he given such a very lavish gift; what female was benefiting from the sum total of their savings? Gloria Somebody – an old flame of his – was a possibility. But then, judging by the evidence, there seemed many flames both old and new in Steve's life.

It was all so horribly banal and expected and exactly like all those jokes on TV. The naughty salesman, the ho-hos and the rolling eyes and the faces pink from beer. Bit on the side, bit of you-know-what. It was all such a standing joke she could hardly believe it was actually happening to her and Steve. She must try not to think about it.

She gazed at the heap of potatoes, unscrubbed on the draining-board. She must peel them one by one; she must gather the cold wet peelings in her hand and shove them into the rubbish bin; she must chop the cabbage and dice the beef and pull off its gristle . . . For the first time in her marriage she thought: I don't like this housework and this cooking.

TWENTY TWO

It was several days since Claudia had opened Alistair's diary; since Saturday she had lived with his fond and watchful secret. It unsettled her, how normally they both behaved. His politeness resembled, uncannily, the politeness of Adrian – Adrian who had passed her the teapot, who cleared his throat and stood aside to let her pass, while on his skin was the scent of another woman. That this time she, Claudia, was the object of passion made it hardly more comfortable. If only Alistair would come out with it. One day he had nailed, across the sink cupboard, a pink piece of cotton to conceal the mops and bottles of bleach. She had been duly grateful; like her husband's fastidious, housewifely ways, Alistair's both touched and exasperated her. It seemed, however, symptomatic. Like her toxic tins, and bottles labelled *Keep Away From Naked Flame*, Alistair's urges were veiled behind the flounced curtain of manners. And what exactly were her own urges? She was still confused.

Something must be said. On Wednesday Claudia brought home a bottle of wine. Alistair had been cooking for them both lately; the menu had been expanded to include chicken portions and breadcrumbed plaice. They would share pleasant, minor discussions upon whether to

175

accompany this with Knorr White, Knorr Cheese or Knorr Parsley Sauce. Claudia as always found herself making the decision while Alistair stood aside, humble in her *Guinness Is Good For You* apron. Her cook, her slave.

After supper he brought the coffee tray into the living-room. At her feet he laid it with devotion. She could see this now. In her armchair she shifted, tucking her trousered legs beneath her. Thank God, she thought, for television. Its coloured window let in the outside world, its chattiness broke the silence.

Later they rose to do the washing-up. Claudia stood at the sink rubbing the sudsy plates. Alistair stood beside her, drying cloth in hand. Now that they were occupied, at work together, she felt bolder. Over-thoroughly scrubbing a glass she remarked:

'You know, it's been more of an upset than it might appear.'

'I beg your pardon?' Alistair's hand stopped.

'The break-up of my marriage.' She finished the glass and started on the grill pan. This was encrusted and congealed; it needed a good deal of scraping. 'I mean that I'm a bit, well, withdrawn from ordinary emotions. Rather in cold storage.'

Alistair cleared his throat. Was he blushing? She concentrated on the slatted metal rack, scrubbing at the greasy lumps that clung. 'I'm trying to become – well, a proper woman again, but it takes time. I can't quite react, yet, as I'd want to. I don't know if I could cope with – well, a proper relationship.' She glanced up. 'Do you understand what I'm trying to say?'

Crimson-faced, Alistair nodded.

'I'm terribly glad.' She eased up the obstinate bits carefully with a knife. Delicately she scraped the corners. 'So, Alistair dear, you mustn't be offended.'

The *dear* hung in the air. She wished he would speak. She lifted the grill out of the water and passed it to him. Heavy

176

metal, it was weighty with meaning; his large, dripping consolation prize. She felt eased by the wine; she was sorrowing, motherly.

Alistair dropped it. Clattering on the floor, it separated into its two component parts.

'*Sorry*.' Alistair fell to his knees. He lunged under the table to retrieve the metal rack. She gazed at his trousered rump. He had tied the Guinness apron at the back in a bow. Rising, he bumped his head against the draining-board.

'Poor Alistair.' She placed her hand upon his head. 'Does it hurt?' His hair was surprisingly soft and sparse; she could feel his scalp beneath. She rubbed his head. 'Poor Alistair,' she murmured, 'don't be hurt.' Her hand remained there for a moment on his warm, needing skull.

He caught his breath; he turned away and bent his head. She felt a gush of pity. 'Alistair,' she whispered and turned him back. She put her arms around him; she was suddenly so moved by his emotions. She pressed his aproned body against hers; he stood rigid in her arms. Behind the thick frontal shield of plastic he was thin and yearning. She ran her hands over his bony shoulderblades. He smelt of soap.

Over his shoulder she gazed at the bright kitchen. Would it not be good to want him, to please him, instead of hankering after unknown married men who forgot her as soon as they stepped into their car? She drew back and looked at Alistair's sandy lashes – for his eyes were closed – and his flushed, passionate skin. Why, indeed, not?

She pressed her cheek against his. It was nice, that he smelt so scrubbed. She took a breath and murmured: 'Would you like to kiss me?'

He was trembling. There was a silence, then he opened his eyes. Pink-rimmed, they kept their gazed fixed on the hot water geyser. He said something but she did not hear.

'What?' she asked, inflamed with charity. Also with a certain itchy desire.

'I couldn't,' he muttered. 'Please . . .'

He disengaged himself from her arms and hurried from the kitchen. She stood still for a moment. His bedroom door closed with a click. She felt awkward but the wine helped this, blurring the edges. And she felt flattered, of course. He knew what she had meant. And what could be greater proof of his love than that anguished cry, that rush from the room?

She picked up the grill and slotted its two parts together.

TWENTY THREE

'Where did you go today?'

'Oh,' said Steve, 'the usual places . . . you know.' He could hardly get through the door nowadays without June starting in on him.

'Croydon,' he said hastily, at random. Why could he not tell her — because she would not understand?

'You're not listening, Steve. I said: I suppose you went to that Timothy White's there.'

'What do you mean?'

'The one with the female assistant that you're always going on about when your coarse friend Bruce telephones.'

'Darling, only once. Anyway we were only joking. You know Bruce.'

'He's horrible. I don't like to think of you two. How you talk together.' She looked at him sharply. 'If you went to Croydon, where's the ice-cream?'

'What?'

'You always bring back some of that Italian kind. You know, from that place opposite the chemist's.'

'Heavens, I forgot. Sorry, Juney.'

'Suppose you had something else on your mind.'

'Hey Junekins, it doesn't sound right, you being sarcastic.' He tried to put his arms around her but she pulled away. She had been pulling away for ten days now.

No I didn't go there, he wanted to say. He had visited no chemists that day, Timothy Whites nor any other. His display stands remained unstocked, the storerooms unchecked, Vince's inflamed face ungreeted. Did Vincent and the others notice his absence? Probably not. Hands reaching for *Liberesse* Body Caress would stop and move instead to the Max Factors. They were all the same anyway, weren't they.

He had walked beside a canal but it was too cold. He had been warmed in a café, gazing out of its steamed-up window. He had gone into a stuffy dark Odeon; there he had gazed at ochre Texan hills and noble horsemen standing on crags, seeking the horizon.

'Steve, I said where did you go after Croydon?'

'Blimey June, what's the matter? You'll force me into whatever-you-think-I-am soon. It's not a blooming interrogation centre.' Guilt made his voice louder. She had got it right, and yet wrong. But it distressed him, that he had to justify a day that no longer quite existed. There she was, forcing him into the sort of person he had nearly resembled in his time, but he was different now.

He had not, in fact, spent the last ten days playing truant. Mostly he had been working, but vaguely, a visit here, a visit there, his heart not in it. But she would be shocked, she would not understand. Lately there was a coldness and a petty sharpness about her; this was new. It must be the effect of being at home all day. And now that she would not let him bury his doubts in her warm body, he realized how much he had relied upon that. She had clung before, but it was nice to feel her clinging.

Still it was odd, this sudden claustrophobic jealousy. He had caught sight of her last Sunday crouched in the corner writing something in a notebook. It must have been something about him – some list or strategic future plan – he could tell by the way she shut it up hastily when he came into the room. He had searched for the book later but he had been unable to find it.

He must tell her something. He tried again, upon a subject that she surely could not find offensive. He would tell her about going to Mr Sims' aquarium shop and finding it all re-developed, and a sauna too. About the reply from the lady at the desk when he asked about the business that had once stood on the premises. That might raise a smile.

'Went to Beckenham today. . .' he began.

'What?' She looked at him, a blush rising. She could be so luminously beautiful.

'Went down to Beckenham –'

The phone rang. By the time he got back, other things had intervened and Beckenham had been forgotten. Anyway, there seemed little point.

He went for a walk after supper. It was a chill, damp night, nearly December now. Through thick bushes he could see into institutional front windows: in one an empty, book-lined room, in another a music stand. Notice-boards, purpose, direction and ideals, occupations that mattered to the person who carried them out.

He doubted if it would do much good, his grand abdication. There would be alarm, recrimination and a docking of his back-dated pay but there would soon be other recruits, what with the prospects and the commission and all that independence, radio thumping, suburbs slipping past. Nature's course would not be altered by his small defiance. No whales would be saved. The plastic display stands would soon be re-stocked. But he himself was going to feel better.

Better? Two in the morning and June had long since gone to bed. In all this he thought of her so little – why could he not include her? He was being so selfish. He stood at the window, the ashtray beside him filled with stubs. In one sense it was simple; he could throw out the filing cabinet that stood in the corner, grey and cold and tinny; he could set his sails in another direction. But what about June – June, to whom he could not tell one-tenth of what was passing through his mind and his heart?

He drew back the curtains. What had Claudia Ensor said? He would like to speak to her now. The fog had cleared; the sky was bright with stars. He could see the bulk of the surrounding houses. They were so solid, those brick mansions with their thick walls and their cellars; built to last. Within them generations had grown up, aged and died; within their gardens trees had matured.

Always he had preferred them to his own flat, a shaky edifice built in haste. Already a crack had appeared across the ceiling of the lounge. So flimsy, his flat. The door surrounds, of frail plywood, had warped under their cosmetic layer of Dulux.

Flimsy as his flimsy young marriage.

Steve lit another cigarette. His throat felt burnt and sour.

'What shall I do?' he said, aloud in his despair. He spoke it to the painted, pretty room.

TWENTY FOUR

Eleven thirty in the morning, and Claudia was at work. In the open-plan office of *Yours*, desks were screened by curved panels. On the inside of hers were pinned notices, letters, reminders, and three different calendars sent to her by rival colour labs. All proof not just that she existed but that she was essential. In fact, her work space was more personal than her own flat. The phone rang more often too.

Claudia put down the phone and sipped her coffee. She could rely on this place, on Chrissy and Grace and Ann, the dyed blonde editress, turning up each weekday, on solid work piling up on her desk. However hectic it became she could cope – arranging schedules with typesetters and printers and colour processors, making up her flat plan for the sections of features and advertisements. She had always been technically rather than creatively minded; she could never work on the more glamorous editing side. Colours, after all, were unconfusing. Though the blue might be subtly merging into something nearer violet, though under the light box there were whole ranges of shades that could not be seen under normal conditions, yet these could be corrected. In this office, at least, she could believe her eyes.

The proof of an advertisement had arrived from the printers. She rose to take it to the light box. Consisting of a slanting metal screen with a strip light above, this blanked out the faulty and impure daylight of the office. It was an ideal to which she would like to aspire – cool, impartial. At work she could almost believe that this, indeed, was her identity. She welcomed it stretching into the shakier areas of her life. Because printers could not afford to stop their machines they occasionally phoned her at night to query something she had said. In her rumpled nightie she would reach over for the receiver. Amidst the blurred confusion of her dreams, so disturbingly peopled, with their eerie tilted landscapes, the man's voice came not as an annoyance but as a relief. Work anchored her.

It was certainly easier than the rest of her life. Easier than the current avoidance of Alistair's eye – since that night last week they had both become even more considerate and polite, managing somehow never to be in the kitchen at the same time, waiting, poised for the click of the other's bedroom door. Simpler, too, than with Wil. The advertisement in her hand originated, in fact, from his agency. Promoting a glosser manufactured by one of Pintaubaum's rivals, this depicted a large pair of glistening lips, proof of the moisture-making nature of the product, with the caption *Have You Been Kissed Today*? Simple bit of paper. 4-colour, Windsor caps. Easy to position this under the white glare – straighten, clip, switch on – easier than avoiding Wil's eye this past weekend in Kent, being as awkward with him as she was with Alistair.

Claudia inspected the photograph, marking with her pencil *less red* in the relevant area. *Have You Been Kissed Today? No*, she would like to scrawl, *I Haven't*.'

More blue, she wrote. *More definition here*.

She whisked Wil's question out of the light box. Why, anyway, the suppliant female? Why not *Have You Kissed Anyone Today*? (*No* to that as well.)

She took the photo back to her desk. *Yours* carried a good deal of cosmetics advertising. The *Liberesse* lady was intimately familiar to Claudia; countless times she had corrected the tan on her legs and adjusted, as it were, the khaki hues of her clothing. Equally familiar were the other glamorous faces that gazed out from the page. Sometimes it struck her as ironic, the sort of advertising *Yours* had to carry in order to finance its features. Some of it was suitable, some less so. An article on executive careers would be set opposite a full colour housewife in a hostess apron; *Do Your Own Vaginal Inspections* would be faced by a misty nude glimpsing, through the foliage, her tuxedo'd dinner date.

Sitting down, Claudia glanced across the office. Over at the far door stood two men. One, deputy promotions on the hi-fi magazine, was pointing out the way; the other man, who was Steven Mullen, appeared to be listening and scanning the room.

Claudia ducked behind the panel. She scrabbled for her powder compact. Today she was wearing her grey silk blouse and black corduroy skirt. Did she look too managerial and unwomanly?

She straightened up, blushing like a teenager. She should, of course, have simply approached him, smiling. It was two weeks since they had met in The Angler's.

Steve had not yet seen her. He walked past the three desks where the subs sat. His hair was wet; it must be raining outside. Today he wore a black suit with wide lapels; with his gleaming sleeked-down hair he looked dark and Latin.

'Heavens,' said Claudia.

'Hello, stranger.'

'How did you know where I was?'

'I remembered, didn't I.'

There was a silence. He looked restive and alert. The shoulders of his suit were dark with rain. 'Are you terribly wet?' she asked stupidly.

'That's right.'

Another silence.

'Nice line in Pentels,' he observed.

She gazed at her china mug full of them, and biros, and efficient sharpened pencils. 'Yes.'

He was carrying his dispatch case. She had an absurd feeling that he had come to sell her something. The way he was standing at her desk. In a moment would he click it open?

'Come to interest me in some mind and body cleanse?' She kept her voice light. 'Come to make me beautiful and all woman? Come to clear my blemishes?'

He grinned. 'Got a lovely new line. Frankly, you're going to go overboard on this one.'

'I can see you're a born salesman.'

'Actually, that's why I've come. I wanted to show it to you.' He rubbed his nose, suddenly shy. 'Is there any chance – I mean, are you really busy?'

She looked at her man's watch. 12.05. Three phone calls to make before lunch, Mr Harris coming in from that agency, four letters to dictate, Zoë to consult about the theatre review artwork.

'No,' she said. 'Not at all.'

184

She unhooked her coat and they made their way back across the office. 'You asked them the way?' She nodded her head towards the hi-fi doors. 'We're owned by the same company but we never meet, except some stuff that I do for them.' They were walking down the stairs. 'It's run entirely by middle-aged men. And our magazine, that's always campaigning for sexual equality, is run entirely by women.' She laughed as they reached the ground floor.

'Don't you ever meet?'

'Just in the lift. And the Christmas party.' She paused. 'The regulation Yuletide fumble.' She smiled at herself; the words were unlike her.

Outside it was raining, heavy but warm for December. Hunched, they hurried across Regent Street. She followed him, weaving around the midday traffic. The cars and taxis were crawling, their windscreen wipers flicking back and forth.

He waited for her on the pavement. A few raincoated figures hurried by; a few more sheltered in the doorways of Dickins and Jones.

'Like a drink? Hungry?' He leant near her, shouting above the noise of the traffic.

'Either. Whichever you like.' She was as putty. She would do whatever he wanted.

There was no pub in sight. The nearest shelter was down an alley to the right. *Nuts About It* was a health food place and at 12.15 just starting to fill up for lunch. Claudia came here sometimes when Verity was up in London, because it was so organic. Claudia paused. Its decor was white and tiled. She must let this place calm and cool her.

They queued at the counter. Upon it stood earthenware bowls of pricey shredded cabbage. People shuffled past. Long-haired, inefficient girls doled out the indicated portions as if they had just dropped in for a few minutes and were doing a tremendous favour. At the cash desk sat a somewhat friendlier, moustachio'd man, *Save The Whale* shifting on his tee-shirt as he leant forward to take the proffered notes. Steve paid.

He was gazing at his plate.

'Do you like this sort of thing?' she asked. Perhaps he was a pie and a pint man.

'Have it every day. Good for the complexion.'

He pulled out two chairs and unloaded the tray on to the table. Despite the business suit there was something raffish about him – gold signet ring, handsome face – though the Mafia look was disappearing with the drying of his hair. The place was full of suits. Though those behind the counter wore faded dungarees, the tables were occupied by office workers – audio typists in Crimpelene two-pieces, well-tailored young men who were lifting forkfuls of greenery from pottery bowls.

'Cheers.' Steve grinned, raising his glass of apple juice. 'Take it easy with this stuff.'

They started eating. She had a vision of their internal organs – hers as unknown as his – churning up this food that appeared, until swallowed, so familiar. She hesitated but did not tell him this rather fey thought. Would he understand? Did she know him?

He said: 'Promise you won't laugh.'

'What is it?' She glanced up hopefully. Thought-reading?

'If I tell you why I came to see you. At least, partly why.'

Her fork stopped with its burden of cole slaw. 'Go on.'

'To cut a long story short, I've given it up. Like I said I would. As from this week. I've had enough, Claudia.'

At her name she lowered her gaze. 'What have you been doing? Does Pintaubaum know?'

'Oh, wandering around, catching up with some films. At least, I did for a day or two but then I decided to do something constructive.'

'What's that?'

'Well, somebody gave me a lot of gen on the things that

186

go into the stuff I sell. Sold. Other stuff too – cat food, clothes, you name it. Thought I'd write something about it. I've started already this last couple of days, been sitting in libraries going through reference books. I spent all day yesterday looking things up. June – that's my wife – she hasn't got an inkling.'

Claudia took a mouthful.

'I brought a couple of books home,' he said, 'but I hid them in my filing cabinet. It's ridiculous, Claudia, but I can't bring myself to tell anybody yet. Not your old man, not my wife. You're the only person who knows.'

Claudia gazed at the abstract arrangement on her plate: beige buckwheat grains freckled with parsley, purple cubes of beetroot. 'That's nice.'

'I just wondered – well, if you could run your eye over what I've written. It's only a couple of pages so far. But, you being a professional and all . . . I mean, that's your line isn't it?'

That is not my line. I'm on the production side.

'Yes, that's my line,' she said, and smiled. She looked down at the tangle of grated carrot, moist with oil.

'Perhaps we can do it,' she said. 'Make a feature of it. *Behind the label*, that sort of thing.'

'Hey, that sounds good.'

'Let's have a butcher's,' she said. Butcher's? She had never said this before.

He opened his dispatch case and passed her a piece of handwritten paper . . . *'contrary to general expectations . . . hitherto doubts have been unfounded . . .'* She did not continue. She longed so much for it to be good and she did not dare to find out.

'Looks interesting,' she said.

'I'm no Bernard Whatsisname. Levin.'

'No really. It looks good.'

'I've got most of the rest down in notes now. Just need to type it. Think I'll go and sit in an Olivetti showroom and pretend I'm making comparisons.'

'You mean you don't have a typewriter?'

'Only at home.'

'And you don't want to . . .'

A pause. She said: 'Look, I've got the afternoon off. I was going to work at home. Would you like to type at my flat? Then I can keep what you've done and perhaps bring it in to the magazine tomorrow. Tomorrow's Friday . . .'

He had stopped eating. 'Really? Straight up?'

Shame at her lie made her cool. 'Yes,' she said shortly.

Outside it had stopped raining. The pavements glistened in the watery sunshine. His wet, red Cortina lay in a back street with a parking ticket under its windscreen wiper.

'You don't mind?' she said as he shoved it, carelessly, into the glove compartment.

'Got a little hoard in there.'

He knew the London streets; she did not have to tell him the way. He drove swiftly and sometimes recklessly, but he turned around to give a thumbs-up to the driver he had overtaken.

Sitting in the passenger seat she gazed at his hands on the wheel and at his heavy opal cufflinks. Adrian had been such a cautious driver, and such a good citizen.

Why had she lied about work? Work was her last bastion of self-respect. Why had she not admitted to her job? She had betrayed it.

They drove across the river. Over to the left stood the power station with its four thick chimneys. They glowed in the pale light of this December afternoon. No, hardly afternoon – it was still only one fifteen.

'Nice car.' She looked at the dashboard with its clock and cassette player. 'I'm glad you don't hang up your jacket at the back.'

He grinned at this. 'Can't bear to give up this motor. I think that's why I keep putting it off.'

'You mean telling Adrian and that terrible smoothie –'

'Henson.'

'Henson, that's right. They can afford it.' She felt a thrill.

'Shall we run away?' He turned to her. She could not tell from his tone. 'I'm boracic but the tank's full.'

She paused. He was joking, of course. She said: 'What's boracic?'

'Boracic lint. Skint. Wrote a cheque a week or so ago and gave all the savings away.'

'What to?'

'Promise you won't tell?'

'Promise.'

'Benevolent Fund for Retired Pornographers.'

'I knew you had a kind face.'

'Headquarters – Nicolette Sauna, Beckenham.'

'They do a lovely Christmas card.'

He laughed. They were in her district now. She gave him directions.

'I'll make you some coffee,' she said. 'Then I'll leave you alone. Or would you like something else to eat? You didn't finish your lunch.'

Didn't finish your lunch? Whoever was speaking, it was a Claudia who had not been revealed to her before. Claudia turned and looked out of the window. Ridiculous. He seemed so impulsive, that was the trouble, he was the sort of person who smoked too much and forgot to eat.

She gazed at the ordinary red-brick houses they were passing. Here she was, an ordinary female in the passenger seat, no longer driving, content to be driven. She had even got rid of her job; she could no longer speak of it, because he would find out she had been lying. Here she sat, longing to cook.

Only cook? She wanted him so much her mouth was dry.

TWENTY FIVE

'I'll pheeze you, i' faith.

    A pair of stocks, you rogue!

    Therefore, paucas pallabris: let the world slide. Sessa.'

June was lost. And she was only on line six.

She turned to Mr Poultney who had just come in from lunch. She herself was on a diet. He was passing the table, a pile of books under his arm.

He stopped. He always had time for her and the library was empty, except for an elderly man who had come in out of the rain and who slumbered at the table.

'I chose *The Taming of the Shrew*,' she said, continuing an earlier conversation, 'because people came once and did it at school.'

He sat down beside her. 'Perhaps I can be of assistance.' He pointed to the page. 'Sly's speaking. He is, as it were, a gentleman of the road, Not dissimilar to our friend at the end of the table.' They turned, smiling, to look at him. 'And the Host says *You will not pay for the glasses you have burst*? i.e. broken. Says Sly: *No, not by a denier.'*

'I know what that means. They have them in tights. 15 denier and 20 denier.'

He explained some more words, indicating them with his long white finger. He had beautiful hands, slender and sensitive, not like a man's really. Perhaps that was why she felt so at ease with him – he was so unhairy and unmale. He never pressed his attentions, spoiling things. She had grown very fond of him.

She wondered if she could tell him about Steve. He would be suitable for this, being brainy yet somehow detached. There was nobody else she could tell – least of all the family back home. Imagine what her brothers would do to Steve if they found out. She shuddered.

'I don't think I'm very good at this,' she began. 'It just goes over my head. I can't shut myself off like Steven, my husband, and forget all the horrible things that are happening.'

He paused. 'It is, perhaps, a rather tempting alternative. Unfortunately so, in some ways. The range of literature is so vast that it can become a substitute for the real thing.' His eyes were lowered, his face pink. 'I'm afraid that this happens very easily. It's rather safer. In books one need have no rebuffs and disappointments.' His face went deeper red. 'And of course no challenges too. One can find in books – well, a rather pleasant refuge. But it's not quite satisfactory, one feels.'

There was a silence. She glanced at him, but he had finished. 'I like magazines better,' she said. 'The stories – you know, the nice ones. They make me feel that everything's going to be all right.'

'My landlady works for a woman's magazine, but I don't think it's quite the type you mention. Rather the opposite, though it's one of those glossy sorts. An uneasy mixture, in my mind. Sometimes I leaf through the pages in the living-room. Rather – well, over-realistic about women's problems and women's rights. No escapist routes there, except in the, as they say, *upmarket* advertisements.'

June wrinkled her nose. 'I know what you mean.' She did like talking to Mr Poultney. With him she felt she had so much to say. But she would not tell him about Steve. He

191

looked the easily-embarrassed type; he liked talking on topics, impersonal ones. She could guess that.

'Getting back to your play,' he said, 'a point illustrates, perhaps, our little conversation.' He leafed through the pages searching for the place. He knew so much about literature. He was her teacher, in his comfortable tweedy sports jacket. His hair was still a little damp from the rain outside. Unlike her other teachers, however, he expected nothing in return.

'Your attention please,' he said with a little mock bow.

He put on his reading voice which had become quite familiar these last few weeks: high-pitched and precise, rather similar to her Aunt Loïs'.

Thy husband is thy lord, thy life, thy keeper,
Thy head, thy sovereign; one that cares for thee,
And for thy maintenance commits his body
To painful labour both by sea and land,
To watch the night in storms, the day in cold,
Whilst thou liest warm at home, secure and safe.'

June let out a sigh. Painful labour, did he say? Very painful she was sure, being rubbed down in saunas.

'You approve of the spirit of this?' he asked.

'I'm not sure. I'm thinking.'

'That's the object of the exercise. Our immortal Bard was a master of the ironic.'

Mr Poultney was called away then. June sat on, gazing at the *Collected Works*. She had understood that bit, but she doubted very much if she would understand any more of the 2104 pages of tiny print without Mr Poultney to pick out the easy parts for her. She fidgeted, glancing at her hands. Too much washing-up; they were dry and rough. She rummaged in her bag, took out her cream and rubbed it in. Enough for today. She would do some shopping.

June gathered her things together and stood up. The Shakespeare shelf was on the top, over in the section to the left. The portable steps were there, where Mr Poultney or one of the others had left them. A wcek or two ago she would have given back the book but she felt at home here now. Friend of the chief librarian, able to find her own way about.

She climbed up, carefully because of the high-heeled boots that Steve had chosen for her in happier days, spending money he could ill afford. Holding the heavy book she reached up, grasping with the other hand the wooden support pole connected to the steps, tottering on her spikes. Slippery with cream, her hand missed its hold.

She grabbed at the shelf, crying out with an absurd little squeak. Three heavy volumes fell as she fell, hitting her on the side of the head.

TWENTY SIX

Claudia had settled Steve at her desk and given him a mug of coffee. Not having any actual work to do, but unwilling for him to see this, she had told him that she preferred working at the kitchen table because it was sunny there and besides they would not disturb each other.

Claudia put her coffee mug on the kitchen table. It was painful, him being so near. She must calm down and be sensible. His reason for being here was purely professional; in fact, it could be said that he was using her quite blatantly to launch his new career.

She wandered around the kitchen, straightening the plates on the dresser, picking dead leaves off her geraniums. She moved the mug of washing-up brushes to the side of the windowsill. It was just the novelty of it, the fact that he was so completely Adrian's opposite. They had little in common. She must think of this; she must think of his wife; she must also think of her own dignity. She must remember that he, Steve, quite obviously felt nothing but a sort of opportunistic respect. The irony, she thought: when Wil and Alistair were there, so eager, if only she wanted them.

It was only a quarter to two. She had better settle down with something which could be interpreted, at first glance, as some sort of work. Besides it would be foolish to waste the entire afternoon.

There were always Alistair's diaries. For days she had been longing for another look, a third glance at them. They would be a boost to her flagging self-confidence. And they were absorbing reading; they could take her mind off anything. They could even be construed as some sort of manuscript, should she be interrupted. And she could fetch them without going into the living-room.

She should not, of course. Countless times she had told herself not to look at them yet again. Every time, in fact, that she had passed Alistair's empty bedroom she had told herself this. In her head the two warring urges had taken on the stylized chant – God, Devil, God, Devil – of some mediaeval morality play. A veteran at this, she knew the words; they bounced from side to side of her brain.

She went and fetched the topmost book, the most recent one. She settled herself at the kitchen table. This time she began at the beginning.

'Most unusual – telephone call at work. The room is mine. Full of excitement all afternoon. Why me? First stroke of luck since arrival in the metropolis.

p.m. Informed Mrs. L. Made arrangements for forwarding of post etc. such as it is. No regrets at leaving this establishment, Kilburn not my cup of tea.

Sunday p.m. Spent yesterday settling in. Still puzzling my selection for this nice flat. At breakfast Mrs E begged me to call her Claudia (henceforth C.) Pleasant little chat about neighbourhood and environs. Cannot yet explain my feelings. . . . .

Wednesday. Since mother, have never lived with lady at close quarters. Last night found little cardboard tube in bathroom. Presume for monthly use. In lunch house, visited Boots on pretext of shaving soap (in fact tube nearly full — with luck will last until end of month). Inspected shelves marked "Feminine Hygiene". Pleasant flower-embellished box labelled "Panty Guards". Puzzled, until closer inspection. Exited in haste, knocking large woman with pram.

Stayed in room all evening. Wrote to Mother . . .

. . .

Saturday. Cleanliness of flat in general: beta minus. When C. out shopping, cleaned bath; black curly hair (note: curly) near plug hole. Sluiced this away with scalding water from shower attachment.

. . .

C. remarked that husband had left her. Is being very friendly, inviting me in for coffee etc. Appears amused at my small jokes. Also appears delighted when I join her for breakfast. Caught her staring at me. Am I being considered as replacement? Pondered this in privacy of room. She does not know, of course. Will allow this to continue — even urge it to. May well be my first and only chance.

. . .

Cooker fused at back plug and had to be shifted. Tried to lift it and failed. C. moved me over and did it with ease. She is strong and capable for a woman. Feelings of inadequacy. If only she knew how I longed to return her feelings.

Disgust at cooker's back regions — congealed and dirty. Volunteered to clean kitchen.

. . .

Wednesday. Disturbing day. New shop opened next to sandwich bar. "Modern Mags". Pretended to be lacing show. Journal covers depicted young boys, mostly of Scandinavian origin.

Went into sandwich bar. Unable to eat my ham roll.'

Claudia heard the ticking of the clock. Her coffee had

gone cold. It was two-forty; outside, next door's washing hung limp from the line. There was no sound from the living-room; Steve did not appear to be typing.

She turned the pages, ignoring the fact that her hands were shaking. She skimmed and paused, skimmed and paused; it was only certain parts that she needed to read and she could recognize them now.

'Purchased "Time Out". Lonely Hearts apparently well-known for this (overheard two juniors giggling on this subject). Correct. "Warm gay, 28, seeks love and companionship, race, age, height no object". Entries of this ilk. (I should, perhaps, have looked for lodgings here rather than the "New Statesman".) Rang "Gay Advisory Bureau". When voice answered, replaced receiver.

"Gay". Word does not suit me. Do I have to alter my vocabulary? Frequently practise "butch" but still does not appear myself talking. Feel there is a set outfit of clothes, words etc. which must try to make fit. Cannot forget Mr Peckersgill – highly esteemed, fine Latin scholar, Branch Deputy etc. – arriving that morning with bruised forehead from fracas with coarse young guardsman. Lengthy, emotional telephone calls in working hours. But for this, Mr P. would be living respectable life with wife, children etc etc. Like myself, perfectly ordinary in every other respect (N.B: Also lost his job.)

...

Just finished "Secret Life of a Victorian Gentleman". Struck by parallels between then and now. Anonymous author forced to resort to partners of wrong class, outlook and interests. The difference: in the nineteenth century this applied to heterosexual adventures.

p.m. Felt generally upset and restive. C. remarked: "You look a bit queer."

...

Something must be done. Am far from sex-mad. If so, would have plucked up courage long ago. My needs are simple: companionship. I would prefer an older man. Above everything I want to talk. It would be a relief. In bathroom, glanced at C's. Bath Gel. "It's Not Just Yourself You'll Be Changing". Felt encouraged. Tackled "Time Out" for second time. Looked for appropriate pub. Found address of one in Chelsea. Idea of "pick ups" most alarming; I can but inspect. Plan trip this Friday.

Can only be grateful towards C. Confidence increased tenfold. A year ago could never have faced Friday's proposed outing. Feel possibility of being loved. Of course, also feel guilty. Long to be of use in other ways – am helping a good deal in the flat, running errands etc. Did all shopping on Saturday.

Also grateful to C. because now finally certain of personal inclinations. If such a presentable, apparently eager lady fails to arouse response, Q.E.D.: none can. This is not C.'s fault. Still feel guilty.

. . .

Friday. Momentous evening. C. said going to party. I mentioned, casually, that I was staying in. When C. departed, washed, shaved, applied newly-bought "aftershave" – "Monsieur Pintaubaum". Pleasant scent. Decided to re-christen myself "Cawley" for duration. Took bus to King's Road, where had cold feet and nearly returned to base. Took courage in both hands.

Pleasant Victorian decor, crowded room, not a female in sight. Made way to bar and purchased small glass of lager. Resolved to make it last, due to a) financial sit. b) embarrassment of squeezing second time to bar.

Stood amidst crowd. Did not know where to look. Worse than first day at alarming school. Unfortunately, mine the only sports jacket in sight. Assembled throng dressed mainly in jerkin-type garments of denim and leather. Beneath these, the ubiquitous "tee shirt". A proliferation of zips. Could not fail to notice tightness, in general, of trousers. Uneasy sensation due, I concluded, to everyone watching everyone else.

This despite almost normal aspect of most. But well-groomed, many with moustaches and "fastidious" mouths. Pictured moustache pressing against moustache. Repeated to myself new name: Cawley.

General atmosphere of transience. Neighbouring conversations concerning New York and Amsterdam, parties, relative prices in "deutschmarks" and "kronen". Had feeling nil percent of company lived nearby.

However, then noticed man with beagle, sitting at a table reading newspaper. Was somewhat older than the rest, with grey hair and pink-striped shirt. Certain he was a resident, because of dog. Looked up and gave me a pleasant glance.

Was pondering how to return this when voice behind me asked if I would like another drink.'

It was a short man, apparently, with a low forehead and a silver medallion around his neck. The two of them started a conversation. Cawley accepted another half of lager and stayed about twenty minutes. The man said he was there most nights.

Claudia skimmed through the next few pages. Cawley returned to the pub the next Thursday. The beagle man was absent but the medallion man was there. A further conversation took place, during which the man invited Cawley to accompany him to a party the following Friday night.

'p.m. Upon return, fear C. noticed something amiss. (Bumped into her with rubbish bag). Told her I would be "out" on Friday night.

Friday a.m. At Returned and Overdue Books counter. Fined pleasant old lady £2.60 (correct sum: 26p). Returned "Kisses Under The Tamarisk" to shelf for Public Hygiene. Must remember Mr Peckersgill. Determined to concentrate but thinking about party; in particular, what must take place when it is over. He is not my type. Has shown no interest in mother, library etc. However, has a) unmistakable intentions, and b) certain squat animal attraction.

Cannot stop thinking, also, about man with beagle. He appeared kindly and intelligent. In every way opposite to tonight's "date".

Friday 11 p.m. Prepared myself and took bus to King's Road. However, got down at Battersea Bridge and walked back home. Severe case of cold feet.

To my alarm, found C. in kitchen in funny position.'

It was twenty to three. Claudia was damp with perspiration. She must turn the page, she knew this.

She turned the page. She ran her finger down the pinched handwriting, searching for the evening when Alistair and herself had drunk a bottle of wine, and he had dropped the grill, and she had held him.

TWENTY SEVEN

Steve sat at Claudia's desk. He was looking out of the window. It faced on to the side of the next house: a brick wall. He had come to a stop. In fact, he had never started.

Claudia had cleared a space for him. Her own papers were piled to one side: letters, a water rate receipt, a garage bill for the servicing of her car. Here was a woman who managed her business and ran her life. Yet these official papers seemed so intimate; even her closest friends, he supposed, did not sit at her desk.

He swivelled round on the revolving chair. It was a large, airy room, uncluttered by frills and small objects. Space to think and to breathe. Some modern furniture, a plant or two, walls of a thoughtful ochre. Some trouble taken but not too much. And the books: rows of them in the bookshelves. They looked used.

He swivelled back to the brick wall. He was a fraud and he must finish it now. He had felt terrible, pretending to go overboard on salads in that health food place. And a worse fraud, taking her in, taking himself in, about his article. Of course he wanted to believe in the subject. He did feel indignant, reading about civet farms and manufacturing processes. No more indignant, however, than your average man in the street. But he had fanned this little flicker, fooling himself it was a blaze. Face it, Steve: you can't organize your thoughts and you're hopeless at writing. Admit it: you just had to see her again.

And she had believed him. She had given him her encouragement and her trust and her lounge, little knowing that it was not her typewriter that he wanted so very painfully.

Steve got up. He gathered his two pieces of paper and his scattered notes. He put them into his briefcase and clicked it shut. He would just think of it as lust, simple lust of the type June was so eager to believe he indulged in. Just a desire to get the ball, as Bruce would say, into the back of the net. Nothing more.

He put on his jacket and went to the door. Leaving his briefcase there, he glanced back at the room he would never know better. There was sunlight at the end of the passage where the kitchen lay. He would explain to her, briefly, that he had second thoughts about his article, that he was going home and that he was sorry to have barged in like that. No foolish revelations at which he could imagine her smiling, eyebrows raised, cool and amused. A woman like that, she was probably immune to declarations by now. She would have everything under control.

Claudia sat at the kitchen table, head in hands. Her fingers were clenched. When he stepped in she raised her head. Her face was crimson and her eyes enormous. She pushed back her chair.

'Oh Christ, Steve,' she said.

TWENTY EIGHT

Mr Poultney had his hands under her armpits. June stiffened, then relaxed. He was lifting her up. She rested against the lapel of his jacket; her cheek pressed against the rough tweed. When she opened her eyes the brown checks blurred and jarred. She felt sick.

'I think, the table. Let us steer ourselves in that direction.'

His voice echoed above her head as if from the far end of a concrete tunnel. He was supporting her, but tentatively, amateurishly, his arm rigid around her. 'Our staff retreat,' he said, 'is up some spiral stairs, I'm afraid. I don't think you could manage those.'

'Let me help, Mr Poultney.' An echoing female voice. 'She's gone quite white.'

'I don't have great experience of damsels in distress.'

'Is she all right?'

June was helped into her chair, back at the table. Eyes closed, she pulled her skirt down over her knees. A silence. They were waiting for her.

She was shivering, her temples throbbed, her head ached. 'I think so,' she whispered. A handkerchief – clean, she hoped – was being held against her forehead.

'We'll need a plaster for that cut,' said the lady's voice,

less echoing now. 'I'll get the first aid box.'

'Marjorie lost the key. Singularly unfortunate.'

'I can go home,' whispered June. 'Please don't worry. I was going home anyway.'

She opened her eyes and gazed out from under the dangling flap of hanky. She felt less dizzy. The other librarians were going about their business; people wandered around the shelves as if nothing had happened. The tramp still slept.

'I'll ring for a taxi,' said the woman. She bent down for a last look at June. With her thick black eyebrows and hairy moles she looked more mannish than Mr Poultney.

'Thank you, Miss Gittings. That would be very kind.'

The woman left. June whispered: 'I get these terrible migraines.'

'Dear dear.' He lifted the handkerchief and bent to look at her cut. His fingers were hesitant. He cleared his throat. 'Felled, as it were, by the weight of learning.'

June tried to smile. Keeping her head against the hanky she reached for her handbag, searching for her compact with the mirror in it. 'Is it bad?'

'No, but you'll need to clean it and put something on it. I'll accompany you in the taxi back to your house.'

'But –'

'Please. I can take an hour or two off – one of the small advantages of – well, relative seniority.'

She paused. Any other man offering to see her home and she would have refused. But she could trust him. He refolded the hanky and put it against her forehead.

Then she frowned. 'I don't have any plasters left. Steven – my husband – cut his leg yesterday and I finished the box.'

'Ah. That puts a new complexion on matters. Unless I'm mistaken it's Thursday.'

'Oh. Early closing.'

There was a silence.

'Might I suggest –' he cleared his throat – 'that we went

202

back to my own humble abode? It's not far – Battersea. I have a good supply of TCP and Band-Aids in my little room.'

She paused, then nodded her head – gently, otherwise it ached. As long as it did not turn into a migraine she could cope. She felt a good deal better.

He removed the handkerchief. 'The bleeding appears to have stopped. No lasting damage, I think.'

There was only a small red stain on the white linen. She felt better, looking at it.

The woman hurried back. 'Taxi's here,' she said.

TWENTY NINE

It was four o'clock. Outside dusk was already falling; the winter afternoon was short. Claudia raised herself on one arm and drew the curtains shut. She switched on the bed-side lamp. Day changed to evening.

She turned back and settled against the pillows. Steve gazed at her. 'I've spent two weeks imagining you,' he said.

'How?'

'Like you are now.'

'I've spent two weeks' she said, 'stopping myself imagining you.'

He hoisted himself up on his elbow. She had such a bare, candid face. Wide brown eyes, messed brownish, reddish hair, the faintest down on her arms. 'You're so delicate.' He touched her. 'And all those freckles here, and here.'

'I used to hate my freckles.' She lay back. She was smiling, watching his mouth as he talked.

'Fragile and helpless-looking.'

'I am helpless, now.'

He touched her cheek; he ran his finger down one side of

her face. He settled down beside her. They lay without moving. She was his size, as tall as he was, her legs as long. They lay body to body, knee to knee, only their toes rubbing each other and exploring.

'Hey, you've got sticking plaster on your leg.' She wriggled down and stretched out her hand. 'I didn't notice it before.'

'Cut it shaving.'

She laughed, burying her face in his hair. Her breath warmed his neck. She mumbled things into his ear. She drew back. 'When Adrian left I stopped bothering to shave my legs. There didn't seem any point. I used to sleep diagonally so the bed didn't seem so big.'

'Claudia, Claudia.' He rubbed his head against hers. Short, brown, messed hair. He wanted to say: I want you as my woman friend, my clever, adult, woman friend. I want you every waking moment.

She said: 'What did you do after you drove me back that night?'

'I didn't want to leave you.' He spoke into her warm hair. 'I didn't want to go home. I drove down to the seaside. Brighton, it was. Walked about a bit.'

There was a silence.

'What's she like?' asked Claudia.

He paused. 'Amazingly unlike you.'

They lay together for a moment.

'You looked so efficient in that office,' said Steve, 'I nearly ran away.'

'You wouldn't.'

'I didn't. I couldn't. You know, I'd been twice to your office the day before.'

'Why didn't you come up?'

'Just looked at your name on the reception desk. That personnel list. Girl must have thought I was mad.' His mouth was in the crook of her arm, his voice muffled. 'C.B. Ensor, Ext. 213.'

He jumped up. 'I'm making us a cup of tea.' He pulled up the blankets around her to keep her warm.

'But you don't know where anything is.'

'Sugar?'

'No. Yes – today, yes. Come back soon.'

He strode to the kitchen, finding things, rummaging about, upsetting the neat rows in the cupboard. He rearranged them carefully on their piece of checked formica – two small tins of tomatoes, salt and pepper side by side. *Smash* instant potatoes – this moved him, he had thought her so sophisticated. They all moved him, her things; they looked so solitary when she was not there.

He found a packet and held it to the light. 'Mmm,' he read the label. 'Lapsang Souchong.'

THIRTY

'A cup of tea might go down nicely,' said Mr Poultney, turning the key in the front door. 'Is my assumption correct?' He opened the door and held her arm as they went down the hallway. 'Ground floor.'

There was a mirror and a table for letters. They stopped at the inner doorway to his flat. June felt all right now but she could see he was enjoying this so she clung to his arm.

He fiddled with the keys, unlocking the door. 'Just settle you in the living-room first,' he said. He opened the door and ushered her into the room to the right, closing both doors behind them. He turned on the lights.

It was a big front room, not her type really, lots of the nothing colours that some people seemed to fancy nowadays and not enough cushions.

'I would advise you to keep on your coat,' he said, showing her to the settee; steel tubes, it had, instead of arms. He bent down in front of the gas fire, fiddling with some matches. 'The central heating, though indeed efficient, can hardly anticipate an early homecoming.'

'Is this your landlady's lounge?'

'She kindly invites me to share.'

June could think of nothing complimentary to say about it. 'She's got the same sort of briefcase as my husband,' was the best she could do.

'She's a career lady. One of these new independent types.'

He drew the curtains above the desk. June got to her feet.

'Could you just tell me where the . . . the . . .'

'Ah, of course.' Pink-faced, he addressed the hearth-rug. 'It's the, now let me see, third door on the right.'

She opened the lounge door and left the room. The passage was dark but the doorway at the end was lit. That was a kitchen, she could tell by a glimpse of fridge. From its direction she heard a faint rattle and someone humming to themselves.

June hesitated. The landlady must have come home early. She stood for a moment, undecided. Should she go straight in and introduce herself, or go back and tell Mr Poultney? There was the whistle of a kettle. The humming continued. Someone, anyway, was happy.

A figure appeared, crossing the kitchen from one side to the other. Naked.

THIRTY ONE

Steve piled chocolate fingers on to a plate. It was icy in the kitchen; he fidgeted on the lino, lifting one foot and then the other. He put the plate on the tray, humming to keep himself warm. He wanted an offering to accompany the tea; he glanced around. A flower. The only thing he could see was a potted geranium, spindly and bloomless, but it was better than nothing. He put it on the tray. Finally he lifted up the tea pot, put it on the tray and carried it to the door.

The passage light, which he had not lit, was lit now.

'Claudia?'

A figure appeared at the far end. It was a man.

'Whoops,' said Steve.

He nearly dropped the tray. Instead, he quickly lowered it so that the tea pot was strategically placed.

There was a silence. He felt such a fool. To hide this he lowered his voice plummily. 'Name's Mullen. Sorry I can't shake your hand, old chap.'

THIRTY TWO

June did not stop until she reached the shops at the end of
the road. She paused, trying to catch her breath. Her head
was throbbing; she pressed one hand against her temple. It
was dark now but the shops were lit – bright blurred colours, people walking past, too close, too many of them.

She did not know this area. Amongst the buses and
lorries she searched for a taxi. Nothing was familiar here
except Steve's red car parked back up that road. Silly not to
have noticed it before, but London was full of red cars
looking vaguely the same.

She hailed a taxi. She managed it all, telling the address,
getting herself in, looking quite normal. She sat down.

The migraine was clamping in; the buzzing light in the
corner of her eyes, the thudding left temple, the gathering
needles of pain, the blunter ache behind her left ear. She
knew so well the order in which they moved in on her.

'You all right miss?'

June raised her head from her hands. 'Oh yes,' she said,
giving him a smile. 'Just had something in my eye.'

A wave of nausea rose. She knew how to bear with it,
pushing it down. *Browse Through Our Bedroom Suites*.
The two seats facing her, the flip-up kind, had advertisements fixed to their undersides. *Make Friends at the Abbey*

School of Ballroom Dancing.

When she got home she made straight for the bathroom. She stood in front of the cabinet with its mirrored door. She managed to open her eyes. Funny that she looked so normal – except for the cut, which had puffed up a little, the skin around it tinged with blue. Funny that she did not mind about the cut at all – she who usually fainted at the sight of blood, who took such care of her face.

She opened the cabinet. Inside were the bottles and ointments with which she had looked after herself, and looked after Steve. Tucked behind them, discreetly, was her diaphragm in its oyster-shaped case. She searched amongst the bottles. It was near the back; she had not had a migraine for weeks.

They were better than aspirins – stronger. Dr Phillips had given her a prescription for thirty that last time and she had only used two. Big tablets, too big to swallow; you dissolved them in water. She picked up the bottle; thick, white, the tablets were wedged behind the glass, promising relief.

She went over and fetched a toothmug. No, both toothmugs. They were in their special toothmug holders on either side of the basin, beside them the toothbrushes – pink for her, blue for him.

She filled the mugs with water. Where should she be found? The bathroom was small and cramped; she might knock her head or fall awkwardly. Ungainly, legs all over the place.

She picked up the bottle and the two mugs. She went into the bedroom, sat on the bed, turned on the beside light and set the mugs down on the little table her side. The lamp gave the room an intimate glow. She started to unzip her boots.

It was only then that she noticed her tights. Great wide ladders all down the right leg, open as spiders' webs with large holes at the top. She was not scratched but the tights were a terrible mess from – when was it, last week? – when she had fallen.

Should she change them? It might be more seemly in a proper pair of tights. They were ruined. But then again, did it really matter? She did not change them.

THIRTY THREE

Alistair had stepped back into the living-room. For a full minute he did not move. From Claudia's bedroom he heard voices. He could not escape to his own room because that would mean passing her door which was open, he could tell by the sounds.

A footstep in the passage. Alistair turned; the man stood there. He was tall and brown-haired. He rubbed his nose. 'Hey, I'm terribly sorry,' he said.

He wore Claudia's dressing-gown – blue with little flowers around the collar. A familiar enough garment, well-worn and womanly, but this time the shins below it were hairy.

Disturbed, Alistair looked away. He paused, then he said: 'I wonder – I was just looking – well, for a blonde lady . . .'

'Lost one?' The man scratched his head. 'Trouble is, they're so badly trained nowadays.' The dressing-gown was only loosely tied around his waist.

'I mean – did you happen to meet a lady in the corridor? She went down to the – you know . . .'

'What?'

'It all must seem highly improbable . . .'

'Perhaps she saw me and scarpered. I have that effect on the sensitive ones." He stopped. 'Hey I'm sorry. It's just that I feel – well, at a social disadvantage.'

210

'No, it's me who should apologize – I mean –'

The man smiled. Alistair saw him again standing in the light, naked, framed by the doorway. He could not speak.

'Perhaps we'd better search for her,' the man said.

Alistair followed him down the passage. Both bathroom and lavatory door were ajar; nobody was inside. They stood in the kitchen.

'She didn't come through here?' Alistair spoke to the lino. 'Er, when you were in the kitchen?'

'Wouldn't have noticed. Not if she was blonde and beautiful.'

'Ah . . .'

'Sorry. I mean, no.'

'She'd cut her head. Not too seriously, but here's the blood.' He pointed to the lapel of his jacket, ashamed that the dry cleaning costs had even crossed his mind.

The man stepped closer to look. He touched it with his hand. Alistair could see he was struggling not to be flippant and switch his role to amateur sleuth. But he would like him to do so; he would like him to be anything. Yet he felt both anxious and guilty about this female, towards whom he felt such surprising affection. Not lust, like now, but affection. He asked: 'Did you hear the door slam? Perhaps she's gone home. She was wearing her overcoat. I'm just a little anxious . . . perhaps she's concussed or lost her memory . . .'

'I don't like to be nosey, but does she do this often?'

'I'm hardly acquainted with her. We just talk together a little at the library.'

'What does she look like? Perhaps we should go out and search.'

'Well. . . .' He tried to picture her. He had never thought of her looks. 'Rather slender, long blonde hair, regular features, neat clothing. Rather attractive, I would imagine.'

'I've been hanging about libraries for days. Why doesn't

211

this happen to me?'

Alistair tried to smile – two-men-together. Not altogether successful. He said: 'Perhaps we should try to find her. I know her name and address because I made out her library ticket.' He paused, gazing down at the man's ankles and beautiful muscular feet – muscular yet sensitive. This man was more sensitive than the way he talked, he was sure. 'At least, I think I can remember it.' He tried to ignore the toes and to concentrate. He tried to picture the card, his own handwriting . . .

'I've got a car outside,' said the man. 'We can go in that.'

We can drive away, thought Alistair. We can drive into the country, we can drive to the seaside. We can drive beyond both of them. Trying to remember the woman's name he was trying to remember this man's; he had introduced himself earlier, hadn't he?

'Well, it was June. J. Mullen, Mrs. I'm just trying to recollect the address. Flat 8, I think, something Elm Road. 9 Elm Road, perhaps. Or was it Alma . . . ?'

But the man's feet had moved.

THIRTY FOUR

The last thing she did, after dropping the tablets into the water, was to take out her contact lenses. She had her little suction extractor with her; one by one she did them, delicately, and put them on the table.

The room was blurred now. She twisted around and puffed up the pillows, propping herself up in a sitting position. She had arranged herself upon, rather than under, the eiderdown. The room was utterly silent; she could hear the rasp of the sateen when she moved her legs.

The light was dim, with only the little bedside lamp. She

leant over and picked up the first mug. She stirred its contents with her finger, bending closer to look. The eight tablets seemed to have dissolved. She sucked her finger; it tasted grainy and very bitter. The water was chalky white and she could see scum around its rim. She remained gazing at it for a moment. It was so quiet she could hear the fridge start to hum, two rooms away. She looked into the waiting whiteness; her quiet drink. She imagined a long black tunnel, then stairs up into a white light. (Light, and a man standing in a kitchen doorway. Light behind him.)

No; white space, echoing. Long dark stairs up and then light, and space, and flowers. She took a sip, and winced. Quickly, before she could think, she drank again, a gulp this time. She lay against the pillows for a moment. No sound but a far door slamming, the creak of the bed as she leant over for the mug.

She took another gulp. She must feel sleepy. She was halfway through the first mug now. Her mouth felt scoured and bitter; a little had dribbled down her chin but she did not want to bother about this. She must push herself into sleep. It must come quickly.

She gulped again; her heart was thumping and there was a ringing in her ears. She must get through these grainy mouthfuls and go to sleep. Sleep and light and flowers. She bent to the plastic rim of the mug and sipped. She urged her eyes to close.

Her heart was thumping louder, louder and louder, like footsteps up the stairs. Higher and higher, the fourth floor, the fifth floor, the fiftieth floor . . . up to the light beyond . . .

Her head swam. She lifted the mug, it felt solid and thick, with a thick rim for her lips. Thick rubbery rim, thick rubbery heartbeats, thumping louder and louder . . . The drink was thicker now at the bottom of the mug, thick as sand . . . she must munch it down and chew it . . . eat herself into sleep . . .

Sleep took so long, with her heart thumping louder. A door slamming. Close your eyes, shut it out.

She opened them. A door opened. Light, and someone there.

'June? *June*?'

The bed jolted, a body flung itself against her. Was this it? Arms were around her, tightly. Her face was pressed against a warm, blue, woolly chest. She lay still for a moment. Was she sleeping now? She put her arms around the body. She opened her eyes. She was not sleeping. Against her cheek were pressed knobbly, embroidered flowers.

THIRTY FIVE

The first flowers have arrived. It is March and there are celandines under Verity's hedge. They are shiny, as if someone has varnished them one by one; the inner sides of their petals are yellow as butter. Their leaves are glossy. On the larch branches bright green tufts have appeared.

Claudia pauses. She is noticing small things now. Tiny shoots, the pattern of growth. When she lived in London she never did. Or perhaps it is the child growing inside her— yesterday in the clinic this was confirmed. She has lived here since Wil left, which was soon after Christmas. Perhaps she is sinking into nature ...

Sinking into the mud anyway. Claudia straightens up from her inspection and moves back on to the path. It is raised concrete, running down the middle of the vegetable garden. It slopes downhill; at the end is a ditch where all three of Verity's children are busy and for a moment quiet. Behind the larches, smoke drifts up from the chimney. The sky is blue, the spring sun warm. Even the chickens are silent.

She feels so well. She has never felt sick in all these three months. She feels strong and alert, she is conscious of her fingertips, her toes, the skin that covers her body.

Verity, too, has paused. She is standing a few feet away. Now she starts working again, her rake scraping the earth back and forth. She is preparing the ground for Claudia's seeds.

Claudia walks slowly, shaking the packet in the way Verity has shown her. Since they have started living together it is Claudia who has the most to learn. She has even taken to wearing Verity's clothes now Verity is too big to get into them; today it is a rust-coloured woollen skirt. Her own London clothes would fall to pieces in a place like this.

Verity works on. She is wearing a big green gathered dress, her hair is tied in a scarf. They are both bending over, working side by side.

'We must look like a mediaeval Book of Hours,' says Claudia, 'toiling in unison.'

'Perhaps *Yours*'ll come and take our photo. You must go up and visit them sometime, Claudia. Give them the idea.'

'*Women Without Men*. How we made them, at last, redundant.'

Verity straightens up and rubs her back. 'Except for fertilizing us.'

'And, I suppose, paying for us.'

'For me, anyway.'

Wil, who now has a bedsitter in Chelsea, sends Verity money; she also keeps the cottage. She is trying to make some cash – she sells her preserves to the local shop, she is trying to get back into fabric design but this is difficult with all the children. She can hardly call herself self-supporting.

Verity pulls off her scarf and shakes her head. She rubs her neck. Her henna dye is growing out; except for the ends, her hair is back to its natural brown. She is still distressed by Wil's departure, but it is final. She is also

215

relieved. She bends to work.

'No ego to protect ...' scrape, ... 'no flirtations to ignore' ... scrape ... 'no waiting up, pretending I'm not ...' scrape ... 'no telling him how young he looks' ... scrape ... 'no feeling inadequate' ... scrape ... 'no pretending *he* isn't ...' The small weeds scatter to either side. She has raked an empty strip for Claudia to plant.

Life with a woman is so simple. They have meals when they want them. Sometimes they sit up talking until two and sometimes they go to bed when the children do.

What Claudia herself should do is something to be thought about, but later. She has given up her job. She has money, for the flat was sold last week. She will have a baby to look after, a child to bring up, but beyond that? She is no painter; she is not going to write the great Kentish novel. She cannot quite picture herself hammering out belts or making candles and selling them in an ethnic London street market, like some of Verity's friends. But perhaps she can. She can become anything; her own picture is changing. She is content just to be here, untroubled, reading books and tiring herself out. After all she has worked hard for ten years. She is fertile and happy; she is needed by Verity, who is now alone, and by her father, likewise alone.

He lives only twenty miles away. She visits him every few days. She brings him plants and takes the plants he offers. She asks his advice. She brings his clothes back to mend (well, Verity mends them). He often visits and comes for Sunday lunch. He seems a different man now; he is no longer her father but an elderly man from whom she can learn, towards whom she no longer has to take a stance. She likes him better. She dreads telling him about the baby in case it puts them back.

Saffron runs up with a jam jar of muddy water. Claudia dislikes Saffron's name but has become fond of the girl. Daisy will take longer. And she can now change Ben's nappies – a small technique this, but necessary. By the time

216

the sun comes out of that cloud ... now ... a million nappies will have been changed.

Verity stands straight and groans. She is too fat for bending.

'Lunch time. Wonder what's Wil's doing now. I know where he goes in the evenings. Those cheap places in the King's Road.'

'Moussaka and candles in Chianti bottles ...'

'African exchange students and loose *au pairs* ...'

'That reminds me –'

Claudia opens her mouth to tell Verity about Heidi. She closes it.

'Wonder what your bloke's doing then.' Verity leans on her rake.

'If only Adrian had found out properly. He's just not interested in people.'

'That's unfair. You never told him why you wanted to know.' Verity shifts on to the other foot; her clogs are heavy with mud. They are always stopping to talk. 'Tossing around on the high seas.'

They gazed into the distance; the greening fields, the murmuring motorway.

'Adrian only *thought* it was the Merchant Navy,' says Claudia. 'Rumour. He said he might be wrong. No one at Pintaubaum's heard a thing.'

'But what did that man Bruce tell him?'

'Something about a shop in London. An aquarium shop – Steve setting it up with some old man. Sounds highly unlikely.'

She scratches her arm. With some research she could find out, but she hesitates from doing so.

'If only I knew he was still with his wife ...' Claudia scrumples up the empty seed packet and pauses. 'I think, I hope he is.'

His lovely body, his lovely leg with the Elastoplast on it. Has his cut healed? What, oh what is he doing now?

217

He had returned to fetch his clothes but she had been out. Alistair had shown him where they were. She envies Alistair, sickeningly.

She walks back and forth, scattering earth through a sieve, covering up her speckled seeds. She will always have a passion for him. His lovely laugh, his lovely shoulders, his flat stomach with its silken skin, the way he grinned, the way he spread the plates and cups all over the bed.

It would have been spoilt if she had seen him again, wouldn't it. Of course, of course.

THIRTY SIX

The July *Yours* carries its usual Pintaubaum single-page four-colour job. Claudia's successor takes the proof to the light box. She notices the model has changed though the combat gear remains. She clicks the switch. A rare face, of great purity and beauty, is illuminated. It is a new girl. She is both child-like and sensual; her hair is long, silky and blonde. It has not been dyed, one can tell by the colour of her complexion (which does not need adjusting; this advert can go through uncorrected). Says the caption (60pt. Univers Extra): *It's Not Just Yourself You'll Be Changing*.

This girl will go far. Later, Claudia's successor is flipping through some agency photos. The face is there. *June Mullen. 34:24:35*.

THIRTY SEVEN

In a small Chelsea pub Raymond is pulling two Tuborgs. He passes them, cool and brimming, to Harry (Gerry? Lenny?) who has brought in a new acquisition. Tonight's young man wears khaki – a pleasantly militaristic little outfit with cheeky epaulettes. Raymond gazes around the bar. Fags in fatigues, how is your war, my war?

'You're a treasure, Ray.' Harry-Gerry-Lenny smiles and turns to his companion. The boy's face is beige and matt; he has applied, discreetly, some tinted foundation over his ever-so-slightly bumpy skin. Just a lad.

Raymond glances beyond them; he wants to get another look at old Philip from down the road. There is an interesting situation developing.

It started when a young man in a raincoat, entering, tripped over that blessed beagle's lead. Apologies, extremely profuse and lengthy, have ended by Philip patting the seat beside him. The young man, after a good deal of fidgeting – should he take off his mackintosh, where should he put his overnight bag? – has finally sat down. Philip has fetched him a lager.

This is unusual. Philip, a regular, is not in the habit of this. He comes here simply for a quiet drink. He is a journalist for one of the literary weeklies; he is getting on a bit, a solitary, amiable old queen, and he has been alone for some years now. A long time ago he had someone – a poet, it was; Ray has forgotten the name.

Sooner or later, in fact, Ray has to clear the neighbouring table. He eases his way through the crowd, for the Saloon Bar is filling up. Nine-thirty on a Friday night, men standing alone and in twos, the atmosphere so casual, so tense.

The young man, pink-faced, is bending to pat the dog.

'. . . just like him. It belongs to our next-door neighbours, actually, in Malvern. Is yours a dog?'

'A lady. Gerty. A touch testy but she's fine when you get acquainted. One of life's more faithful friends. Look at that – you ought to be highly flattered.'

'I'm fond of dogs.'

'We can safely assume she's taking to you. Did you say Malvern, by the way? I'm partial to it around there . . .'

A burst of laughter drowns the conversation. Ray picks up the glasses and pauses. He is needed back at the bar.

'Let me introduce myself,' he hears the older man saying. 'Philip Tring.'

'I'm so pleased to meet you. The name's Cawley.'

'Sorry, didn't catch that.'

A pause. 'My name's Alistair. Alistair Poultney.'

Dec 2, 2016

Deborah Moggach

STOLEN

'If you knew Ashford, which I wouldn't recommend, then there was nothing more shocking than to set up house with a Pakistani.'

Always a rebel, Marianne was the first girl in her class to bleach her hair and learn how to smoke. A few boyfriends and one abortion later she falls in love with Salim, the proud and elegant Pakistani with eyes like treacle.

East meets West in a passionate mixed marriage. However, Marianne knows little of the Islamic view of motherhood. When his wife proves unfaithful, Salim reasons that she is morally incapable of bringing up her children and kidnaps them while she is at work. There follows nightmarish flying visits to Karachi, and protracted legal battles for wardship of the children.

Terse, wry and compassionate, Deborah Moggach explores the emotional upheaval caused by a woman's adultery, and how children can be used as weapons for vengeance. Now a major TV series with LWT, *Stolen* is a controversial look at life at its untidiest.

Deborah Moggach

YOU MUST BE SISTERS

Claire – a model daughter, an imaginative teacher, as clear and legible as her handwriting.

Laura – a student, a beauty, as vital and rebellious as her parents could ever have feared for.

As children they had shared everything – so much so that later, neither sister could quite remember to which one of them some long-distant adventure had happened. Far from the leafy respectability of Harrow where they grew up, each are now going their distinctly separate ways in this warm, funny and poignant novel of coming-of-age.

A Selected List of Fiction Available from Mandarin

While every effort is made to keep prices low, it is sometimes necessary to increase prices at short notice. Mandarin Paperbacks reserves the right to show new retail prices on covers which may differ from those previously advertised in the text or elsewhere.

The prices shown below were correct at the time of going to press.

☐	7493 0003 5	**Mirage**	James Follett	£3.99
☐	7493 0134 1	**To Kill a Mockingbird**	Harper Lee	£2.99
☐	7493 0076 0	**The Crystal Contract**	Julian Rathbone	£3.99
☐	7493 0145 7	**Talking Oscars**	Simon Williams	£3.50
☐	7493 0118 X	**The Wire**	Nik Gowing	£3.99
☐	7493 0121 X	**Under Cover of Daylight**	James Hall	£3.50
☐	7493 0020 5	**Pratt of the Argus**	David Nobbs	£3.99
☐	7493 0097 3	**Second from Last in the Sack Race**	David Nobbs	£3.50

All these books are available at your bookshop or newsagent, or can be ordered direct from the publisher. Just tick the titles you want and fill in the form below.

Mandarin Paperbacks, Cash Sales Department, PO Box 11, Falmouth, Cornwall TR10 9EN.

Please send cheque or postal order, no currency, for purchase price quoted and allow the following for postage and packing:

UK   80p for the first book, 20p for each additional book ordered to a maximum charge of £2.00.

BFPO   80p for the first book, 20p for each additional book.

Overseas   £1.50 for the first book, £1.00 for the second and 30p for each additional book
including Eire thereafter.

NAME (Block letters) ....

ADDRESS ....

....

....